The Best Laugh Last

a novel by

John B. Rosenman

Treacle Press

To the Mona's

THE BEST LAUGH LAST
Copyright © 1981 by John B. Rosenman
All rights reserved under International and Pan-American Copyright
Conventions. For information, write the publisher, Treacle Press, Box 638,
New Paltz, NY 12561. Publication of this novel is assisted by grants from the
New York State Council on the Arts and National Endowment for the Arts.
Manufactured in the United States of America. Design by Bruce R. McPherson.

LIBRARY OF CONGRESS CATALOGING IN PUBLICATION DATA

Rosenman, John B., 1941-
   The best laugh last.

   I. Title.
PS3568.0825B4   813'.54   81-12990
ISBN 0-914232-44-4   AACR2

Typeset by Open Studio Ltd., a non-profit literary facility supported in
part by grants from the New York State Council on the Arts and the
National Endowment for the Arts.

The Best Laugh Last

One

WELL, THIS TIME it looks like I finally did it. Even though I got up at seven, bolted my Rice Krispies, and roared into Green Town with five minutes easy between me and the opening bell, I was still late to class. Out of nowhere comes Engine Jack blowing his whistle like a maniac, and I'm stuck there watching fifty-eight cars drag across the tracks fifteen minutes ahead of schedule. And damned if there isn't this burrheaded buck waving at me from the caboose when it's all over, grinning like he knows I have a chat with Bledsoe all tucked away even before the sun's turned up.

Naturally, I do my best. Gun Big Red and whip him to a turn before the red white and blue WELCOME sign, grab my books and haul ass into the Fine Arts center just as three of my students make an early break. Never saw such a change in my life. Grins turn to groans before you can hum a note from "Sweet Georgia Brown." One kid's so sad he calls me 'Massah' and begs me to let his people go.

7:45. I guess I know then there's no getting around it. Bledsoe and I are definitely headed for another rendezvous with the embers from our last one not even cold yet. The trouble is, it's just the kind of thing he's been waiting for.

As usual, the rest are sitting there quietly in the dark. Not one has taken the trouble to get up and turn the lights on. It's as if they don't care, as if some essential spark has been canceled out of them. This is freshman English, and if there's anything harder than selling grammar to these kids at a quarter to eight in the morning, I sure haven't heard of it. I flip on the lights.

"O.K., gang! Let's go! Dig out those good old *Harbrace Workbooks* and turn to page 27 where we left off last time." I clap my hands, paroxysmal with enthusiasm. "Fine! Now that we're bright eyed and bushy tailed, volunteers are gratefully accepted. All right, number 13, who wants it?"

Silence.

"Please! Let's not have everyone press forward at once. It's difficult to breathe." I feign indecision, acting like there's a forest of hands out there. "Hmm, let's see. It's so hard to choose. How about—Carmelita!"

Groaning, Carmelita bends over her book.

Every student (is, are) surprised by the teacher.

Carmelita looks up. I wait. She looks at the sentence again. "Uh—are?"

"No. 'Every student' is singular and takes a singular verb. It should be 'is.' All right, Willy, grab the next one."

Many in the class (was, were) surprised to find that their teacher came from a distant land.

"Was?" says Willy.

Well, it looks like it's going to be a splendid day. Not only have I probably screwed myself out of a job, but they've already forgotten what I taught them last time, which was next to nothing. But what the hell, maybe I'm a slow learner too. You know, when I first came to Ashland College two years ago, I had your typical white liberal's missionary zeal. God, was I going to awaken them and lead them out of the darkness. You would have loved me then. I was Galahad to the rescue in my shining armor, courageously determined to save dem po' darkies.

Then I found out what all new teachers do: the students here are uneducated, can barely read, write, or think, and more to the point couldn't care less about your noble sentiments. The administration is mostly concerned with the money it gets from the government for each warm body that comes through the turnstile, and doesn't really care about undoing the damage of years of lousy preparation. Faced by these facts, the new teacher passes through predictable stages. First, he experiences shock. Then comes disillusionment. The students aren't responding and don't care. They come to class late, creating disturbances. They talk and yawn, go to sleep with their heads laid flat on their desks. If the teacher believes in his own special calling and charisma, he is likely to redouble his efforts to reach them. He experiments. He stands on his head and spits educational nickels. He cracks jokes and talks only about black heroes in an effort to make them like him. In short, he does everything he can think of to be another Sidney Poitier in *To Sir With Love*. And in the end, when all his efforts accomplish little or nothing, he gets smart and stops trying. After all, why break your butt when no one wants what you're selling? Or to put it another way, why walk the last mile when you're underpaid to begin with?

By the time a teacher reaches this stage, you can usually spot him. He stops spending hours honing and polishing his lecture notes and commences dragging a phonograph to class to eat up the clock. His complaints about students start to resemble healed wounds. They acquire a detached, encrusted they-can't-do-anything-right quality. If he is a white liberal whose disenchantment has been severe, he may even become a racist. He cynically reminisces about his former idealism and jokes about the time when he had been young and naive.

The trouble with me is I still care. I feel it's my job not to give up but to keep trying. Duffy in Math and Hart in Music are slow learners too, and I bet Bledsoe has their numbers.... But if there's anywhere in this world where good teachers are desperately needed, Ashland's the place.

Splitting the class into halves, I pit the left one against the right and pick up the pace, theatrically stalking about to hover menacingly over students whose turns have come. I get mild results. A few students laugh and once I even get three straight correct answers. But does picking the right verb help them much in learning to speak and write? The trouble is, teaching is based on intangibles. How do you ever know if you're getting across or if what you're achieving is worth it?

Whatever the answer, it's for damn sure that Dame Rumor hasn't been letting any grass grow under *his* shoes. No sooner do I get back to my office after class than he's rapping at my door to give me the Good News. Dame Rumor. That's what I call Farnsworth, Chairman of what passes for the English Department around here. In some old play there's this dude by that name who's always the first to get the dirt and pass it on. That's Farnsworth, all right. Toad sucker. Lizard licker. Farnsworth suffers chronic overbite from love of other people's miseries and is always bloated with sympathy when he lets you know your ass is up for grabs.

"David?"

"Yes?"

"Mind if I come in?"

"Not at all. Please do."

So in he comes with his outdated tweed jacket and his phony buddy-buddy look, and I slip into the role of polite host, hamming it up extra fine to spoil it for him. I even make it a point to put the coffee on. Naturally he sits down like he's on a social call.

"How'd your weekend go?"

"Great. Spent it angling for the big one out at Lake Marion."

"Really? Catch anything?"

"You bet. A striped bass and a couple bream. Some were so small, though, I just tossed them back."

"Well, it's a mite early for Marion. Fishing's only good there in May and June."

"That's what they say, but Bagley in Psych caught an eight pound bass there last week. Used a twenty pound test line with a spin beetle lure. Snagged it just off the point, way I heard."

Now, the point of all this crap is that I despise fishing and would no sooner be caught in a boat than sober on a Saturday night. And Farnsworth knows it. Yet we go through with the charade, smiling our dislike at each other. God, I hate the sonofabitch.

All at once he whips out his pipe. When Farnsworth does that it's a sure sign he's going to hand you someone's head on a platter. As long as I've known him, he's never fired up without dispensing ill tidings.

4

"By the way," he says. "Puff...puff...received a call from...puff...puff...Dean Bledsoe a few minutes ago."

"That so?"

"Hmm hmm." Cherry blend fills the room like napalm. He snaps his lighter shut and leans back, savoring the moment. "It was about you."

"Really? What did the Dean want?"

"Didn't say. Fact is, it was Mrs. Sharp who called. All she offered is that your presence is required immediately."

"I see." Mrs. Sharp is the Dean's secretary, who will be reincarnated as a barracuda. "Well, I 'spect I ought to mosey over there when I get the time."

"I 'spect." Farnsworth takes a puff and for a moment the look he gives me would chill your liver. Clearly, I'm not playing the game right. I'm robbing him of his fun. Bledsoe is Torquemada, the Grand Inquisitor, and my banter is like a red flag in Farnsworth's face. One sweats and soils his pants when he receives a summons from Bledsoe. One does not dismiss it as an RSVP or a sign of having made the Social Register. Certainly not at a private black college like Ashland where all the administration and two-thirds of the faculty are black, and where teachers—especially white Uncle Toms such as Farnsworth—enjoy all the rights and authority of house niggers.

Farnsworth's look lingers. "You know, Dave," he says, "you really ought to take things more seriously."

"What things?"

"Well, like you should get your hair cut, for one thing. It's far too long, and you know how the President feels about that. But even more important, you should stop criticizing the way things are done around here. At faculty meetings you practically come right out and say the Administration's incompetent and doesn't care at all about educating students."

"Why shouldn't I say that? It's true, isn't it?"

That, of course, goes nowhere. He removes his pipe and pokes its stem at me.

"That's not the point. This is a black Methodist college, Dave, and you ought to tone a lot of things down. People here

5

just don't appreciate your views and strong language."

"Quite frankly, Doug, I don't give a damn what they appreciate."

"Well, you better learn, or be prepared to suffer the consequences. Your friend John Hart just got fired for causing difficulties, and the same could happen to you if you're not careful. Believe me, I've—

"John?" I sit up. "He's been fired? Why?"

"Probably for doing the same things you do, like trying to force teachers to join the AAUP and clamor for more rights."

"Yeah, but even Bledsoe won't fire you for that, he just lays in a warning." I think it over, suddenly rattled. "And John's got too much class. He's the best black faculty member here."

Farnsworth smirks and pokes his pipe at me again. "Now you know better than that. Around here they don't want trouble from anybody. Believe me, Dave, I've just got your best interests at heart. The Dean and the President don't approve of—"

"Troublemakers?"

"You could put it that way—"

"Rabble-rousers?"

"Uh huh. That's—"

"Bolsheviks? Agitators? Wavemakers? Tub-thumpers?"

"Yes, and that's another thing, Dave. You're too flippant. Like just now or when you criticize the school for being backward and unprogressive. At the last meeting you sounded like Trotsky when you gave that speech about Ashland cutting itself off from the community and not trying to attract local students, whites, and adults. Sure, this isn't Harvard, but a lot of us make our living here. You should be more discreet."

I clear my throat and crank up the old smile. My hands ache, whether for a drink or to wring his neck, I'm not sure. What's certain is that I don't have to sit here and take this. So I say I'm grateful for his comments and get up.

He does too. His overbite comes out and caresses the pipe again, but the feast is over. Besides, he realizes he's gone a bit too far. Guys like Farnsworth: I've seen them before. They have to maintain a delicate balance and stay behind their nice-guy veneers. Otherwise they let their scurvy hides out of the bag.

"Well, I didn't mean to be critical, you understand—"

"That's O.K.," I say. "I'll just accept it in the spirit it was intended. You're a prince of a guy, Farnsworth."

"Uh huh. Well, hope it goes all right with the Dean. If there's anything—"

"Thanks. If there is you'll be the first to know."

"Good."

He probably *will* be the first to know. A guy like Farnsworth, he's got his tentacles everywhere. Five seconds after I leave The Man's office, Mrs. Sharp will probably be on the blower to him. I don't know how he does it. I watch him go, wishing I'd thrown caution to the winds and told him what a prick he is.

Two

I KICK THE DOOR shut and pour myself some coffee. Over the years folks have told me that if I made it any stronger I could mortar bricks, but as far as I'm concerned it tastes fine even without the Golden Cup Award. Too bad Farnsworth didn't stick around to sample it. I'd have liked to have seen his face after the first swallow.

I should get over there at once, of course. Keeping The Man Waiting is extra bad form, but I'm not the young Turk or kamikaze I used to be, so I take a moment to savor my brew.

For some reason I'm thinking of the farm in Middlefield, Ohio where I grew up. Twenty years. Twenty years since I blew up at my father and left the place, all because I preferred reading books in the hayloft to manure and hard work. Well, here I am. Twenty years and umpteen jobs later. If I'd only stayed put I'd have a red neck and a dozen kids by now, not to mention a one hundred and twenty acre farm.

After a minute I finish my cup and leave the place. Funny, it looks like it's going to be a Cracker Jack day. The sun is shining and pigeons are hopping around the cupola on top of the Ad Building. Yep, in an hour it's going to be another splendid South Carolina morning. By then I ought to know if I still have a job for next year.

The campus, if that's what you want to call it, is slowly coming to life. Students and teachers head listlessly to class, and a few cars enter along the hedge of flaming pyracantha fringing the one driveway into the place, almost stopping halfway to climb a speed trap hump. As you turn off Wade Hampton you can already see the red white and blue WELCOME sign. The campus itself is absolutely flat. There are no rolling hills. No green commons for couples to lie on in the sun. No spread blankets transistor radios raspberry frisbees gliding through the air. In short, nothing. It's a long time since the Elysian Fields of Kent State University for me. Here and there a few modern buildings fight a losing battle against shacks from the early Paleozoic.

Take the Music Building, for instance. According to rumor, it was once an army barracks up North. The school got it free, dismantled it, and reassembled it here piece by piece. Mason Hall, where I keep my digs, isn't any better. The spitting image of The House of Usher, its second and third floors are officially condemned and there are no lights in the hallway. Three or four times a year Orkin men spray for termites and roaches.

Crossing the driveway, I pass some janitors who are already busy doing nothing. Maintenance is spelled mañana around here. At Ashland almost everyone, from the Head of Maintenance on up, seems to have his title and love it, but only a few are willing to work. They've even got one ace who infected by the pervasive torpor and inefficiency of the place, spends his days sweeping the same flight of steps. Upkeep elsewhere is the same. Some toilets haven't worked for years and the new Fine Arts Center is already going to hell. Never use the johns there, by the way. They don't lay in any soap and the towel dispensaries have been ripped out of the walls.

Outside the Ad Building I run into Duffy and tell him the good news.

"Say, that's a dandy way to start the day. Worried?"

"Naw, I've been to The Man before. Just spread 'em wide and keep a loose sphincter."

"Ha ha ha. But you've been in to see him a lot lately. Hope there's no trouble."

"You and me both."

"Well, my heart's in your corner, Dave. I've logged a few visits to the Dean myself."

"Who hasn't?"

"Yeah, but when you're Chairman of the Math Department you get blamed for everything." Cautiously he looks around. "The bastard. He hits you like a cyclone and won't listen to a word you say. Irrational, incompetent, sadistic—"

"Mr. Warmth."

"That's him. You know, everyone hates him. I don't know how he stays in power. If this were Africa, there would have been a coup years ago."

"Wait till you hear my plan."

"Count me in. I can pass out the ammunition. Oh, by the way, have you heard about Hart?"

"Yeah, Farnsworth said something about him being fired. What's the dope?"

"Well, it's all hush hush and quite mysterious. Seems the Dean called him in for a special meeting, and the word is that he's not going to be back next year."

"No kidding. Maybe he didn't do like he was told and kept taking his music classes all the way into Columbia for concerts." I squint into the sun, thinking what a queer bird John is for Ashland. In a way he's even odder than me. A handsome Ph.D. from Princeton who radiates class and always wears a suit and vest, he believes students need cultural exposure they can't get here. Such people don't score many points at Ashland, believe me.

Duffy frowns. "No, I don't think it was another of his trips that did him in. Like I said, this is hush hush. The impression I get from the source I talked to, and this is deep background, you understand, *very* deep, is that Hart has done something so bad they don't want it to get around."

"Sounds murky."

"Murky enough to be a cover-up, my friend." Duffy taps his head. "You know, I've got my own little shit detector up here and it's picking up fumes from all over the place."

"Wonder what it could be? I mean, what could be so bad that they treat it like a state secret?"

"I don't know, but you've got that look in your eye again. Take my advice and stay away from it. You've got enough problems with your track record at faculty meetings." He slaps my shoulder. "Anyway, let me know how it goes with the Dean, huh? Give me a buzz."

"Right. See you."

Duffy, he's all right, one of the few people around here I can stand. Too bad about his wife, though. According to the grapevine, she's a real hot number and likes to play around.

I go inside and climb to the second floor, feeling like it's Mount Everest. Outside his office I pause. Suddenly I want to go back to my pad, pour myself a stiff one, put on Dylan or Elton John, and wait for Connie. I'm really tempted to leave. Emptying my mind, I open the door and go in.

Inside, Mrs. Sharp hustles around her desk, aiding the mismanagement of the place. She shoots me a look like a bright bird.

"Yes, Mr. Newman?"

"Would you tell Dean Bledsoe I'm here to see him?"

I watch her disappear through the open door of the Dean's office. After a moment she returns and without looking at me continues what she had been doing. I find a chair against the wall and sit down.

He's using psychological warfare, of course; making me cool my heels. And the thing is it always works a little, even though I know what he's doing. What I've got to do is a number on myself, get an erection or practice transcendental meditation. Anything to fight back. Maybe I should ravish Mrs. Sharp. How about it? Can I get a bone up over her? Suddenly I see myself clambering over the counter with a hard on, interracial rape in mind. What will it be like to hump a tarantula? Will I make the Alumni Newsletter? I see the photo now, Dean Bledsoe pulling me off. Caption: Ashland Instructor Runs Amok, Attempts Rape Of Local Witch. Services To Be Held...

Enough of this. Mrs. Sharp is hustling about the file cabinet now with her long, bright red, and sharply filed nails. They're filing nails, envelope slitting nails, nails filed for speed and accuracy. Yet for all her seeming efficiency, Mrs. Sharp is kin to the speed king of the stairs, a cog in an antiquated system where everything must be made out in triplicate and signed by at least two people before it is lost. I guess I knew what to expect from this place when I sat here waiting to be interviewed by the Dean for a job. There was Mrs. Sharp rapidly typing away while above, hanging down so they could fall on her head at any moment, were three tiles that had come unglued. Like the Chinese say, a single picture is worth a thousand words.

Here's a story you can have for nothing: years ago, so legend has it, the school acquired a computer to improve its record-keeping, only to learn they had no one who knew how to run it. So they got rid of the thing. At Ashland, *teachers* keep the records. Every semester I get misspelled memos from the Dean, asking for the number of students in my classes. Is Willie Clyde in English 101? Don't ask the Registrar, ask David Newman. At the end of each semester I fill out 180 separate grade slips for the 90 students I teach.

Suddenly The Man says something in his office. Mrs. Sharp darts me a look.

"Dean Bledsoe will see you now, Mr. Newman."

I go in. The Man is behind his desk. He gets up and he keeps on getting up. He gets up for what seems the longest time, growing until he fills the room. Six and a half feet worth. He reminds me of what Idi Amin would be like if he were semi-civilized by a Ph.D. in Education from Columbia. He waves at a stiff wooden chair.

"Sit down, Mr. Newman."

I sit and he gets right to it.

"It has come to my attention that you were late to your seven-thirty class this morning."

"Yes."

"Mr. Newman, after our last conference, I'm rather surprised to see you here again. I thought I had impressed upon you the importance of proper conduct, not only as it relates to faculty meetings but also as far as other things are concerned as well."

"Yes, you did."

A frown crosses his pecan features. "Then I'm puzzled as to why we've gathered here this morning."

I clear my throat and take a crack at it, sensing it won't make much difference.

"Well, you see, I had allowed for plenty of time to get to my class this morning. But when I got to the railroad tracks the train was there fifteen minutes early. By the time it passed, which took over ten minutes, I was late."

"Why weren't you there sooner?"

"I beg your pardon?"

"Seems to me you could have *anticipated* that the train might be early and have allowed for it."

I take a deep breath and try again.

"But I *did* anticipate it. I was there a full fifteen minutes before the train was due. I have a copy of the railroad schedule at home. I think that being there that much ahead of time, especially so early in the morning, is more than adequate preparation."

Well, I can see I'm still not there. He sits massively impervious to reason, and I feel my fear of the man begin to gather. Like some elemental, crackbrained force he gets to you, overwhelms like a steamroller. Add to that a vicious cruelty and you've really got something. Ask Duffy, for example, who speaks of him in a stage whisper with facial tics and had whatever initiative he once had bled out of him by the fear of another confrontation. It's been said that sooner or later almost everyone gets invited to see him, with no advance warning why. You simply open your mailbox Friday to find a typed memo requesting your presence in his office Monday morning. It's a splendid torture tactic. During the weekend you have plenty of time to fret and brood about which sins you're going to get crucified for, only to go in and get plowed under over some piece of simple-minded fluff like your course syllabi. And more often than not, you find your Department Chairman there too, sitting with your dossier perched on his knee and ready to nail you on inconsistencies.

Still, despite his Reign of Terror, it's damn hard to get fired. That is, unless you've gone energetically to the mat with him as often as I have. Right now I can hear him gearing up for an early pin.

"I'm afraid I can't agree with you, Mr. Newman," he says.

13

"It's been my personal experience that trains are frequently *more* than fifteen minutes off schedule. Besides—"

"But fifteen minutes is quite a—"

"Besides, you could always have gone around it—"

"But there's no convenient—"

"...rather than simply sit there doing nothing. Your decision—"

"Sir—"

"...just to sit there indicates a resolve *not* to meet your class and a reluctance to fulfill your duties—"

"That's not—"

"...as they are defined in your contract. In addition, let me remind you that this current dereliction on your part—"

"But it's not—"

"...is only the latest of a *protracted* series of incidents that I personally find most alarming. Dr. Farnsworth informs me that you fail to start your classes promptly and that he has heard you criticize our policies not only to other teachers but to visitors to Ashland as well..."

Believe me, Dave, I've just got your best interests at heart. You two-faced bastard, I should have kicked your balls in.

"You have also disrupted faculty meetings, especially the last one where you stated that we should introduce a costly remedial reading and writing program and recruit regular students, adults, and whites from the community—"

"This school's too insular," I manage to break in. "Besides, such students would add a desperately needed variety to a student body consisting mostly of black kids from South Caro—"

"...You have even deemed it fit to denounce faculty meetings as a waste of time—"

"We've rehashed the same pointless subjects again and—"

"...and have demonstrated a persistent failure to show respect to Dr. Farnsworth, to your other superiors, and to hand your course syllabi in on time..."

So it goes. I go under while the cultivated accent rolls numbingly on. Once he gets going, the only real way to stop him is with a bazooka or an elephant gun. To distract myself, I glance cautiously around at (for Ashland) his luxurious office, taking in the freshly painted walls, the plush carpet, four or five cushioned chairs, and a row of morocco-bound law books in a bookshelf. I have been informed by several teachers that he failed the New York Bar Exam twice but never could bear to part with them. Also, despite his professed concern for Ashland's welfare, it's almost common knowledge that for years he has interviewed without success for positions at better colleges.

Near a jade name plate engraved with the name Luther Bledsoe, his massive fist wears a ring with a diamond the size of a golf ball. At the President's Reception, which is held once a year at the President's mansion (impressively named Westminister), I heard The Man comment that it was a gift from his wife. Apparently she's loaded. Also, she's almost white. This combination plus his being a Bostonian with a taste for three hundred dollar leather coats, has caused some blacks to resent and to be suspicious of him, to regard him as an outsider and carpetbagger. Looking up, I notice again the steel rim spectacles against his light brown skin, and, as always, I'm surprised to discover that he's a handsome man. Not only don't his good looks seem to fit, but he's handsome in a crude way like some refinement has been left out.

Throughout this, snatches of what he's saying keep slipping through. "Terms of your contract...professional misconduct...need to set an example for your students..." It's only when I hear that my "tardiness this morning results in a failure to use class time fully," that something revives in me from the old days. Before I can stop, I let it pop that *their* tardiness makes it impossible to start class on time anyway.

"That's not true. Students take their guidance from the teacher. If you show up late they feel it's proper to do the same. It's your responsibility—"

I shake my head. "They come in ten minutes late, twenty minutes late, whenever they feel like it. I could start my classes every day at the sound of the bell and it wouldn't make any difference."

"*I* don't have that problem."

"But you're the Dean. With all due respect, they know—"

"It has nothing to do with my position."

"With all due respect, I think it does. Besides, the problem's only aggravated by your reluctance to establish a firm rule. If students knew, for example, that they could only be ten minutes late to class without—"

"You need not concern yourself with administrative matters, Mr. Newman. And let me remind you that at Ashland, students acquire good work habits primarily from their instructors, whose duty it is to maximize the potentialities inherent in the classroom environment and to evaluate pupil progress in terms of behavioral objectives."

Christ, cut the educational bullshit. Aren't you aware of anything? At Ashland, student discipline is a standard joke. I've had them come to class forty minutes late, grinning and disrupting everything. Often they put their heads down on their desks and go to sleep with their tongues hanging out. But I can't say this to Bledsoe. To him, it'll sound racist, like I'm putting them down. Then I'll be out of here like a shot. Button your lip Dave! Sweating, I realize I've gone much too far. I'm digging my grave with my mouth again. Actually it's amazing he's put up with it, what with the run-ins we've already had. Maybe he can't afford to fire people. Turnover is already high here because teachers hate the place. Also, he gets his share of weirdos. Dukes, for example, the black dude I replaced, taught all his courses the same way. Whether it was Shakespeare or Freshman Comp., you got Black Lit. After a while he stopped coming to class. Then one day he loaded his girl students into a U-Haul and carted them off to the Holiday Inn where he set up a prostitution and drugs franchise. I guess next to Dukes, I'm O.K. At least with me he knows what to expect.

Still, The Man hates sass. Years ago a teacher named Baxter threatened to shoot him, so Bledsoe bought a German luger. When Baxter came in, he drew on him and chased him all the way down to the first floor, where he cornered him behind the Coke machine. At the last moment he held back, but the luger lies in his desk still, loaded and ready to go.

Right now something else is coming down the tubes. He flips open a folder and delicately adjusts his steel rim spectacles.

"Mr. Newman, do you know what this is?"

"No."

"It's your file. I took the liberty of pulling it."

"Oh."

"Very interesting. Let me see. Says here you're thirty-eight years old. Received your baccalaureate from Oberlin in Political Science and your M.A. in English from Kent State."

"That's right."

"But you never received your Ph.D."

"No."

"I see. Why is that?"

"Well, at that time there was the war in Southeast Asia and other things, and I guess I—that is—I guess at that time I felt they were more important. Anyway, a doctorate didn't seem to mean anything. Just a piling on of useless knowledge."

"I see. And now?"

"Sir?"

"Well, you've had eleven years to think about it. You could have gone back."

"Yes, well..." I wave my arm in the air. "I guess I didn't."

"Hmm, I see. Just gave up all that work."

"You could say that."

"Just quit."

I don't say anything.

"And gave up the opportunity to contribute something to your specialty, perhaps something that would prove of value to your students."

"Dean Bledsoe."

"Yes?"

"Just how much do you think students here would benefit if I *had* finished my study on 'Seduction and Resistance in *Paradise Lost?*'"

I've scored a hit, at least a slight one. He pauses for a moment.

"That's not the point. I'm trying to discover a pattern in

your past behavior that will explain your present conduct. For example, I notice here that subsequent to your graduate work you have held *several* positions. Penn State, The University of Texas, Wheatfield—"

"Yes, well, it's a mobile profession."

"But six jobs in ten years? It almost looks as if you couldn't hold a job."

I move a little in my chair, which I suddenly realize is rock-hard, unlike the other cushioned chairs in his office. He prods my file as if it's a living, breathing human being he's got there.

"Tell me, Mr. Newman. Just out of curiosity, why did you leave your last place of employment?"

"Oh, the usual reasons."

"Care to amplify?"

I shrug, feeling like Baxter cornered behind the Coke machine.

"Let's just say I wanted to spread out a little. At Farmington, they had me teaching strictly Freshman English."

"I see. Is that the *only* reason?"

By now, sweat's running down my sides. The bastard's toying with me. Any moment now he's going to pounce with something.

I hedge a little. "Well, that's *part* of the reason."

"I see. Part of the reason. Well, Mr. Newman, I took the liberty of contacting Farmington College. Would you like to hear what Dean Shrike wrote back?"

I find a spot just over his shoulder and stare at it.

"Since you don't indicate a preference, I assume you have no objections. 'Dear Dean Bledsoe,' he begins:

> Pursuant to your letter of March 21 concerning Mr. David Newman, who is currently employed at your college. Mr. Newman was an employee at Farmington two years ago and taught courses in first year English. At the end of the year, his contract was not renewed because it was felt not to be in the best interests of the College.

As Dean, I found it necessary to confer with Mr. Newman on several occasions, but my efforts to reach him proved totally ineffectual. Mr. Newman was an agitator who was sharply critical of administrative policies and openly contemptuous of the rules. His effect on faculty members can only be described as highly disruptive. While I can only speculate as to the reason for your inquiry, I assume it involves some similarity to my own experiences with Mr. Newman.

In the event I can assist you further, please feel free to contact me again.

Sincerely,

Robin H. Shrike, Academic Dean

"Comments, Mr. Newman?"

"No, except..."

"What?"

What's the use? It'll be a waste of time to say it to him. Still, it should be said.

"Except that the rules I was 'openly contemptuous' of were stupid and wrong. You know what they wanted me to do? They wanted me to get my hair cut and wear a suit and tie. As far as I'm concerned, that's not only a violation of my personal freedom, but it has nothing to do with teaching. I mean, how's a polka dot tie going to make me a better teacher? And as far as criticizing policies is concerned—"

"Finished, Mr. Newman?"

Cut off, I want to ask him if he knows about the teachers who bore and rip off their students with canned lectures or who simply play records to entertain them. Those who play the game right and draw their pay for doing nothing. But it's a waste of time. He's one of them.

"Finished."

"Very well. Dean Shrike's letter seems to confirm my own assessment of your conduct, but I'm inclined to give you one last chance. If you prove remiss in the future in any way, however, I will find it necessary to dismiss you. Is that clear?"

"Yes."

"On the other hand, perhaps you'd rather *not* teach here next year. Perhaps you have another teaching offer? I rather doubt it, but if you do, let me know now and we can terminate your employment at once."

"No, I'd like to stay."

He leans forward, pretending not to hear.

"What's that? I didn't quite hear you."

This is it, the real cruncher. In rounds one and two I took my knocks but stayed away from him. Now it's round three and time to eat crow. This is what it's been about all along, what he's really been after. He wants to see me crawl.

"No," I repeat, thinking of how I prefer teaching to being a garage mechanic. "I want to stay." I swallow. "I'll follow the rules."

A smile slits his face, and he gazes at me for a moment.

"Thank you, Mr. Newman," he says. "That will be all."

Three

LEAVING THE BUILDING, I come out into the most beautiful
day you ever saw. Birds are singing, and the sun is nailed up
there like a magnet. Seems it should lift my spirits right up to it,
but it doesn't.

To tell the truth, I took quite a banging in there. The Man
can dazzle you when he's in form, and today he was a young
Cassius Clay. Best I can do now is to head home and grab a
couple stiff ones. I've earned them.

Seeing Big Red parked by the WELCOME sign lifts me a little.
When I was a kid, I learned to drive in my family's 1953 stick
shift fire engine red Chevy station wagon. For some reason I'd
always missed it after I left home, and when I finally wound up
here, midway between Dogpatch and nowhere, I was lucky to
find one just like him. A few hundred dollars worth of parts, a
week's work, and presto! he springs like the phoenix out of my
past, although a little the worse for wear and more than ever a
rattling crate. Connie calls me foolish whenever she sees him,
but for me Big Red still delivers the goods.

On my way out, I notice the monument's still down. The
monument is—or was—a pedestal dedicated to Ashland by
the "Class of 1929," and six weeks ago it was destroyed by our
school bus in what has become known as the "Crash of 1929."
It still lies exactly where it fell, a pile of debris.

Crossing those damn railroad tracks again, I turn south past
the green glare of a magnolia and a plantation-style mansion
that's run to ruin. Green Town in early April is pink, red,
white, violet. Azaleas, dogwood, wisteria saturate its streets.
Azaleas especially, great gorgeous globs of them. Wisteria
climbs and intertwines itself to the tops of the tallest trees.
Leaning back, I drink it all in and gun Big Red along the tracks.

Railroads: that's the South. Half the towns started as whistle stops and are cut in two by nowhere tracks to other towns.

And the signs! South Carolina must be the fireworks mecca of the world, for outside the towns you find gaudy cartoons on billboards a hundred feet long advertising goodies for the simple-minded. SILLY SALLEYS. CRAZY CLEMS. NUTTY NEDS. Inside, there's firecrackers and cherry bombs and enough munitions to wage another Civil War. Obscene playing cards and ashtrays. Nutcrackers shaped as women with opposable thighs, just insert it and crunch! I have a theory. It's my personal belief that to future historians, the dominant art form of the twentieth century will be the road sign. That's where we're really at. Not cubism or expressionism but Colonel Sanders with his Golden Arches.

I rent a house ten miles from town, and the scenery on the way is typical of S.C. Fields and telephone poles are swallowed up by kudzu. There's a white Baptist church with a scraggly cemetery and shacks on stacked blocks with rust brown tin roofs. Black kids play in dirt yards. They swing in tires hung from trees, and some are nearly naked. Where I live is itself no prize. It leaks and the door doesn't lock. But I'm not choosy. The way I see it, it's like a lot of places I've been. Connie complains when she visits and hounds me to get an apartment in town, but I'll be damned if I'll pay $50 more for a dump the size of a shoebox.

When I get home I head straight for the hooch and pour myself a bomber, and by the time Connie comes in, I'm doing a slow backstroke in my second drink and dining on Manischewitz Matzo Crackers. The corners of the day are pleasantly rounded, and Elton's waving good-by to that "Yellow Brick Road" again.

Connie does what she always does when she drops in. Starch white in her dental assistant's uniform, she places her cleaning equipment on a chair and starts straightening up the place, putting this here, that there, acting just like she's at work arranging instruments on a tray. She's compulsive that way and I bet when she goes to heaven, she'll start by straightening

St. Peter's halo and checking the Pearly Gates for dust.
Still, she has a figure that would make a corpse salivate.
When she gets within striking distance I make a grab and pull
her into my lap. My hand leaps up her sleek nyloned thigh like
a salmon.

"Hey!"

I don't give her a chance. I press my lips to hers and drink in
her softness and warmth. Beneath the medicinal veneer her
woman smell comes through. Her arms come around me and
we get close. I can feel her breasts against my chest, her
eyelashes flicker against my own. Her thighs are smooth and I
nudge them apart, maneuvering for the inside where there's no
nylon. She opens them, and I dive for pay dirt.

Then she's off my lap and laughing.

"Whoa, partner, why in such a rush?"

Abandoned, I take in her luscious figure and crisp auburn
hair.

"We've only got an hour."

"Not today. Dr. Snyder's taking the whole afternoon off."

"No kidding! Why's that—he got something going on the
side?"

She laughs, showing teeth she likes to nip me with.

"If you knew Snyder like I do, you wouldn't say that. He's a
real family man, taken his boy fishing."

"Why bless me. In that case, let's get it on. As the poet says,
'Gather ye rosebuds while ye may—' "

"Not so fast. I want to straighten up here first. Besides, you
couldn't last five hours."

"Slanderer."

"David?"

"Hmmm?"

"What's this?"

She stands with a shirt in her hand.

"A shirt."

"I can see that, but what's it doing on the floor? Oh, David,
don't you *ever* clean up? How can you stand to live in all this
confusion?"

"Confusion? What confusion? I know *exactly* where everything is." I take another belt from my drink as she stands there in exasperation, her white uniform already coming unhooked as a result of running around to put my life in order. I'm feeling superb-o. I flop lazily over to execute a slow Newman Crawl, thinking of an hour from now when I have her white stays off and can negotiate on *my* terms.

Suddenly her brown eyes register horror.

"David! What's that?"

"What?"

She goes to the sink. "My god, are these the *same* beans we had Thursday? Why didn't you *refrigerate* them like I told you? How can you *stand* to let them just sit here?"

I take a sip and a bite of cracker, beginning to get annoyed by her nit-picking. Christ, it's like Bledsoe all over again.

"Now look, Connie," I say, "if you don't—"

But she's already off again, tackling a pile of dirty clothes over by the john and slipping them into a laundry bag she brought with her.

"Say, Connie…"

"What?"

"Where do you do my clothes, anyway—a laundromat?"

"No, at home."

"At *home*? But what about your husband?"

"Arnold? What about him?"

"Well—doesn't he notice?"

"Notice what?"

"The clothes. I mean, they're not *his*. Doesn't he ever *see* all those clothes and ask questions?"

"Arnold?" She laughs and neatly snaps the strings of the laundry bag shut. "Not Arnold, he never notices anything."

So she's been doing my stuff right under Arnold's nose. Poor slob's even paying for it. I muddle the thing over in amazement before discovering my drink's dead. I hold the glass up, offering it backward over my shoulder.

"Connie."

"What? Oh." Quickly she takes it and goes to the fridge. Super-efficient Connie. For all her neat-as-a-pin-let-me-put-

24

your-life-in-order-mentality, she'd make a lovely geisha for the right man. A thought strikes me.

"Say, Connie?"

"Yes, love?"

Why is it, do you suppose, most of the women I see lately are married?"

"What do you mean?" Behind me, I can hear her wrestling with the icetray in the prehistoric Kelvinator that came with the place.

"Well, you for example, and about sixty other women in the last couple years. All married, slipping away to see me on the sly. Why is it, do you suppose?"

A cold drink is deposited in my hand from behind. Connie appears in front of me.

"Maybe it's because you're such a fantastic lover. Married women really go for that, you know."

"No, seriously, I want to know. You don't mind my asking?"

"Why should I mind?"

"Well, you haven't told me much about your marriage, and the question *is* kind of personal."

She shrugs. "It's O.K. Anyway, I can't answer for the others, but speaking for myself, well, I want someone who's not tied down or about to get tied down. Someone without roots who I can do something for."

"A tumbleweed, you mean."

"Something like that."

Somehow I don't like the idea of me as a tumbleweed and sensing this, she kneels beside the chair.

"Hey, cheer up."

"Sorry."

"That's O.K." She strokes my hand, looking up. "How's your drink?"

"Drink?" Remembering it, I take a sip of what proves to be gin and tonic. "*Bellissimo.*"

She laughs, tilting her head to one side. "Thank you, kind sir."

"Connie."

"Yes?"

"Sorry about that."

"That's O.K., honey. Anyway, the other thing's true too. You *are* a fantastic lover, and married girls like that. Believe me, I know."

Suddenly everything's all right again. I put the glass down, and we go into a marathon kiss. This time it's like a cool swim on a hot summer day with her hand caressing my hair in waves. I feel like diving into her and never coming up. Then the phonograph gets into it by getting stuck. Sighing, she draws back, and I get up to flip the album.

When I turn around she's in her apron at the sink clashing pots together like cymbals and scraping macaroni off the previous weekend of my life. The water's going full blast and for a while I just stand sipping the fine drink she's made me and watch the neat bow she's tied in back bounce like a wind-up key on some big-as-life mechanical toy. She's a regular dynamo, Connie is, and for a moment I get to wondering what it would be like to be married and, as they say, settled down, and to come home to someone like her every night. Maybe I've been missing something all these years. But then she'd probably be doing someone else's laundry right under my nose and I'd be too much of a jerk to notice.

Come to think of it, what's a hot item like her doing with him anyway? Whenever she mentions Arnold, which isn't often, it's to dismiss him as a nonentity. Seems to me she said once he was in PR for some local company.

"Covington Tool," she says when I ask, not turning around. "He's their Director of Advertising and Public Relations."

"Sounds exhilarating."

"It's O.K."

"Pay much?"

"About thirty."

Thirty thousand. As an instructor I get nine nine. The bastard, he can pay my rent too if he wants.

"So why work? With that kind of bread you could eat bonbons all day in bed and I could come over to service *you*."

"Male pig."

"You like your job, then, I take it."

She shrugs. "It's all right. Anyway, it gets me out of the house."

"And you've got no kids."

"No."

"Intend to have any?"

She turns partly around while drying a plate. "Why do you ask?"

"Just curious. You don't talk much about ol' Arnie, and I was wondering if you two had any plans in that direction."

Even with as much as I've stowed away, I know I'm being nosy. Connie's nice about it, though. Or indifferent: a classic case of an inactive ego. Outside her sanitation fetish, she just doesn't seem to take things personally or to have any drives or ambitions. Except her sex drive, that is, which can frazzle the doughtiest of drivers on the hairpin turns.

"No, we don't plan on any kids," she says. "Couldn't have them anyway."

"Why's that?"

"Arnold had a vasectomy last summer."

"A vasectomy? No shit. Was that his idea?"

"No, mine."

"And ol' Arnie just sat still for it? The snip snip routine and all?"

"Uh huh." A lazy smile grazes her lips. "Better watch it, big boy, you could be next."

I make a show of covering my crotch.

"But don't you want any kids?"

"Not particularly."

"What about Arnold?"

"Arnold?" She laughs. "'Ol' Arnie,' as you call him, is too tired when he comes home to care about anything except watching Starsky and Hutch. Besides, if you want to know the truth, he's—well, he's impotent half the time, and I, well, we just don't..."

She lets the sentence hang in the air.

27

"You mean the bloom's off the rose?"

"Something like that."

"So why don't you get a divorce?"

"Why should I do that?"

"Well, if you feel there's not much left..."

"I still don't get you."

"Well, if you feel there's not much left, why don't you bail out? Try for something better?"

"Better? You mean like another man?"

"Maybe."

"Like you?"

"Well..."

She laughs softly. "You see, David, it's not always so easy. Besides, it's not *that* bad with Arnold. We get along, and in our own way we understand each other. Believe me, plenty of women have it a lot worse."

"And he never suspects?"

"Oh, I think he does. Beneath the surface, he probably knows everything. But it's part of our...agreement not to say anything."

"I see." My drink's empty, and the phonograph is stuck again in the middle of "Goodbye Yellow Brick Road." I lift the needle and not too steadily plonk it on its way. Something about the song jars my memory.

"Connie, ever see *The Wizard of Oz?*"

"Sure, all kids do."

"Remember the beginning where Dorothy leaves the land of the Munchkins and starts off on the Yellow Brick Road to get to the Emerald City?" Something in me squeezes into a fist, gets mad at her. "The part where she seems to feel it isn't good enough, that she has to find something better? Well, I guess that's me. If things aren't good enough, I try to improve them."

"And if it doesn't work, or no one listens when you complain?"

"I move on."

"Where to?"

"To...to..."

Again she laughs. "Poor David, it's time to grow up and come down to Earth. Accept Kansas. There is no Yellow Brick Road or Emerald City. And the Wizard's..."

Yeah, I know. The Wizard's a phony named Bledsoe behind a curtain of power.

She goes back to her dishes and I watch her from behind. Scrub. Scrub. Bounce. Bounce. Spurning diplomacy, I attack from the rear and put my arms around her. She presses back against me.

"Come on, baby, let's go."

"Sure you're up to it?"

"When have I ever failed you?"

The back of her neck is warm and fragrant. My hands develop minds of their own and work beneath her white blouse. Each is blessed with more than it can hold. Her nipples feel like soft spear points.

Still, she doesn't stop with the dishes but continues to scrub away. I swear, if a rapist ever gets hold of Connie, he'll have to wait until everything's squeaky clean.

I'm biting her ear lobe when she finally finishes and puts the towel away. In a second her breasts are against me and she wraps her arms around my neck. Her tongue sweetens my mouth and she starts moaning.

Enough. I take her hand and pull her toward the bed, my mind bent on carnage. At the last moment she draws back.

"Wait—let me straighten it first."

"The hell with that!"

I push her down and instantly I've got a tiger by the tail. Hot as I am, I'm holding on for dear life. Connie aroused is a four alarm fire, a bucking bronco, moans in my ear and legs coiled around my waist squeezing the breath out of me. Before I know it, I'm on my back, shirt and pants open while she does all sorts of naughty things. Kicking my shoes off, I slough my duds and turn her over. She peels her panties. I don't even wait. I enter immediately and answer her thrust for thrust. Almost instantly she has her first orgasm. Her legs rise to my shoulders and she makes sounds like a man. I'm on Cloud Nine. Swelling

29

with pride and power, I drive her up toward the brass design work of the headboard. Again she comes, using the words I love to hear and calling me baby, stud, telling me she loves me, she wants it, raking my back with her nails. Her legs squeeze and scissor-lock my rib cage and she does all sorts of things with her hands to bring me pleasure. I drown in her colors, approach the cliff. Then she's begging me to join her in a great leap beyond ourselves: "Come with me, now, baby, come. Come with me now, Come with me, Baby, come, Come!"

Blast-off. My whole body puckers in pain as I gather the world's honey. Then I avalanche. Her legs rise to my shoulders again, and this time her nails rake me as we fall.

Four

AFTERWARDS SHE'S FULL of mischief and still frisky as a rabbit. I feel like a breather, though, and roll off to gaze up at the ceiling, which reflects my thoughts like a giant mirror.

Bledsoe's face is up there, threatening, his logic as madly irrefutable as Big Brother's. Then there's Hart. What could he have done that made the Dean call him in and fire him on the spot? Must have been pretty terrible, whatever it was, especially when you consider what Yours Truly and others have gotten away with. Maybe Duffy's right about a cover-up.

All of a sudden Connie nips my ear. I squirm away but she's too fast and whispers into it.

"Five minutes? You don't give a Yankee much time to recuperate."

"Yankee? I thought you were a Southern boy."

"Hardly, ever hear a Reb speak this way? No accent?"

"Then where *are* you from?"

"You mean last year or the year before last?"

"Originally."

"Originally? That takes me back a long way. Hard to remember. Let me see—Ohio."

"Ohio! Well, what do you know. It's a small world."

"How so?"

"I'm from Ohio, too. As a matter of fact, I graduated with a B.A in Sociology from there in 1970."

"Yeah, what school?"

"Kent State."

"Kent State?" I look at her with interest. "Well, fancy that. It *is* a small world. I crashed that scene too."

"Well well."

"Well well well."

"Well, hi."

"Hi, yourself."

"Old Home Week."

"Yeah."

The fact that we both went to the same school is a bond. I turn over on my stomach and stroke her hair. Above her upper lip runs a line of tiny beads of perspiration.

"Funny."

"Hmmm?"

"I just mean it's funny that after all these years, you and I both wind up here. In Green Town, South Carolina, of all places. My God, the chances of that happening must be astronomical."

"Sure is hard to believe."

"You're darn right it is. And look at the questions it raises. I mean, we're two different people. You're steady, reliable. I'm..."

"A tumbleweed."

"Yeah, a tumbleweed. Which makes it all the more unlikely. By what special providence do two people like us, so completely different, arrive here at the same time in the same place? I mean, what is the common element that unites us? Is there some hidden resemblance, greater than the sum of all our differences, that accounts for it? Maybe if we could just see beneath the surface of things—"

She stops me by tapping my shoulder. "Hey, you're doing it again."

"Doing what?"

"You're *analyzing* again, like all you intellectuals do. You know, David, it's not really as mind-boggling as you make it sound. In the first place, like you say, I *am* a steady person. I married Arnold right after graduation and moved down here to his home town. And I've been here ever since. And you..."

"What about me?"

She smiles. "Well, like you said, you're a 'tumbleweed'. Sooner or later you were bound to pass this way."

Her matter-of-fact attitude annoys me, but I'm suddenly struck by something else.

"You know, when you think about it, it's surprising we

never met. Kent State isn't all that big, and we were there at the same time."

"Ships that pass in the night."

"Yeah, and who knows, if we'd met maybe we'd have gotten together. Maybe you'd have taken the wind out of my sails and there would have been no Arnold and we would have spent the last eleven years in Middlefield, Ohio on my father's farm. I'd have been respectable as hell and every Saturday night we'd go into town for an all-you-can-eat fish fry at the Cartwright Inn and watch the Amish ride their wagons up and down Main Street. How does *that* grab you?"

She makes a face. "Thanks, but I'll stick with Arnold. Anyway, it could never have happened."

"Why not?"

"Well, you're too much of a drifter. I can't imagine you ever settling down on a farm."

"I see. Bet you never had that kind of problem. You were probably *born* domesticated."

"Oh, no, I wasn't. It may interest you to know, Professor Know-It-All, that I was once a hippie who was into *everything!*"

"Aw, go on!"

"No, I mean it, I hit the whole scene. Sex. Pot. Vietnam. I was in more sit-ins and occupied more buildings than you ever did. And drugs. I've had enough acid, coke, uppers and downers to turn on for a lifetime. I was always running around trying to overthrow the Establishment and yelling how corrupt it was."

"Oh, come on, you don't even like it when I smoke!"

"Well, it's true. I was a regular revolutionary. Revolution For The Hell Of It! Roast A Pig! Burn Baby Burn! Free The Chicago Seven!"

It's too much. I try to swallow it, but it's like a watermelon. All I can do is ask "What happened?"

"Happened?"

"Yeah, how come you changed? What happened to you? Look, you remember the May 4th massacre, don't you?"

"Sure."

"Well, so do I. In fact, I was there."

"You mean you were actually—"

I close my eyes. It's a beautiful sunny day in early May. Guardsmen on the hill. Students at the bottom, throwing stones that land fifty feet short. Kids against kids. Then I hear crackling sounds. What's that? Five feet away a student vomits blood and goes down, looking at me with stricken eyes. Everyone's screaming—

"David, you're trembling!"

I open my eyes. "I was there," I say. "I saw them die. I could have gone too."

She touches me. "But that was eleven years ago."

"One of them put a flower in a guardsman's rifle the day before. She was a nice kid. I knew her."

"David—"

"You know, Connie, I think it was that day which really put direction into my life. Up to then I was always trying to change things, and when I got to Kent State there was revolution in the air. The SDS and other groups were involved and I knew their leaders personally and learned how to operate from them. But it was that sunny day with kids dying around me, that I think I first really began to understand how the system works and what I had to do. You know, those kids weren't within a city block of them and they just mowed them down like weeds. Sure, it's perfectly all right to invade Cambodia, but protest a little and it's the Firing Squad for you. And talk about cover-ups!"

"I know, it was a complete whitewash, wasn't it?"

"You're damn right. And the whole rotten system hasn't changed a twitch since then, either. It's still phony and hypo-critical. Politicians spout pious morality on the one hand and plan Watergates and foreign assassinations on the other. They lock you up and throw away the key for possessing an ounce of grass while taking bribes and humping secretaries who can't type at taxpayers' expense." I pause and look at her. "You know, what I can't understand is how you could forget all that, Connie, how you could give up the fight completely and settle down here with—Arnold."

For a moment I think she's going to let me have it. Then her eyes soften like she's trying to remember. After a while her words come back from a long distance. "You know, at one time it did mean a lot to me. It was almost my whole life. I *did* care. And I took risks for what I believed in, tried to change—"

"That's what I can't understand. Why—"

"Why did I give it up?" Eleven years peel from her gaze in seconds. "But it all seems so *unreal* now, so childish. I mean, all that protesting, what did it ever accomplish? Nothing. If there were any changes made, it was by people who couldn't care less what we felt, and who changed things for their own selfish reasons. I mean, it was all just a waste of time, a fad of the sixties to let off steam. An excuse to get stoned, get laid, and get on the six o'clock news. An ego trip."

"Well, I don't feel that way. I haven't—"

"I know you haven't," she says. "You're still fighting the dead fight. Oh, David, no one cares, it's all just bullshit and business and money and politics. Look, you're always complaining about where you're working now, how poor the school is, how those who run the place are only interested in ripping off the students. You're still crusading. And what progress have you made? Have you even got an organization started? No. And the upshot of it all is that you'll probably be out in a year, and the school will grind on without even missing you."

She's right, of course. Dead right. Damn her, not only has she fooled me with her spikey past, she's also told my life story. God knows I've packed more suitcases than you can shake a travel sticker at. Turning away from her, I lie back and look up at a plumbing discoloration on the ceiling.

"Hey, Connie, get me a stick, will you?"

"Sure, hon, where are they?"

"In my pants, along with my lighter."

She gets up and picks up my pants from the floor. For a moment I think she's going to say something about my smoking or how sloppy I am, but she doesn't. That's one thing about Connie: usually she knows when to keep silent. I watch her fish through my pockets. Her buttocks are delicately rounded and the sun, streaking through the pinch-pleated draperies she picked for the place, turns to gold the even more delicate hairs that fleece her body. After a minute she finds a pack of Camels and comes back to the bed.

"I didn't know anyone smoked these anymore."

"They don't. I'm a relic. Actually, I started smoking these back in Ohio behind the barn, and I've been ruining my lungs with them ever since. Take my word for it, they're poison."

"You don't have to convince me. I've seen what tobacco does to teeth."

She places it between my lips, lights it, and starts playing with the hair on my chest. "Tell me," she says, her hand straying lower, "how did a farm boy like you ever wind up teaching literature?"

"Good question. I guess I overreacted to the notion of spending my days ankle deep in manure. Anyway, I've always hated physical labor. In other words, I'm lazy."

"I see. How's that?"

"Oooooh, yummy. Where'd you learn to do it that way?"

"I've had lots of practice."

"You don't have to convince me. Hmm, that's super. I like the way you—"

Right then the phone rings.

I lie there while John bangs out "Rocket Man," wanting only the launching pad of her fingers and my cigarette. But Connie, natch, is too tidy to let a phone go unanswered. Rising, she hops across the floor and rescues the receiver on the third ring.

"Hello. —David? Just a moment, please."

I get up reluctantly and take it from her.

"Hello?"

"Hello, Dave. How did it go this morning?"

Duffy. With his Bledsoe fixation I might have known he'd call.

"It went fine, Duff. He was Sodom, I was Gomorrah."

"Really reamed you, huh?"

"Let's just say he threatened my job for about the eighty-seventh time and then broke my bones for emphasis."

"Did he give you a chance to explain *why* you were late, or did he just blow you down like he usually does?"

With Connie listening, I don't want to go into details. God knows, I've said enough already. Also, I've had it with the subject. One way or another, it seems like I'm still stalled at the tracks at 7:25 A.M. and everyone keeps bringing it up. Any minute now, I expect Amos 'n Andy to barge in. "Hey, der, white foaks, was dis I hear 'bout you bein' late ta class dis mawnin'?"

And Duffy. He'll want to know *everything,* up to and beyond the look on The Man's face the moment he cut 'em off and presented them to me as a memento. For my own sake, I better cut it short.

"Look, Duff," I say, "do you mind if we go into this later? Right now, I've got company."

"Oh sure, I noticed the voice. Sexy."

"I'll tell her."

"Why don't you put her on and let me do that?"

"Sure thing. Want me to tell her first you're married?"

"You bastard. Anyway, why don't you come over tonight for a free meal and fill me in on the latest episode of the Bledsoe Blitz? Sylvia would like to meet you."

"Thanks, but I'm whipped out. How about tomorrow if it's not inconvenient?"

"No, that'll be fine. Anytime around six. And bring your secretary with you."

"Maybe I will."

"Right, see you then."

I hang up, and Connie jumps right in.

"What's this about your job being on the line again?"

"It's nothing."

"It didn't sound like nothing." She looks at me suspiciously. "David, are you in trouble with the Dean again?"

"Leave it alone, will you? It's nothing."

"Then you are in trouble again. Oh, David, what did you do this time?"

"Nothing, I was just late to class."

"Oh, David!"

"It wasn't my fault. The train came early and by the time it passed—"

"David, you know the Dean has it in for you. Why do you *insist* on provoking him? If I didn't know better, I'd think you wanted trouble."

"That's ridiculous. The train just came early, that's all."

"But you're always doing things like this. If it's not a train—"

"Look, drop it, huh? Don't make a federal case out of it."

"But I can't drop it. Oh David, you're so intelligent and gifted, I can't stand to see you throw it away all the time and waste it. If you just planned things better and took a little care—"

I go to the window and gaze out at the pond in back. Damned if it isn't like facing Bledsoe all over again. Turning, I start to tell her to get off my case in stronger terms, but decide against it. Instead I go over and try to put my arms around her.

"Stop it, David, I'm in no mood—"

"Come on, pet, forget about—"

"No! I don't think it's right."

She pushes away and I'm treated to the sight of Connie pouting. What the hell is this? First she switches me with her Patty Hearst track record, and now she's acting like a little girl. And all because I've outraged her sense of neatness and order. People like Connie, I realize again, take loose ends in the lives of others as a personal insult. It's like a stain on the blueprint of their existence. Everything has to be in its ordered place: husband, job, lover, dental instruments, dinner dishes. And God help you if there's any dust in your closets.

In a last effort at salvaging things, I take her hand. She snaps it away.

"Stop it!"

"Why are you acting this way?"

"Because you've let me down!"

"Let you down? What are you talking about? I'm not your husband. Who gave you the right to come in here and—"

"I'm just saying you should be more careful what you do

and stop giving people a chance to hurt you."

"Yeah? And I suppose the train was my fault. Maybe I should have *pole*-vaulted over it."

"No, of course not. I'm not saying that."

"Then what are you saying?"

"I don't know. Maybe you should start by buying a suit and getting yourself a haircut."

"Aw, hell!" Suddenly I'm sick of the whole thing, Connie, Bledsoe, everything, and start getting dressed.

"Look, David—"

"Damn it, who are you to lecture me about anything? Messing around while the guy you practically castrated sits at home home." I look for my other shoe and find it under the bed. "You know something? You're just another phony, like everyone else."

She's beside me now, all reconciliation. I move away.

"David, what's wrong?"

"Nothing." I stuff my wallet in my pocket and grab my keys.

"David, please don't go. Can't we talk this over?"

Outside, her Toyota glitters in the sun beside the green blades of a yucca plant. I ram the key into Big Red and gun him for all he's worth. *Arrrrrr...Arrrrrr...Arrrrrr...* No dice, the sun has cooked him to death. Sweating, I crank the window down. Connie comes outside and the screen door spanks shut behind her. She stands in a pair of panties in the brilliant sun with her arms folded across her breasts. Looking straight at her, I try the ignition again. *Arrrrrrrrrrr!*

Momentarily I waver as common sense batters against my anger. Then the engine catches and before I can stop, I've shifted into reverse and Connie goes wheeling past. My right foot stabs the brake and as the back wheels struggle for a purchase on gravel, my left foot hits the clutch and I slip the gearshift into first. In the corner of my eye I see Connie, sensuous and spurned. For an instant I'm two people, sanity to stop and create, madness to be wreckage forever. Then Big Red shoots forward onto the highway churning gravel, and I floor the pedal for town.

Five

THE DAY IS bone-white hot. To my right I pass the fairgrounds where they race stock cars on weekends. Every year at the county fair they have a freak show there. Two-headed babies and other assorted goodies. Come one, come all. Inside I recognize the symptoms. I'm an impulsive person by nature, and sometimes when I get worked up I'm like a paratrooper who jumps without a parachute. Occasionally I don't even know what I'm going to do and it turns out to be dangerous.

Once, in Canada, I damn near killed myself. I was riding in a ski lift with a long-haired girl of smashing looks, and the furthest thing from my mind was to do something chancy. We were flirting in a casual way and I asked her if she had ever made it on a lift before. Above us were the mountains, white-capped, serene, and beautiful. I could see every rock crag, every birch tree in the clear chill winter air. As we rose toward them, her breath kept clouding before my face. She had very white bright teeth and I remember thinking that she was beginning to get interested and if I played it right I could be in Nirvana by nightfall. At the top we got off the lift and headed down one of the intermediate slopes. The snow was pure powder in spots, absolutely first-rate, and as I worked the first moguls I felt the excitement take over and burst into a kind of somnambulistic prayer: Please, God, don't let me do it. Whatever it is, don't let me do it. Let me reach the bottom in one piece.

Near the base of the slope, just before it levels out toward the lodge, there's a mogul that hot-doggers like to hit. It's not for the geriatric set but for someone with a twenty-year old spine and the split-second reflexes and coordination of a gazelle. Riding up on the other lift, I've passed practically right over it and seen kids attack it and rise 15, 18 feet off the surface. Once, the timing was such I could almost have touched the kid. If you misjudge things just a pinch and come down askew, you can snap your legs like twigs and plow up half of Ontario with your face.

Anyway, coming down the slope I find myself skipping the christies and driving the poles into the snow. I pass the girl, who yells "Hey!" and a moment later, apparently knowing something I don't about my intentions, she screams. I hit the mother dead center and flat out, planting the poles and unweighting just before the summit. Then I'm climbing off the edge of the world and fighting to keep my skiis together. Suddenly sane, I try to scream. My guts go cold to my knees and ram out right through my ass hole. Far far beneath me is the snow and I'm still rising Jesus still rising and there's no way to apply the tips I've read in *The Canadian Ski Technique* to *this*. Just before I swallow my heart, I stop rising and hang suspended above the mountains. Then, Sweet God, I'm coming down down down and manage to hit first the left ski then the right at an angle so that I shear to the left and hold an instant before losing it as my right ski and boot come off and I break my left ankle rolling over and over and over... Later, the doctor tells me how lucky I am to escape with an injury that will sideline me for only six weeks.

And what will it be this time? Usually, when I get this way, I simply tell people what I think of them rather than engage in daredevil shenanigans. But you never know. Right now, if externals mean anything, I seem to be opting for the nonviolent route, cruising sedately into town well within the speed limit. I'm curious as all get out as to what I'm going to do, and somewhere within me a voice is saying, don't do it. No matter how revved up you are, stow your death wish and get your head together. For God's sake, sit down and take a stress pill.

I'm on Jackson Street now, in what used to be the heart of the city but which has since run a bit to seed. Some of the stores are vacant and up for rent, and the business section faces increasing competition from two modern shopping malls to the north. The square, as I enter it, is numb and silent in the heat. Sweat fills my eyes, and I wipe it away as I pass the Court House, Penney's, station WNVB, and Banker's Trust. Abandoned on his pedestal, the Confederate soldier keeps his vigil aloft over nothing, an ancient flintlock pointed down at his feet.

Two blocks past the square, I turn the wheel over to the curb in front of a pawn shop and kill the ignition. Around me the soulful street-talk slurs and slips and eludes my understanding, defiant alike of Northern liberals and Standard English. Approaching my mogul, I get out and start walking. A couple of them look at me in curiosity. Then I'm out of the sun and standing at the very heart of darkness, the Parable of the Cave operating in reverse. Suddenly I know what my mission is and blazing with enlightenment, move past a thousand false forms. An emerald green juke box. A Pabst Beer sign. A faded mural from the 60's with men and women in afros and African clothing. Faces turn, look at me blankly. Moving around the pool table, I pluck a stick from the rack and chalk its tip.

"Belly up, boys, who wants to be the first to hand me his money?"

Silence. They watch me.

"Boys," I say, twirling the stick, "let us not be bashful. I'm a bad-assed hustler from the white side of the tracks, and I sho' would like the priv'ledge of sep'ratin' some of you dudes from your hard earned food stamps and welfare checks."

That gets the natives restless.

"Hey, man, what's this shit?"

"Yeah, who let the honky in?"

"Cat's smashed on dope."

"Gotta be, come in here."

"Ooooo-Eeeee! Who's gonna let 'im out?"

"Shit, man, he come in here, let *'im* see he can git out."

In my hands the pool stick is a living thing.

"Four ball, corner pocket."

Whack! Bull's eye!

"Hey man."

"What's that, Rufus?"

"Name ain't Rufus, friend. That was *my* shot ya just screwed up."

"Gee, that's too bad, Rufus." I move around the table. "Six ball, bank." Plink. "Right in the old apple basket."

I stand up and grin at him with satisfaction. He's fat as a slug and jet black. Sports a jagged scar on his left cheek. Each of his ear lobes is pierced by a gold round earring. Obviously a mean customer, he's the kind you cross streets to avoid meeting.

Studying the table, I pick my next shot, a hairy one with the eight ball partly concealed.

"Eight ball, corner pocket."

Wap!

His hand shoots out and spears the cue ball before it makes contact. He stands tossing it up and down.

"You've hijacked my ball, capt'n," I tell him.

"In a minute I'm gonna *cut* 'em off, man. Maybe ya don't hear so good. I said—"

"Let *me* have 'im, Reggie."

"Unh unh, Eddie. This dude's all mine. Wanna see he's so cool with that stick pokin' up his ass."

"Aw, Rufus," I say, "is that any way to treat a guest? Where's your Southern hospitality?"

"Right here, man." A switchblade snaps open in his hand. "I got all the *hos-pi-tal-i-ty* here ya wants."

Suddenly I laugh. My God, I haven't seen one of those things since James Dean in *Rebel Without A Cause*.

"I don't know, Reggie," Eddie says. He's a cool dude with shades on and a t-shirt that reads In and Out Car Wash. "Maybe ya ought to let 'im go. He's fuckin' crazy."

"Yeah, Reg," another says. "I don't want no part of this. Let's kick 'im out."

I straighten up. They're getting away from me, and if I don't make my point soon I'll be back on the street. Placing my hand on the table, I vault onto it and swing the stick like Cyrano. Crack! The switchblade clatters across the room and thrusting quickly, I poke his fat gut. Touché!

Yells. Shouts. Cries of "Get the mothah!" Swinging the stick

43

about me in an arc, I drive them back while the voices rage inside me, one screaming for sanity and counseling a fast break for the door, the other on fire with its fierce purpose. Raising my staff, I suddenly achieve absolute silence, a transformation not unlike Moses' parting of the Red Sea. Through the window I see them packed outside on the street trying to see, and as I savor the moment, a revelation flashes upon me. It is a vision of my final confrontation with Bledsoe on the field of Armageddon when news of *this* caper gets out.

"Gentlemen," I say, "I'd like to speak to you today about a part of our heritage of which you are the most recent but by no means final flower. I speak, of course, of that testament to American Idealism and Initiative: the three hundred years of systematic exploitation of the black man."

"Aw, jeez," someone says, "do we gotta stand here—"

"No, don't listen!" I shout, raising the staff. "Get real skunked up and don't listen. Act like any other ignorant mob and show me how smart you are with your beer and fifth grade educations and your dead-end jobs. Come on! I bet if you put your minds to it, you can get real tough and beat the hell out of one white man."

I've got them now because they don't know what the hell's going down. They stare at me uncertainly, like sailors on the verge of mutiny. Reggie's recovered his knife and stands looking up at me searching for a place to stick it. His face gleams with sweat. His dime-sized nostrils flare. Pointing a finger at him, I use a trick I've used in class lots of times.

"You, Reggie, so hot to stick me with that thing. As a representative of those gathered here, do you know why you can barely read and write, why you can't get a decent job? *Do you?*"

I wait for him to answer, then shout at the room: "Do *any* of you?"

"The white man—" one of them says.

Warming up, I cut him off and turn back to Reggie whose face is filled with hate. "Sure, blame Whitey," I snap. "That's always easy. But check any history book and you'll find that the first slaves were sold to this country with the aid of black men. In other words, your *own* people first sold you out. For money. And they're *still* doing it! Tell me, Reggie, did you know *that?*"

He's mad as hell now and even more dangerous than before because of his shame. He doesn't like not knowing the answers and he doesn't like what I've been telling him about blacks. In his face two emotions rage back and forth. Hate. Shame. Hate. Shame. Like some intense, emotional drum solo.

"Let me tell you something else, Reggie. Let's skip three hundred years and jump from Africa to what's happening right now in this very room. What do we find? I'll tell you what we find. We find that the centuries-old rip-off of the black man is still going on. Just look at yourselves. You can barely read and write, and because of that you can't get decent jobs and make decent money so you can hold your heads up with pride. You're losers, ghetto rats, and this same town you live in couldn't care less what happens to you. To it you're niggers who can never be any better because you're born stupid and second-rate. And you want to know the worst of it? This is all aided and abetted by corrupt blacks. Only now they don't wear tribal robes but three hundred dollar suits with precision cuffs. In others words, they're socked into the system more than *this white man* will ever be. They're whiter than white, pal, and their hearts and balls belong to Exxon, General Motors—"

"That's a lotta bull!"

"The hell it is!" I shout back. "Take this college in town, for example. Supposedly it exists to educate poor blacks. But it doesn't. It's just a business, part of our national bureaucracy. The school gets federal juice for each student, so all it cares about is numbers. To hell with education. To hell with students. To hell with Green Town and the boys in the Rainbow bar. Do you think it even cares what you feel or what happens to you? Hell, no, all it wants is more money so it can introduce more government programs that coddle students whom this state has never taught to read and write and drown them in

45

soul-expanding exercises of gibberish that destroy forever their last chance to learn. And it's all done with black support, man. Black presidents, black deans—"

But I've lost him, lost them all. I've gotten too highfalutin and over their heads and before I can even start on the nuts 'n bolts of how to organize and change things, Reggie jabs his blade at me, trying to skewer me like a kebob. I yell "Stop!" but he won't listen. Won't any of them listen. Furious, I raise the cue stick and bring it down like an ax on top of his head. Crack! It breaks right in two. Reggie doesn't even blink as he climbs up on the table to get me.

I jump back and trip over a pool ball. Then everything's slow motion as I go over backward with Reggie coming after me. For a long time I watch him come, just he and his switch-blade as I fall inch by inch like I'm dazed or drugged or caught in the quicksand of one of those dreams where you try to get away and run and run and look back and it's getting closer and emerald green light gleams on the knife blade as he brings it down...

Then my arm's seized in a terrible grip and I'm erect and awake again. Reggie's still there but whoever's got me, has him too. A huge hand holds him at bay, its fingers pressed like bars against his chest.

"Come on, Mr. Newman."

I try to see who it is, but I'm propelled through the crowd like a leaf. My feet hit the door step and instead of falling, I'm borne upright into the blinding sun. The hand holds me so hard it hurts, and again I try to see who it is. But all I can do is blink sweat and see stinging red slits of color.

A door opens; I'm at my car. Finally I can see and gaze up at a familiar face. It's a smooth, pecan, handsome face. Who is it? Oh, yes. He's six feet six, as tall as Bledsoe. Basketball Center. One of my students. Solomon. Solomon Wise.

"Thank you," I manage. "I—"

"Go home, Mr. Newman," he says politely, holding the door open. I get in and he closes it and presses the button down

46

with a massive, rubbery thumb. "Drive careful, and I'll see you in class tomorrow."

I nod and try to say something, but he steps back from the car. Somehow, I get the key in the ignition and the car started while he watches. The last thing I see before turning off Jackson Street is Solomon Wise in my rearview mirror standing just where I left him, still looking after me.

Six

 T HE QUESTION IS: Will I *ever* get over those damn tracks?

Right in the middle of class, just when I'm beginning to get Othello's act together, along comes the first Whoooooo! Whoooooo! from middle distance. Courageously I press on, hoping to make a crucial point or two before it sneaks close and blasts the place to pieces. When I started teaching here, I damn near filled my pants the first time I heard it. There I was innocently prattling along when the Gates of Hell opened up. WHO-OOOOO! WHOOOOOO! Bursts so loud I thought the whole thing was coming right through my classroom. I could even hear those ancient rickety-rackety tracks crack asunder as the cars derailed one by one and headed in my direction.

Shakespeare 302, though, ain't worried. Sitting in open-eyed slumber, they're indifferent alike to the Bard and man-made catastrophes. As I watch, two put their heads down and drop off to sleep. Another sits etching "J.N. + E.K. Aquarius" on a side blackboard. That's one thing about them. They may not be able to speak or write a correct sentence, but they sure as hell know their signs. Hey, foxy mama, what's yo' sign? Aquarius? Oh, wow, say, das all right!

Now it's a matter of strategy. Should I opt for the silent route or take a poke at it and lay Iago's hang-ups on them? Either way, I lose. The dude who runs the train's a better fencer than I am. If I clam up he slips past the college soft as velvet and I lose a couple minutes. If I pipe up he bongs my eardrums till my brains rattle.

I wait, think, reflect. What the hell.

"Many of you probably wonder why Iago—"

Right then Engine Jack lets loose a perfect ripper, the kind Excedrin thrives on. It's so loud a few students even achieve

48

consciousness. The room shakes; venetian blinds rattle against windows.

Tired of trying to educate kids with a fifth grade education during an earthquake? Then lie back a while and enjoy a smoke. Yeah. I fish in my pants and resurrect a crumpled pack and a safety match while he lets loose three more corkers and starts playing with the bell. Lighting up, I discard the match through a broken window.

The free entertainment gives me a chance to think about Hart again. What could he have done that could have been so bad? Badmouth the President? Screw a student? Maybe I ought to go and ask him, just walk in and—

"Mr. Newman?"

The voice is so close I jump. Bledsoe—he's heard about yesterday! But when I turn around it's only another kid with one of those *Excuse of Absence* forms The Man hands out like chewing gum to any student who cuts class for a week or two and then tells him he had open heart surgery. Relieved, I scribble my initials on it and pretend to record the change in my grade book. This keeps everybody but the teachers happy, who are reduced by these things to slip signers, attendance takers, babysitters.

"Well," I say after the train has passed, "can anyone tell me why Iago hates Othello?"

Silence.

"Let me put it another way. What has Othello done that makes Iago seek revenge?"

Blank stares.

"O.K. Let's try it one more time. On the basis of reading the first act, which I assigned to you over a week ago, what do you think of *Othello* so far?"

In the back of the room, Elvira chats openly with Mary Lou, a smile on her face.

"Elvira."

"Huh?"

"What do you think of *Othello* so far?"

Blank stare.

"What do you think of the play, Elvira?"

"I ain't got the book yet."

"I see. Mary Lou?"

Mary Lou shrugs her shoulders.

"Doug?"

"I haven't got to it."

"Willy Clyde?"

"Huh?"

"What do you think of *Othello*?"

"Who?"

"Carolyn?"

"I started to read it, but…"

So it goes. After a few more names I give it up. What should I do? Not one of them has read it. For that matter, some don't even have their books or read off someone else's right in class. After all, it's stupid to spend $1.95 for something as useless as a play when you can buy a Big Mac and fries with it and still get some change back.

Thinking it over, I've about decided to have them read the play aloud when Carolyn Waters raises her hand.

"Yes, Carolyn."

"Uh, this novel, *Othello* —"

"Play."

"Say what?"

"*Othello's* a play, Carolyn, not a novel."

"Well, is it true it's about a black dude who gets it on with a white chick?"

"That's right, Carolyn. Lots of juicy sex. You ought to read it."

A couple students laugh. Willy Clyde, wearing cut-off jeans and a red tank shirt, breaks out in a grin.

"Sex? Hey, man, that's all right!"

More laughter. Carolyn looks at him.

"You would say that."

"What you mean?"

"Don't you all go saying, 'What you mean.' You know where I'm comin' from, Willy. Sex is *all* you ever think about."

Willy's grin cracks wider. "Aw, mama, I didn't say nothin'."

"Huh, don't you go pourin' none of that 'mama' jive on me, neither. Maybe that stuff's O.K. for the streets but it don't cut no ice with me, honey. So just keep yo' mouf shut and don't say *nothin'*, y'hear?"

Half the class is in stitches and the English language is on its knees. Willy Clyde, grinning, overmatched, and loving every moment of it, retreats into mock protests of innocence. Naw, she's got him all wrong. Sex ain't his thing at all. Infinitely scornful, Carolyn attacks and overkills his frail defense, calling him a male pig, a locker room hero, and then in a burst of supreme contempt telling him he's "all talk cause you ain't got no balls."

Pandemonium. Except for Carolyn and a few horrified girls, we're all laughing so hard we can be heard clear across campus. Willy leads the pack, aided by a pal who keeps pounding his back like he just won a prize. One thing's certain: for the moment at least, they're all awake. Now if I can just turn it in the direction of the play and spark their interest. Flicking my butt through the broken window, I hold up a hand.

"Actually," I say, "*Othello*'s a play which is steeped in sex. Desdemona—"

"She the white chick?"

"Uh huh."

"And don't she get married to this black dude Othello?"

"That's right."

"Wait a minute," says Willy. "How does her daddy feel about this?"

"How do you think?"

"Man, just knowing how white folks thinks, I bet he wants to string 'im up by the—"

"Uh, dead on, Willy. And what about Othello?"

"What you mean?"

"Well, if you married a white gal, how would you feel if a white dude named Iago kept telling you she was cheating?"

"Guess I'd be pretty mad."

"At who? Iago or the girl?"

"Both, I guess."

"Yeah? Why the girl?"

"Shoot, man, cause she was cheatin'—"

"But she isn't. She loves Othello and is completely faithful to him."

"Wait a minute," says Carolyn, "you mean Iago's *lyin'* to Othello?"

"Bull's eye."

"What he want to do that for? Don't he like blacks?"

"Naw," says Willy, "he wants Des— uh, Des—"

"Desdemona."

"Yeah, he wants Desdemona for hisself."

"Well, which is it, Mr. Newman," says Carolyn. "Does he lie cause he don't like blacks or cause he's got the hots for Desdemona?"

I shrug. "Maybe he's got the hots for Othello."

"No lie!" says Leroy Drummond. "You mean Iago's *queer?*"

"What do *you* think, Leroy?"

"How should I know? I haven't read the play."

"Ah, that's the point. You were supposed to."

"Shoot, you mean you're not gonna tell us?"

"Bingo!"

"Awww!"

"That's unfair!"

"Eat your hearts out, gang. And next time I'm going to give you a quiz question to make sure you've read the first act. The question is—"

"Wait."

"Hold on!"

Quietly I wait while they drag out their notebooks, thinking that if there's one way to fan their interest and get them to read the play, it's Race + Sex + A Pre-Announced Quiz. As it turns out, the rest of the class is one of my best. I get a discussion going and some are beginning to see the differences between a play and a novel. When the bell rings I head outside feeling like I've made a breakthrough and run into Rinehart, who wears a three-hundred dollar suit with an ascot. He plunks down an alligator guitar case next to me on the sidewalk.

"I'm Bledsoe's hit man," he says.

"The torpedo from Detroit?"

"Right on. You seen Alex?"

"You bonging it with him these days?"

"Yeah, he's on cello. We gets together out at the Poppies and boogie a bit."

At the moment, Jacqueline Carter, a bright student of mine who was just elected Homecoming Queen, passes by. Rinehart's eyes track her.

"Ma-an," he says. It takes him two seconds to say the word and he does it in a way no white cat can match.

"Jiggle your jewels?" I ask.

"Man," he says, still watching her. "I've known her since she was jailbait. She was a real together chick then, but now she's just suckin' it in. I'd like to give her some dope and bring her down."

We stand there a minute, Rinehart in his hand-knit vest, me in my cotton shirt, watching Jackie twitch her tail toward Moulton Hall.

"Half the foxes there are knee deep in grass," he says.

"Wonder who supplies them."

Rinehart gives me a slow wink.

"Still working your way through college, huh? Ever think of opening up the faculty trade?"

Another wink, this time a mock one.

"Funny you should mention that."

By now Jacqueline's disappeared into Moulton and Rinehart splits.

Rinehart. He's some operator. Pot. Smack. Covers the waterfront. Last year I had a girl named Dorothy in one of my classes. Sweet, bright thing. Well-dressed too, which is a rarity around this place. Now, thanks to Rinehart, she sits stoned in class in those ass-tight cut-offs some of them wear, Rinehart's initials embroidered where her back pockets used to be.

I find Hart working at his "post," which is right where the

53

Dean says we're supposed to be when we're not teaching. When I rap his open door he looks up from behind his desk, smiles, comes over, and escorts me to a chair. Talk about courtesy. This kind of treatment is unheard of at Ashland.

As usual he's wearing a suit and vest and reminds me of a black Richard Cory. Tall, imperially slim, and handsome as you can get, the guy almost radiates enough class to make you think Ashland has a chance. Of the school's seventy teachers, forty-five of whom are black, twenty white, and the rest foreign, not all are bad but sometimes it sure seems they are. Many are semi-literate and can't write or express themselves much better than their students. Most have views as fossilized and narrow as those at the top. John, like Duffy, Ambrose A. Abernathy in Art, and a half dozen others, offers a hope that things could improve if only he were given the opportunity.

When we first met—John joined Ashland just this year—I was put off by his impeccable mustache and glittering ways and dismissed him as a phony Princeton missionary down here on an ego trip to save his poor brothers. Then I found that beneath the obvious differences we had a lot in common. Both of us feel the same way about the place and get into trouble, though I've got to admit he does it with a lot more style.

"John," I say, plunging right in, "I'm going to ask you a nosy question. If you don't like it, you can tell me to take a hike."

"Go ahead."

"I hear you've been fired."

For a moment he just sits there. Then he laughs.

"You never pull any punches, do you?"

"You can always tell me to leave."

"No, it's all right. It's your way, even if it is a bit too *fortissimo* for my taste." He smiles, "You know, I like it when you get up on your soapbox at faculty meetings and preach that we spend too much time talking about petty bureaucratic matters and not enough about education. We've rehashed the same old issues like student tardiness and attendance a dozen times without once deciding anything or talking about something important."

"It's not going to change, either."

"Sure, because everything's structured at us when we go in and we don't have a chance to debate or introduce anything of our own. Oh, they say we do, but we don't. You know, I've been thinking a lot lately."

"Yeah?"

"Yes. I've been trying to figure out why Ashland's so poor. Is it the Administration's fault? Everyone in it—the Registrar, the Business Manager, the Head Librarian, even the Head Cashier—is an empire builder with his own pocket of power he jealously wants to protect and expand. So they all work independently and at cross purposes with each other. Is it the faculty's and staff's fault? Or is it the students we always complain about? Sometimes I think that if we just had good students Ashland would be transformed magically over night into a kind of Princeton of the South. Other times I think the only way to save this place is to sweep it all away, the good with the bad, and start over. But it seems a bit extreme to throw the baby out with the bath water."

"So what have you decided?"

"That it's ultimately the Administration's fault. Of course the students are terrible, the faculty largely incompetent, and the staff lazy and unsupervised. But in the end it's the Administration, especially Bledsoe and the President, who bear the responsibility for the way things are. I mean, someone has to be accountable, and from where I sit those two men are only interested in getting more power and more money."

I scratch my neck and wait a second. "Then it's true?" I ask.

He sighs and leans back. "Yes."

"And they bounced you because of your trips to Columbia?"

Something crosses his face but it's gone before I can read it.

"Yes. Our leaders evidently feel that culture is a waste of time, especially when students have to travel a hundred miles and the school gets stuck with the tab. I tried to tell them that music majors need the experience only live concerts provide, that listening to Beethoven's 7th through a set of headphones is no substitute for the real thing. But they weren't impressed."

55

"They must have warned you."

"Sure, but I thought if I took only a handful in my own car rather than used a school bus, and paid for the tickets myself, it would make a difference. It didn't."

"Sorry."

"Well, I've had it. You know, I left an excellent job at Princeton to come here. I wanted to do something to help black students. My friends kept telling me I had water on the brain and they've turned out to be right. Like I said, the real bottom line on this place is that they don't give a damn about students. They just don't care."

He picks up a conductor's baton and then drops it in disgust.

"Anyway, I've written Princeton and my old job's still waiting. I'm going back where people treat you like a white man."

I start laughing. He does too, and in seconds we're howling. When we finally stop, though, it still seems that what he did wasn't bad enough. Maybe he's holding something back. That's one thing about John. Classy as he is, he has always seemed a bit of an enigma, like he's hiding something or somehow isn't complete. Remembering what Duffy said, I give it one more crack.

"And that's all there is? That's why they sacked you?"

I get the look again—fleeting, unreadable. What else could it be? I shrug and get up as heels come tapping quickly down the hall. What happens next is one of those things that happens once in a lifetime. A pretty girl with honey blonde hair rushes into the room. Hart jumps up and moves toward her. "Oh, John, he—" Then she sees me and stops. We all freeze. My eyes go from her, delicate, white, and beautiful, to him, frozen with one arm around her. My brain clicks, skips six steps, sees a light. Aha!

"You're—married?"

Hart moves closer and puts his other arm around her. Her blue eyes, electric with panic, move questioningly between us. He looks at me.

"Yes, since spring vacation. We were married in Myrtle Beach."

ers I'm going to see a fella in my department
ll. I think he might support us. Right now, we
acking we can get."

o you really think John has a chance?" Carol asks.

," I say, my heart pounding like a triphammer.
I was really born for, I guess, combat for a just
charged up, primed to go. All I need now is Hart.
hpin. I look back at him. He smiles and holds his
hank you," he says. "We'll wait till we hear from
's soon."

be," I say. "The way it looks, we may not have

"And you've kept it secret?"

"We tried to," he says. "At least until we could find the right time to tell people."

I believe I see it all now. "Only they found out first and that was the real reason they axed you." I consider the implications. So the old taboo is still alive and kicking. A big black buck makes the beast with two backs with a beautiful blonde belle and they sound the alarum. And I thought it was all gone with the wind. But the moonlight and magnolia blossoms, the pickaninnies and colonels in their ice cream suits are still alive and well in South Carolina. Not to mention those mint juleps served on verandas. However, this still doesn't explain the girl's terror or the way she holds him.

Hart starts to provide the missing piece. "Marrying Caroline might not have been bad enough in itself, though the Dean was very ugly about it. But as my wife will tell you, there's something more."

I turn to her. "Hi, I'm Dave Newman."

"Hi, Dave. I'm Caroline Sanford. And my father is—Brantley Sanford."

"I don't—"

"He's the Chairman of the Board of Trustees."

"And rich," says Hart.

"And very rich," says Caroline. The fear has left her and what I see now is a young woman very much in love clinging with concern to her man. "When my father found out, he became furious. He treated me like I was—like I was something horrible—and ordered them to fire John. He's used his power just like a club."

"The one time I met him," Hart says, "he all but burned a cross in my face. I think he'd kill me if he could."

"Oh, John, he would!"

"What do you mean?"

"That's what I came to tell you. I heard him on the phone and I think he's hired somebody to hurt you."

"Nonsense. He's the Chairman of the Board, not the Godfather. Things like that don't happen."

"John, you don't know him like I do. He means to break us up, and he doesn't care how he does it."

"Maybe you'd better believe her," I say, thinking of Brabantio. "The question is, what are you going to do about it?" Suddenly it occurs to me how quickly I'm getting involved in all this. Minutes ago I was a casual friend of Hart. Now I'm knee deep in their lives. What's more, they seem to welcome me there, maybe because it gives them a chance to share the strain of their secret with someone.

"Do about it?" says Hart. "What can I do about it?"

"Fight."

"How? By going through channels?"

"No, that would be a waste of time. You'd only face the same people who fired you to begin with. What you've got to do is something big. After all, it's the squeaky wheel that gets the grease."

"Meaning?"

I place my hand on his shoulder. "Meaning, my friend, you may have to see a lawyer or go to the newspapers."

He considers it and shakes his head. "No, I've had enough. They've made it clear I'm not welcome around here, and I've got a job waiting up north where they judge you on your merits." He kisses Carol on the forehead. "Besides that, it's been hard on her. It's not easy being caught between your husband and your father."

"Don't worry about me, John. It's you I'm worried about."

Despite her delicacy, I'm getting strong vibes from her. If she is Desdemona, I bet she's also a tough lady who can handle herself in the clinches. The question is: is Hart up to her? He looks the part, but will he fold when the chips are down? Now's the time to find out.

"Look, John," I say. "They fired you because you're black and some rich white man didn't like it. Damn it, I wouldn't take it. If it was just because you broke some petty rules — well, O.K. Then I'd say it was a stupid system and to hell with them. But this is some ante-bellum bigot who's decided to crush you. Damn it, that's not right. I wouldn't take a slap like that from God's own hand."

"That's easy enough for y
"Don't give me that. I've
times. And had it chopped o
"Look, it would be stup
already made it clear they d
"Who the hell cares what
here because *they* wanted y
wanted to teach black kids
and go back to Princeton
money, where the students
because they're already th
then you can sip martinis
lounge and reminisce abou
year of your life to your l
appreciate the gift you off
you going to knuckle unde
and fight?"

For a long moment he's
"Honey?"
"Whatever you want, Jo
"Even if it means challe
"Yes."

He turns to me. "And w
get out of this?"

"I want to help."

"Why? Why stick *your*
father's being dangerous,
"Let me worry about th
"There's something els
director. I don't know th
ness."

"Really? I thought all
ghetto."

He grins. "Want to kn
been to a ghetto is the thi
"That's O.K., I've ha
us."

"What are you going t

"For o
named Si
need all t
"David
"Yes, I
This is wl
cause. I'm
He's the l
hand out.
you. Hop
"It bett
much time

Seven

TEN SECONDS AFTER I've left I've got a plan cooking. What we've got to do is hit them big, use the media. And that means a piece in the local paper, perhaps followed by an editorial. Coverage by the local radio station if we can get it. Also, it wouldn't hurt if we got a petition signed by Hart's students and submitted to Bledsoe himself by a delegation from Hart's classes.

All this has got to be organized. First I have to find Sitwell. If we're going to get anywhere, it's important to get faculty support. That, of course, is going to be tough. At Ashland teachers are mice concerned only with holding onto their jobs, political ostriches with their heads in the sand. What I've got to do is shake them up and make them care. They have to be shown that the rights of one are inseparable from the rights of all. And Dick should be the place to start. Talking to him last semester, I got the impression he's been screwed more than once by the Big Boys and loves them about as much as I do.

I find him at once, squatting outside of Mason Hall, which like an old whore can be entered only from the rear. Dick's a human burglar alarm, a sentinel who always reminds me of those stone lions guarding the entrances to libraries and museums. He's one of a broken set, though, and is gifted with a redneck's ability to squat for hours, preserving inviolate the English Department's abode of luxurious isolation.

Early as it is, Dick is already at his post outside the Fountainbleu.

"How's Miami Beach, Dicky boy? Been in for a dip yet?"

Hefting a handful of dirt, Sitwell considers the matter while pigeons flutter through broken windows on the third floor.

"Been thinking about it, Davy," he says.

I squat next to him, eager to get to the point but not wanting to seem anxious. After all, we're not exactly buddies.

"Say Dick, did you know—"

"Heard there was some excitement on Jackson Street yesterday," Dick says.

"What kind of excitement?"

"Some English teacher walked into The Rainbow and stirred up the natives."

"Why'd he do that?"

"I don't know. Didn't get all the details."

"Huh." I dig out the Camels and find there are only two left. "Smoke?"

"Thanks. Didn't know they made those anymore."

I light us up. "Anyway, Dick, there's something I'd like—"

"Shhh. Listen."

From the distance a sound reaches us, unhuman but with a definite beat to it.

"Good God, what's that?"

"Dragon."

"Dragon?"

"Watch."

After a minute the sound resolves itself somewhat, but I still can't make it out. Then the dragon comes into view. It's purple and yellow and has three heads. Six legs stamp like pistons and its six arms roll and pitch from side to side. Watching closely, I notice it also comes with sunglasses and that each of its heads is shaved bald except for a braid which is arranged in back in the shape of a horseshoe. In front, a large club insignia jerks up and down.

"Jesus Christ."

The pledges are no more than fifty feet away now, and up close their yellow shirts, purple pants, and black boots sparkle in the sun. But I still can't make out their chant. It seems right out of the jungle, endlessly illusive until sheer repetition and an educated guess provides the last piece to the puzzle.

OMEGA PSI PHI! OMEGA PSI PHI! OMEGA PSI PHI!

"And they wonder why this place is for the shits," Dick says.

"Personally, I'd like to slay that dragon.'

"Go to it, pal." Dick flicks off some ash before going on in that expressionless voice of his. "You know, last semester I had a kid who would have sold his mother just to get into that frat."

"No shit."

"Yeah. Needed a C average in his courses and he didn't quite have it. It was all he cared about. Not his studies, not even his Kawasaki 900. Anyway, he kept sucking after me to give him a B so he could make it, pressing me after each class and leaving me notes signed "God Bless You" on my windshield. Then he started hinting he'd run me down with his motorcycle and break my legs if I didn't deliver. Got so bad I was even thinking of going to see the Dean."

"Why didn't you?"

Dick shrugs.

"And did he get his B?"

"Hell, no. I flunked him. That kid didn't know anything."

"Well." I launch the butt into a rut and watch the pledges turn past Moulton. "It would sure as hell improve this place if they'd just get rid of these damn clubs," I say, trying to move the conversation back to where I want it.

"That's where you're wrong. Ain't nothing going to improve this place except urban renewal."

"Still, you've got to try."

Dick turns and looks at me for a moment. "Is that what you were doing in The Rainbow yesterday?"

I pause. "Maybe."

"Jesus."

"Someone has to try. Otherwise, we could all get screwed."

"What do you mean?"

Looking at him, I break the news about John Hart and Caroline Sanford, placing particular stress on her father's use of power to get Hart fired in an attempt to split them up. Before I've finished, Sitwell has begun to let a thin high-pitched whistle escape between his teeth.

"That's real juicy," he says. "So King Sanford doesn't like having a coon for a son-in-law."

"No, and it looks like he doesn't mind using a little muscle to scare Hart off. That's why—"

"I know that Caroline Sanford," Dick observes. "She's real

table pussy. And I sure go for all that blonde hair. Wouldn't mind seeing it spread out on a pillow."

I frown, not liking the direction things are going. "The point is, Dick, if it can happen to Hart, it can happen to any of us. What we've got to do is mount a counteroffensive."

"What are you talking about?"

I swallow with excitement. Here it goes.

"Well, the first thing we've got to do is expose them for what they are. So I thought that at the next faculty meeting I'd make a little announcement. That's where you come in."

"Come in?"

"Yeah, we're going to need a little support among the teachers. So after I announce how Sanford has used his position to get one of us fired, it would sure help if I had at least one fellow teacher to back me up, especially if he's—"

But Sitwell's looking at me like I'm some kind of bug. "Jesus, Newman," he says. "You're a real special case, you know that? I've never met anything like you before."

"Look, it can work, I know it. All we—"

"Christ, you're a real bleeding heart, aren't you? A regular do-gooder. They ought to stick you in a cage and display you in a zoo somewhere."

"Don't say that. We can change things here if we all pull together."

"Well, count me out, daddy. The whole thing sucks. I found that out a long time ago."

Effortlessly, Dick rises from his crouch and walks away. From the back he reminds me now of a wooden Indian, rigid and imbued with life only from the waist down. He does not look back.

"And you've kept it secret?"

"We tried to," he says. "At least until we could find the right time to tell people."

I believe I see it all now. "Only they found out first and that was the real reason they axed you." I consider the implications. So the old taboo is still alive and kicking. A big black buck makes the beast with two backs with a beautiful blonde belle and they sound the alarum. And I thought it was all gone with the wind. But the moonlight and magnolia blossoms, the pickaninnies and colonels in their ice cream suits are still alive and well in South Carolina. Not to mention those mint juleps served on verandas. However, this still doesn't explain the girl's terror or the way she holds him.

Hart starts to provide the missing piece. "Marrying Caroline might not have been bad enough in itself, though the Dean was very ugly about it. But as my wife will tell you, there's something more."

I turn to her. "Hi, I'm Dave Newman."

"Hi, Dave. I'm Caroline Sanford. And my father is— Brantley Sanford."

"I don't—"

"He's the Chairman of the Board of Trustees."

"And rich," says Hart.

"And very rich," says Caroline. The fear has left her and what I see now is a young woman very much in love clinging with concern to her man. "When my father found out, he became furious. He treated me like I was—like I was something horrible—and ordered them to fire John. He's used his power just like a club."

"The one time I met him," Hart says, "he all but burned a cross in my face. I think he'd kill me if he could."

"Oh, John, he would!"

"What do you mean?"

"That's what I came to tell you. I heard him on the phone and I think he's hired somebody to hurt you."

"Nonsense. He's the Chairman of the Board, not the God-father. Things like that don't happen."

"John, you don't know him like I do. He means to break us up, and he doesn't care how he does it."

"Maybe you'd better believe her," I say, thinking of Brabantio. "The question is, what are you going to do about it?" Suddenly it occurs to me how quickly I'm getting involved in all this. Minutes ago I was a casual friend of Hart. Now I'm knee deep in their lives. What's more, they seem to welcome me there, maybe because it gives them a chance to share the strain of their secret with someone.

"Do about it?" says Hart. "What can I do about it?"

"Fight."

"How? By going through channels?"

"No, that would be a waste of time. You'd only face the same people who fired you to begin with. What you've got to do is something big. After all, it's the squeaky wheel that gets the grease."

"Meaning?"

I place my hand on his shoulder. "Meaning, my friend, you may have to see a lawyer or go to the newspapers."

He considers it and shakes his head. "No, I've had enough. They've made it clear I'm not welcome around here, and I've got a job waiting up north where they judge you on your merits." He kisses Carol on the forehead. "Besides that, it's been hard on her. It's not easy being caught between your husband and your father."

"Don't worry about me, John. It's you I'm worried about."

Despite her delicacy, I'm getting strong vibes from her. If she is Desdemona, I bet she's also a tough lady who can handle herself in the clinches. The question is: is Hart up to her? He looks the part, but will he fold when the chips are down? Now's the time to find out.

"Look, John," I say. "They fired you because you're black and some rich white man didn't like it. Damn it, I wouldn't take it. If it was just because you broke some petty rules—well, O.K. Then I'd say it was a stupid system and to hell with them. But this is some ante-bellum bigot who's decided to crush you. Damn it, that's not right. I wouldn't take a slap like that from God's own hand."

"That's easy enough for you to say. You're white."

"Don't give me that. I've put my head on the block lots of times. And had it chopped off too."

"Look, it would be stupid to charge into battle. They've already made it clear they don't want me."

"Who the hell cares what *they* want? Damn it, did you come here because *they* wanted you? Or did you do it because *you* wanted to teach black kids? Sure it's easy, you can pack it in and go back to Princeton with their Persian rugs and big money, where the students don't need you much to begin with because they're already the best in the world. And now and then you can sip martinis with friends in some plush faculty lounge and reminisce about the time you sacrificed a precious year of your life to your less fortunate brothers, who didn't appreciate the gift you offered them. But the question is, are you going to knuckle under and run, or are you going to stand and fight?"

For a long moment he's silent. Then he looks at her.

"Honey?"

"Whatever you want, John. Do what you think is right."

"Even if it means challenging your father?"

"Yes."

He turns to me. "And what about you, David? What do you get out of this?"

"I want to help."

"Why? Why stick *your* neck out? If you're right about her father's being dangerous, we could both get hurt."

"Let me worry about that."

"There's something else," he says. "I'm a pianist and a band director. I don't know the first thing about this kind of business."

"Really? I thought all you people learned to deal in the ghetto."

He grins. "Want to know something? The closest I've ever been to a ghetto is the third row in a theater."

"That's O.K., I've had enough experience for the both of us."

"What are you going to do?"

"For openers I'm going to see a fella in my department named Sitwell. I think he might support us. Right now, we need all the backing we can get."

"David, do you really think John has a chance?" Carol asks.

"Yes, I do," I say, my heart pounding like a triphammer. This is what I was really born for, I guess, combat for a just cause. I'm all charged up, primed to go. All I need now is Hart. He's the linchpin. I look back at him. He smiles and holds his hand out. "Thank you," he says. "We'll wait till we hear from you. Hope it's soon."

"It better be," I say. "The way it looks, we may not have much time."

Seven

TEN SECONDS AFTER I've left I've got a plan cooking. What we've got to do is hit them big, use the media. And that means a piece in the local paper, perhaps followed by an editorial. Coverage by the local radio station if we can get it. Also, it wouldn't hurt if we got a petition signed by Hart's students and submitted to Bledsoe himself by a delegation from Hart's classes.

All this has got to be organized. First I have to find Sitwell. If we're going to get anywhere, it's important to get faculty support. That, of course, is going to be tough. At Ashland teachers are mice concerned only with holding onto their jobs, political ostriches with their heads in the sand. What I've got to do is shake them up and make them care. They have to be shown that the rights of one are inseparable from the rights of all. And Dick should be the place to start. Talking to him last semester, I got the impression he's been screwed more than once by the Big Boys and loves them about as much as I do.

I find him at once, squatting outside of Mason Hall, which like an old whore can be entered only from the rear. Dick's a human burglar alarm, a sentinel who always reminds me of those stone lions guarding the entrances to libraries and museums. He's one of a broken set, though, and is gifted with a redneck's ability to squat for hours, preserving inviolate the English Department's abode of luxurious isolation.

Early as it is, Dick is already at his post outside the Fountainbleu.

"How's Miami Beach, Dicky boy? Been in for a dip yet?"

Hefting a handful of dirt, Sitwell considers the matter while pigeons flutter through broken windows on the third floor.

"Been thinking about it, Davy," he says.

I squat next to him, eager to get to the point but not wanting to seem anxious. After all, we're not exactly buddies.

"Say Dick, did you know—"

"Heard there was some excitement on Jackson Street yesterday," Dick says.

"What kind of excitement?"

"Some English teacher walked into The Rainbow and stirred up the natives."

"Why'd he do that?"

"I don't know. Didn't get all the details."

"Huh." I dig out the Camels and find there are only two left.

"Smoke?"

"Thanks. Didn't know they made those anymore."

I light us up. "Anyway, Dick, there's something I'd like—"

"Shhh. Listen."

From the distance a sound reaches us, unhuman but with a definite beat to it.

"Good God, what's that?"

"Dragon."

"Dragon?"

"Watch."

After a minute the sound resolves itself somewhat, but I still can't make it out. Then the dragon comes into view. It's purple and yellow and has three heads. Six legs stamp like pistons and its six arms roll and pitch from side to side. Watching closely, I notice it also comes with sunglasses and that each of its heads is shaved bald except for a braid which is arranged in back in the shape of a horseshoe. In front, a large club insignia jerks up and down.

"Jesus Christ."

The pledges are no more than fifty feet away now, and up close their yellow shirts, purple pants, and black boots sparkle in the sun. But I still can't make out their chant. It seems right out of the jungle, endlessly illusive until sheer repetition and an educated guess provides the last piece to the puzzle.

OMEGA PSI PHI! OMEGA PSI PHI! OMEGA PSI PHI!

"And they wonder why this place is for the shits," Dick says.

"Personally, I'd like to slay that dragon.'

"Go to it, pal." Dick flicks off some ash before going on in that expressionless voice of his. "You know, last semester I

62

had a kid who would have sold his mother just to get into that frat."

"No shit."

"Yeah. Needed a C average in his courses and he didn't quite have it. It was all he cared about. Not his studies, not even his Kawasaki 900. Anyway, he kept sucking after me to give him a B so he could make it, pressing me after each class and leaving me notes signed "God Bless You" on my windshield. Then he started hinting he'd run me down with his motorcycle and break my legs if I didn't deliver. Got so bad I was even thinking of going to see the Dean."

"Why didn't you?"

Dick shrugs.

"And did he get his B?"

"Hell, no. I flunked him. That kid didn't know anything."

"Well." I launch the butt into a rut and watch the pledges turn past Moulton. "It would sure as hell improve this place if they'd just get rid of these damn clubs," I say, trying to move the conversation back to where I want it.

"That's where you're wrong. Ain't nothing going to improve this place except urban renewal."

"Still, you've got to try."

Dick turns and looks at me for a moment. "Is that what you were doing in The Rainbow yesterday?"

I pause. "Maybe."

"Jesus."

"Someone has to try. Otherwise, we could all get screwed."

"What do you mean?"

Looking at him, I break the news about John Hart and Caroline Sanford, placing particular stress on her father's use of power to get Hart fired in an attempt to split them up. Before I've finished, Sitwell has begun to let a thin high-pitched whistle escape between his teeth.

"That's real juicy," he says. "So King Sanford doesn't like having a coon for a son-in-law."

"No, and it looks like he doesn't mind using a little muscle to scare Hart off. That's why —"

"I know that Caroline Sanford," Dick observes. "She's real

table pussy. And I sure go for all that blonde hair. Wouldn't mind seeing it spread out on a pillow."

I frown, not liking the direction things are going. "The point is, Dick, if it can happen to Hart, it can happen to any of us. What we've got to do is mount a counteroffensive."

"What are you talking about?"

I swallow with excitement. Here it goes.

"Well, the first thing we've got to do is expose them for what they are. So I thought that at the next faculty meeting I'd make a little announcement. That's where you come in."

"Come in?"

"Yeah, we're going to need a little support among the teachers. So after I announce how Sanford has used his position to get one of us fired, it would sure help if I had at least one fellow teacher to back me up, especially if he's—"

But Sitwell's looking at me like I'm some kind of bug. "Jesus, Newman," he says. "You're a real special case, you know that? I've never met anything like you before."

"Look, it can work, I know it. All we—"

"Christ, you're a real bleeding heart, aren't you? A regular do-gooder. They ought to stick you in a cage and display you in a zoo somewhere."

"Don't say that. We can change things here if we all pull together."

"Well, count me out, daddy. The whole thing sucks. I found that out a long time ago."

Effortlessly, Dick rises from his crouch and walks away. From the back he reminds me now of a wooden Indian, rigid and imbued with life only from the waist down. He does not look back.

Eight

Aɴᴅ ᴀꜰᴛᴇʀ ʜᴇ'ꜱ ʟᴇꜰᴛ I go inside and put on the java. Jerk! What
were you thinking of when you went to see Sitwell? Did you
really expect him to risk his job for someone he didn't know?
Just because you care about the Harts is no reason to assume
others will. Nor can you expect to trot down to the local paper
and have them join your crusade or the town radio station to
leap at the chance to blast Sanford. Even back in the sixties up
north when Black was Beautiful, things weren't *that* easy!

I take a sip of my coffee, which has attained the sludge-like
properties I prefer, and try to figure what to do next. Suddenly
the phone rings at the end of the hall. A chill rips through me.
What if it's Bledsoe calling about my escapade at The Rainbow? Maybe he's found out. After all, Sitwell knew! Or maybe
my visit to Hart's office has been duly recorded and reported.
Either way, it could be the old ball game. By this point in my
life you'd think I'd have learned the rudiments of self-
preservation. But no, with my job hanging by a thread, I have
to go galloping around the landscape, trampling taboos wherever I go.

What makes it all especially bad is that I know the damn
phone's likely to ring on to the crack of doom because Mason
Hall's a place where no one ever answers anything. What
should I do, let it sing itself to sleep? If I do, it will probably
ring for minutes and the caller might call back. On the other
hand, if I try to cut my agonies short by answering it myself,
it'll fizzle just as I reach it from my office all the way at the end
of the hall.

This time someone claims it in the middle of the fifth ring. I
wait.

Footsteps.

Coming my way.

I close my eyes, trying to will them to stop. Stop at 106, 108, knock on *Sitwell's* door. Stop!

Footsteps.

I wait, sweating like a bastard. Go away!

They halt outside my door. There's a pause.

Tap tap tap.

I go over and open the door, wishing the floors above me, which are officially condemned, would collapse and bury my visitor. Outside Dame Rumor stands in the unlit hallway.

"Phone, Dave."

"Thanks."

I try to see if Farnsworth's got his pipe out, but it's too dark. His voice doesn't give anything away either. Sometimes if you listen closely to it, you can hear a guillotine blade fall. This time, though, it's either neutral or protectively self-colored like the darkness around him, which swallows him from sight as he leaves.

Courageously, I follow him all the way to the phone, my footsteps sounding hollow in the dark. Like a black fist, the phone hangs down by its cord. I take hold of it and snap the receiver up into my palm.

"Davy?"

Davy? What the hell is Bledsoe calling me Davy for? "Davy," the voice repeats, "is that you? Why don't you answer? Are you all right?"

I swim up toward the light. After a moment I realize the voice is feminine and that I'd been certain all along it would be The Man. I clear my throat.

"Hello, Connie."

"David, is that you?"

"Yeah."

"Are you all right?"

"Yes."

"Then why didn't you—"

"We must have had a bad connection."

"Oh. Anyway, I'm calling from work. I've been concerned about you, you know."

"No, I didn't know. Why the concern?"

Her efficient voice wavers. "Well, after yesterday..."

"Yesterday?"

"You did run out on me, you know. Practically like a crazy man. I was afraid you might, well, do something rash."

By now I'm plugged in again and feel like my old self.

"I did."

"What?"

"Do something rash."

A slight pause.

"What did you do?"

"My God, Connie!"

"What?"

"They think *I* did it. The cops..."

"The cops? David, what is it? What about the cops?"

"When I came to, there was this woman, and, *My God, Connie!*"

For the first time ever, her cool shatters.

"For Christ's sake, David, what is it? What did you do? Don't just keep saying 'My God, Connie.' What—"

"There was this woman..."

"Yes, yes. You've already—"

"And when I came to, she was just *lying* there."

"Just lying where? Go on!"

"In the street, Connie. Just lying. And I was..."

"Yes?"

"I was naked and tearing at her clothes in a frenzy. And then this police dog, a doberman named Ralph, seized me by the ankle—"

At the other end she starts to laugh, helpless peals that race up and down the musical scale before stabilizing at a point midway between deafening and mind-boggling. Most uncharacteristic of Connie, I must say. I have a mental image of everyone there turning white. In one of the rooms, Dr. Snyder swivels his head around from a root canal in bloody progress to listen in disbelief. Dear Lord, what's that? Surely not *our* Connie! And all the time Connie laughs on, shattering the bullshit of neat procedures we divide our existences into, the instruments arranged on trays, all our root canals. Laughs at what she does not know but which I do, standing here in the darkness: that we are all alone, ultimately and inevitably alone in our separate traps, divided and sealed off from each other by our own shortcomings and incompleteness, by circumstances almost without limit. Some, like Rinehart and Dick, never know or suspect or are capable of caring that they are cosmic orphans. Others slice their days into schedules and projects to shield themselves from the horrors.

Like a balloon, Connie's laughter gradually settles to earth. The metal snap on her purse opens and I hear her blow her nose.

"You bastard," she says.

"Ain't it the truth."

"Here I'm worried about you and you're playing games like a little—oh, David, what am I going to do with you?"

In a moment she'll be completely composed again and I'll be a wayward child for her to clean up and set right. I move to kill the thing.

"Look, Connie, I've got—"

"Still, in a way, I suppose it was my fault. I did upset you. Well, I intend to make amends."

"That's not necessary."

"Oh, but it is," she says brightly. "Tell you what. Tonight I'll come over—"

"Tonight I'll be at Duffy's."

"Well, tomorrow, then. I'll be over at five-thirty and cook you the best veal scaloppini you've ever—"

I stop listening and step on a roach that's nuzzling my shoe. The trouble with Connie and women like her is that they think food is a cure-all. Have a fight? Eat something and it'll all be patched up. Suicidal? Can't get your shit together? My special recipe will clear the vapors and soothe your dyspepsia in no time. If I don't watch it, she'll have all my psychic sores breaded down into a veal cutlet with garlic bread and tossed salad served on the side. And for dessert there will be all the pussy I can handle to complete my rehabilitation.

Except for one ingredient: wine. Eminently practical, Connie's not one to slight the benefits of self-therapy, so I'm entrusted with selecting a bottle of the old bubbly, "something not too heavy, you know, but anyway, I'll just leave that up to you."

"Sure."

"And please *try* to relax, honey. Don't let things bother you so much. Promise?"

"Yup."

"Good. Well, I've got to hop now. See you tomorrow at five-thirty."

On the way over to the Ad Building I ponder the wisdom of her words. Just take it easy and accept things as they are. Don't let them get to you. Sure. And Dick's right, too. The order of things sucks. The world's a sewer. It's not worth the caring, and the first thing you should do is to look after number one and forget all about John Hart and his problems. Get smart. After all, if the shoe were on the other foot, he wouldn't do anything for you. Let Hart and his new bride fight their own battles.

What the hell. If you can't lick 'em, join 'em.

Trying to achieve Nirvana, I think of waving fields of grain, a metronome, cod fishing off the Atlantic Coast. Teacher, tranquilize thyself. Soothe sorrows into serenity.

In the President's Parking Space outside the Ad Building, the Mercury Grand Marquis glitters with chrome a block long. The bastard. I'd like to be the Tooth Fairy and leave Big Red under your pillow in exchange. Or take your pompous Westminister and swap you my suite at the Palace. Even Steven. Your mansion for my plugged up toilet with its—

Peace, David.

Peace.

The President. The word conjures up the image of a fat man with a roly-poly face, hard as granite beneath the jowls. Unlike Bledsoe who's a northerner, he's a local boy who originally was just another of those poor half-naked black kids you see in yards outside of town. Except for one thing: ambition. At

Ashland he put himself through school by being a cook and doing other odd jobs. Later he taught at Ashland before becoming its president, a position he has held ever since as if by Divine Right.

Today that scrawny black kid has grown plump and prosperous. A born fund raiser, he displays a deliberate, precise, ultra-correct speaking style which he spent years acquiring. Still, despite the fact that he only cares about money and new buildings and has done next to nothing to help students learn or to improve the academic atmosphere, you've got to give him a few points. After all, in the twenty-eight years he's been in charge, Ashland has doubled the number of its bricks. At least French classes are no longer taught beneath a makeshift gym with basketballs bouncing overhead.

Good start, Dave. A trifle cynical, but not bad. That's the ticket, think on the bright side, think sunny. If there's a silver lining in the system anywhere, sniff it out, expand it into a religion. Above all, emulate "Happy" Ray, who'd be proud of you right now. Be enthusiastic, be a booster, be a politician with an organ voice charged with optimism. And always remember: seen from the right angle, even Medusa has her good points.

"Happy" Ray, my old buddy, yang to my yin, grin to my groan. For the joy of it I buzz by his hive but he's gone.

Think on the bright side.

Take the President, now. Seen in the right light, he's even admirable, and if he lets Sanford make him fire Hart, maybe it's all for the best. After all, Princeton's paradise compared to this place, and if these young lovers can't stand the heat, they better find out now because a mixed marriage is difficult even under the best of circumstances.

34 ... 18 ...

So intent have I been on becoming a Pollyanna that I've started the combination without knowing it. By the time I come around, I've already ticked off the first two numbers. Suddenly I stop.

There may be a love note from You Know Who inside.

My fingers freeze on the dial.

Confucius say, the first step toward inner peace begins with not caring. So forget about your mail, let them stuff your box till it explodes. To be invulnerable means to be indifferent.

Start now.

My fingers itch.

Now.

Start and reverse the pattern of the last thirty-eight years. Take it easy and drop out. God knows, you've earned your rest. If Bledsoe wants to reach you, he can write Bartleby at the Dead Letter Office.

Now!

Turning away, I head out into the sun, my car keys already in hand.

Nine

Sʏʟᴠɪᴀ ᴅᴜꜰꜰʏ turns out to be the kind of arty, intellectual broad I thought I'd left behind, meeting me at the door with more gimmicks than a guru. Inside, waiting for Duffy, all I can do is absorb the bombardment. An airy, diaphanous, ankle length dress out of *Zorba*. Brass ear loops and bracelets that swing and chime constantly. Around me, sitar music twangs in endlessly formless, convoluted chords that compete with jasmine incense for my attention and one of those huge rattan fan-back chairs woven out of reeds you find in the Phillipines. Above all, there's the dark hunger of her gaze. Her eyes make you feel you're the center of things, as if when they touch you, you become profoundly important while everything else fades into insignificance.

Blitzed by her reception, I try to handle the sensory overload so I can get a fix on her, making small talk which leaves her dissatisfied and looking for more. Despite the strawlike throne she sits in, she's no beauty. Her mouth's too wide and her eyes, striking as they are, are too far apart. Also, she's done nothing with her hair, which is black. Strands of it loop down the sides of her face, and I'm reminded of Connie's crisp hair style with every strand in place. God knows about her figure. Beneath the teasing folds of her dress she could be flat as a board for all I can tell.

Still, if she's no stunner, she is—striking. She's got a dark, exotic look and when her eyes…

"Dave—sorry to keep you. Where's your secretary?"

I start to get up but Duffy waves me back. Tucking his shirt in, he goes over to a side table.

"What's your pleasure?"

"What have you got?"

He runs his eyes over the array of bottles. "How about scotch?"

"No offense, Duff, but scotch rots my shorts."

"You sure? I've got a virgin bottle of Chivas Regal here. Nothing finer this side of the grave."

"Max," says Sylvia, "why don't you try David on ouzo? I bought some just last week."

"Ouzo?" Vaguely troubled, he pauses with the Regal in his hand. It's the first time I've ever heard anyone use his first name, and it sounds dead wrong. Max. I repeat the name in my mind but it still doesn't fit. Duffy is just not a 'Max' kind of person. Names, I've always felt, carry their own meanings and exist in a Platonic realm of pure, incorruptible ideas. When we name someone we simply choose a name from that realm, and if we pick the wrong one we stand a good chance of screwing that person up for a lifetime. As long as he lives, something in him tries vainly to conform or shape itself to that name. No, Max doesn't fit. Max is for the cigar-in-the-teeth bruiser with the plaid shirt sleeves rolled up over brawny tattooed forearms. Mild, likable, vulnerable Duffy with his soft body and stooped shoulders could never *be* anything but Duffy, or Duff, or just plain 'Good Old Duffy'.

Duffy puts the bottle down and quickly checks his stock. Bottles clink. Frankly, I'm surprised he has so much. From where I sit I can see rye, bourbon, a madeira, and several brands of gin and vodka. The list goes on.

"Ouzo? That's funny. I can't seem to..."

"Here, let *me* do it."

She gets up off her throne, which gives a stiff, creaking sound, and moves gracefully to the table. For a moment, against the light, I catch a glimpse of the smooth curve of her thigh outlined beneath the fabric of complex, flesh colored, flower-like patterns. Without even looking, she reaches between his hands and extracts a bottle, which she pours into some ornamented goblets.

"Have you ever had ouzo before, David?"

"Can't say that I have, Sylvia."

73

"Then my advice is to go slow. Don't jump in all at once."

She hands me a glass, which contains about two ounces of colorless liquid over several ice cubes.

"What is ouzo, anyway?"

"It's a Greek liquer, an apertif, very bold. Greek men regard the consumption of it in an undiluted state as a test of their manhood."

"Hear that, Dave?" says Duff, winking at me from his chair with a twin goblet in his hand. "This is a macho brew, so don't pop your buttons."

I laugh and gingerly wade in. The stuff burns like fire and is mean as a bull. Tastes like licorice. I take a deep breath and watch Sylvia toss half of hers off like it's mother's milk.

"See that, Duff? Looks like she wears the pants in your family."

He takes a sip and shivers as it goes down. "So tell me, how did it go against the champ of the Philistines?"

"Philistines?"

"It's Max's little joke," says Sylvia, turning her dark eyes on me. "As you know, in the Old Testament Goliath was the champion of the Philistines, a word which Arnold used later to refer to the middle class, who were culturally impoverished, ignorant, narrow-minded, materialistic, and selfishly indifferent to the sufferings of the poor and those beneath them."

"Oh, I see. And I'm—"

"David, of course, with a humanistic sling in your hand."

"Man, that's heavy. Well, to tell the truth, wee Davy here didn't have a stone for his sling and Goliath ate him alive."

"Good heavens, what for?"

"David couldn't make it to class on time yesterday," says Duffy, "and Bledsoe isn't exactly the kind who listens to reason."

"I know. You've told me that often enough." She turns her eyes on me again. "Max tells me you've socialized a lot with the Dean."

I shrug and take another swig, wishing they'd drop the subject like I did, once and for all, a few hours ago. Around us quadraphonic sitar chords twang through the incense.

"So what did happen?" says Duffy.

"Not much. I tried to reason with him and make him see that I couldn't get to class on time because the train came early and blocked the tracks. But he said I should have anticipated it and been there earlier. Talk about *non sequiturs*."

"Just wouldn't listen, huh?"

"You've got it, pal." I finish my drink and lean forward, aware that if I'm not careful, I'll flush my resolution and the New Me right down the toilet bowl. As if on cue, Sylvia rises and takes my glass, which she goes to refill. I stab the air with my finger. "It was just like shouting into the wind, and then..."

"What?"

I pause, goose-stepping over the part where Bledsoe read the letter from Farmington and made me grovel. "And then he said that if I so much as sneezed in the future, he'd arrange a *permanent* vacation for me."

Sylvia returns with the goblet; Duffy nods.

"That's Bledsoe all right, sadistic and mean. I remember one time at a meeting of the Academic Affairs Committee—"

"Oh, Max, you're not going to tell *that* one again, are you?"

Duffy looks at her like he's been slapped.

"So what if I do?"

"Nothing. It's just that it wears thin after a while." She waves a wrist on which hoop bracelets slide and ring. "But if you must, go ahead."

Duffy frowns and tosses his drink off.

"Anyway, there was this meeting and we were discussing revised course descriptions for the new college catalogue. I had taken the job really seriously, going through catalogues from a dozen schools to get some ideas and make sure I covered the most important points. Then, out of the blue, do you know what Bledsoe did?"

"What?"

"Suddenly he started talking about this particular chairman who had simply *copied* course descriptions from other catalogues and passed them off as his own. Oh, he never mentioned me by name, but he did it in such a way that everyone knew just who he was talking about. That's a tactic of his, you know, something he probably learned at law school before he failed the bar exam and decided to make his fortune here. Believe me, he's really good at assassinating someone's character indirectly without coming out honestly and confronting him face to face. I just had to sit there and take it. And it wasn't true. I hadn't plagiarized. Those course descriptions were good, and they were mine."

"Then you should have told him that."

Duffy's face registers surprise. "You know, that's just what I wanted to do. But I just couldn't."

"Well, you should have."

"But that would just have made it worse. Then he would really have torn me to pieces."

"Not if you got mad enough and didn't back down."

Duffy shakes his head and gets up to pour himself some more ouzo.

"I don't know. You know, I did feel something inside driving me to speak out. But..." He makes a gesture with his glass, something suggesting hopelessness and frustration. "But I just stopped short, couldn't do it. Anyway, I've never been able to get anywhere with people like Bledsoe."

I stretch my legs out and take another belt of the ouzo, which goes down as warm and silky as a kitten. "You know something?" I say. "When I saw The Man yesterday I told him face to face what I thought of his policies."

"You did?" Duffy's face colors with awe and admiration. "What did you say?"

I gaze back at them both in satisfaction while a small voice keeps telling me how full of shit I am. Big Bad Dave. Muy Macho and Bulging with Ouzo. Why don't you tell them how tough you were when you left his office? Still, part of it's true—I did say what I thought about one of his rules.

"I pointed out to him that it was a waste of time to start class when the bell rang anyway since they don't start to arrive until five minutes later. I told him if he really wanted to do something about the mess here instead of just blaming teachers, he should begin by requiring students to be on time."

"You did? You said that? And what did he say?"

"He didn't say anything."

Duffy shakes his head back and forth. Perched on the edge of his chair, he holds his goblet in both hands. "You know, there's one thing in particular I can't get out of my head."

"What's that?"

"The way everyone just sat there and didn't say anything. I mean, they all knew I hadn't cheated. They all knew the kind of person I am. But they just sat there. That really hurt. I thought they were my friends."

I wave my glass, aware of Sylvia's eyes. "They were just afraid to stick their necks out. People are like that."

"Still, I don't know." Duffy shakes his head again and I realize he's beginning to get drunk. "You know, I've never been able to figure some people out. Take that phony chairman of yours, for example. Know what Farnsworth did after the meeting? Came up to me in his tweed jacket and smoking that pipe of his and told me in this real sincere voice how dreadful the whole thing was and how unfair Bledsoe was to treat me that way. Stood looking me right in the eye, not even blinking. And you know what I found out afterward? *He* was the one who told Bledsoe I'd filched those course descriptions. Can you beat that? I mean, why would he start such a lie and then tell me how sorry he was? Why would he do it? What did he have to gain?"

"Kicks, maybe," I say, thinking how Farnsworth had just reamed me the same way with Bledsoe.

"Yeah, maybe the bastard just doesn't like people and gets off hurting them while pretending at the same time to be their buddy. Anyway, I really wonder about some people, especially about what happens to them when they get in groups. Before, you think you know them. But when they get together…"

"You find out they're bastards."

Sylvia laughs. "You have an earthy way of expressing yourself, David."

I look at her, feeling the detachment of the last few hours

crack like make-up. For a moment I think of the Harts with their arms around each other. "Well, it's true, no matter how I say it. I remember one time, at Benton, I tried to get the teachers organized and form a local chapter of the American Association of University Professors. Everyone was gung ho until the brass got wind of it. Then I got sacked and all my friends just turned their backs on me."

She smiles. "I'm sorry to hear that. It must have been distressing. But you do the same thing Max does, you let mundane things trouble you. As I've tried to get Max to see, as living entities we are all contaminated by this material world, and it would help him if he avoided entanglement with it. Now, in the *Bhagavad-gītā*, it says—"

"The what?"

"The *Bhagavad-gītā*. It says that we must purify our activities in order to achieve *mukti,* or freedom from material consciousness. Only by so doing can we attain a state of pure consciousness and transcend our problems."

"I see." She's beginning to sound like a hip version of Connie in her advice on how to stay cool, an intellectual flower child left over from the sixties. I look around the room, smelling the jasmine and listening to the inexhaustible permutations of the sitar. The only things the room lacks are junk antiques, strung beads for a curtain, and an abstract painting or two. To tell the truth, she's beginning to get on my nerves. I don't like her calling him Max or what she does to him or the way her eyes keep hammering at me. Sylvia. At work I hear rumors about how "special" she is. Wonder if "Max" knows. Probably not. Or maybe he's just another Arnie who keeps his mouth shut and looks the other way.

Sylvia's deep into *karma* now, and Duffy slips me a wink. This gets to Sylvia who puts the cosmos on the back burner for a moment.

"What's so funny?"

"Oh, nothing, dear."

"What is it? Am I getting too mystical for you?"

"No, it's just…"

"Go ahead, say it."

"Well, it's just that I expect you to have us in a nude encounter group any minute."

Sylvia looks annoyed. Then she laughs.

"Well, *I'm* willing!"

"Me, too!"

"What about you, Max?"

"Hey, I think I'm getting short-changed here."

"Oh, come on, Duff," I say. "Where's your spirit of adventure?"

"In the same place my adding machine is. You forget I'm head of the Math Department."

"What does that mean?"

"Just that I can count. You're one short, so ante up, Bub."

"Can't I use my credit card?"

"Not in this kind of game. Call your secretary."

I grin. Sylvia looks from him to me and back again.

"What's going on here? Somebody knows something I don't. What's this about a secretary?" She pauses. "Oh, I get it, David has a—"

"Let's just say I circulate."

"Hmm."

"So you see, I'm not much for avoiding this what-ya-call-it material entanglement of yours, though I might go for a nude grope."

"Yeah, tell us how that works, Sylvia."

" 'How that works,' " says Sylvia, determined not to let us get to her, "is that men and women take off their clothes and touch each other in order to discover who they really are. They try to get in touch with their true feelings and strip away the walls that separate them from themselves and from each other."

"We have quite a bit of that going on up at the school," says Duffy.

"I'm not talking about *sex*, Max. I'm sure Ashland's faculty is randy as goats. No, I'm talking about seeing ourselves and each other as we really are. Total honesty. Complete self-expression. And now that you mention it, that's something your school could use a lot more of."

"What do you mean?"

"Well, the blindness, for one thing. Do you know, whenever I've been up at Ashland, I've had the feeling that the blacks there just don't see me. It's like I'm invisible. For example, have you ever noticed that when you greet them their answers don't match? You say, 'How are you?' and they say 'Right,' or you say, 'Nice day, isn't it?' and they say 'O.K.' Once I even asked one of them for the time and he just looked right through me and said 'Fine.' "

"You've got a point," I say. "But often that's the way they talk to anybody. It's subcultural."

"For sure," says Duffy, getting up to pour himself a drink. But he says it in such a way that I know he's thinking of the Academic Affairs meeting again.

"Haven't you had enough to drink?" says Sylvia.

"I can handle it."

"All right, but I don't want you getting sick again like you did at the Cramers."

Duffy reddens and starts to say something but stops. He glares down at her and then, not too steadily, goes back to his chair.

"Well, I better look after dinner." She gets up and goes into the kitchen.

"Any cigarettes, Duff?"

He waves his hand at a table beside me. "Check the drawer."

Inside I find a pack of filter-tips and a lighter. Lighting up, I rise and pour myself some bourbon and stand watching Sylvia through one of those windows with the louvered shutters you close toward the middle. From the living room, the window provides the only view into the kitchen.

"You're not going to *drink* all of that?" asks Duffy.

I glance at my drink and take a belt. "Why not?"

"My God, if I tried to polish that off they'd have me in formaldehyde. You must have a hollow leg."

"Nope, just plenty of practice." Framed in the window, Sylvia looks at me for a moment.

Duffy laughs. "Well, I practice too, but it doesn't do much good." He takes a sip of his drink. "And sometimes, as Sylvia not too nicely revealed, I guess I—I guess I go overboard."

"Maybe you should stay within your limit."

"That's what she keeps telling me. In fact, she says I only drink to..."

"What?"

Duffy blushes. "She says I only drink to prove I'm a man. You know, Dave, to be honest, I don't even like the stuff."

"Then why..."

"I guess something inside me just makes me do it."

Awkwardly I touch his shoulder, searching for something to say. Sylvia appears at the window again.

"Come and get it, boys."

Dinner turns out to be something I've never seen before which has taken up residence on my plate. Cautiously, I prod it with my fork.

"What is it?"

"Eggplant provençale."

"Oh."

Surprisingly, it's not bad. I'll have to tell Connie about this one. The dandelion salad, though, is something else. Ugh. Might have known that along with everything else, she'd be a vegetarian.

Halfway through the eggplant I surface for air and find her dark eyes watching me.

"Hope you like it. It's good for your endogenous balance."

"You see how I'm wolfing it down."

She laughs, and for the first time I notice her laughter is just like her eyes.

"You know," she says, "that's just what you reminded me of just now. A wolf. And I imagine you like your cuisine the same way. No frills. Meat and potatoes and no waiting."

"Lady, McDonald's is my patron saint."

"You're a bachelor wolf too, and I hear they're the hungriest kind."

The chatter's getting a bit choice. Is she coming on or what? Lifting my glass, I toss off the rest of the bourbon.

"You sound like I'm some savage just out of the jungle."

"Are you?"

I look at Duffy, who just sits there.

"What do you think?"

"Well, I do find you a bit basic, like the way you keep drinking without letting it show. Max can't do that."

"Uh huh." She'll be examining my teeth next like I'm a horse or asking how I like living in trees. Bitch. Smug snobby arty bitch. Inside me a struggle's going on, and I'm not fully sure why. Duffy's battered look has something to do with it, though, at least enough to make me want to include him in the conversation on something approaching an equal footing.

"By the way, Duff, you were right about that detector of yours."

"Detector?"

I give the old bean a tap.

"Oh." It takes him a couple seconds to catch on. Then his eyes light up. "You mean Hart? So there *was* something." He leans forward. "Well, come on, man, give. What is it? What have you found?"

"You know Caroline Sanford?"

"Brantley Sanford's daughter? Sure. But what's she got to do with Hart?"

I pause. It's like I'm being dragged slowly but surely out of some safe shady place where I had ceased to care and hoped to rest. Warning signs flash like confetti around me. Stop now, Dave. Stop now!

"Not much," I say. "Only that Hart married her secretly and her daddy found out about it."

Unlike Sitwell, he doesn't whistle. "Jesus! Are you serious?"

"Yes. I went to see Hart in his office and Brantley's daughter burst in like the devil was after her. Before I knew it they were laying their whole story on me. Caroline said she heard her father talking to someone on the phone about rousting Hart and came running to warn him. The way it looks, the Chairman of the Board will do just about anything to break up their marriage, even if he has to use violence."

"Incredible. An interracial marriage at Ashland!" He nods to himself. "Yes, that explains everything, especially the cover-up. And Sanford used a little friendly persuasion on the President and he got Bledsoe to fire Hart."

"Right."

"Well, it figures. Sanford's got money and clout. The President has to please him. If *he* goes, he'll take four or five other trustees with him." A pleased look enters his face. "So I was right. It wasn't just Hart's trips."

"You're sharp as a tack, Duff."

"Yeah. Anyway, what's Hart going to do? Think he'll stick? Or will Sanford make him run?"

"I don't know, except..."

"What?"

I try to shrug casually. "Except that I kind of promised to help them."

"Help them? What can you do?"

"Nothing, I guess. Go to the newspapers, maybe. Anyway, I thought it over after and realized I was just being stupid. If I get involved in this it will be my job."

"*Now* you're learning. Haven't I been telling you all along to keep a low profile? Still, your idea about going to the newspaper isn't bad."

"Oh, come on. The local gazette wouldn't even let me through the turnstile."

"Who said anything about them? They stay away from top local dirt like it's the plague. Besides, their idea of a hot item is who won the blue ribbon for marmelade at the county fair. No, I'm thinking about something big: the paper in Columbia."

"*The Enquirer?* You're pulling my leg."

"No, I mean it. As a matter of fact, Bryce Courtland—he's the managing editor—has run stories against Sanford before. Seems they're old enemies and genuinely hate each other. Courtland was even forced once to settle a slander suit out of court. From what I've heard, he's been itching to even the score ever since."

Sylvia picks this point to butt in. "But he'd hardly be interested in a personal matter like this, especially when there's no proof."

"I'm not so sure," Duff says. Although he's fading from the liquor, his eyes are suddenly shining. "You know, if the Harts were to go and tell Courtland their story in person, he just might run it. Sure it's personal. But it's also a beautiful case of racist corruption in higher education, and that's news!"

"You really think so?" I ask.

"Sure!" Duff says, figuring the angles. "You know, all this is marvelous. Just marvelous. Gad, what a story! Why, if this thing broke, Sanford, the trustees, the President, they'd all be caught in it and trying to stick the blame on each other. Especially—Bledsoe!"

Thinking of my latest interlude with The Man, I grin. "You know, you're a sharp strategist, Duffy. We'd make one hell of a team together."

He smiles back. "Maybe. But you're not thinking of getting involved in this, are you? Because let me tell you, if you do you're liable to find yourself caught between a rock and a hard place. Not only will you lose your job, you might have to kiss your ass good-by. Believe me, if Sanford wants to get his daughter away from Hart badly enough, he won't care who he hurts. One more won't make any difference."

"Don't worry, I'm staying out of this."

"You sure? Because..." Suddenly he stops and turns ashen. "Gee, I feel sick. Must have had too much to drink."

"You going to be all right?"

"I don't know. Better lie down."

"Here, let me help you."

"I can handle him," Sylvia says. Getting up, she helps him through the living room and into the bedroom, where she maneuvers him onto the bed and removes his shoes.

"Sorry about—I—Dave..."

I move closer. His eyes are closed and as I look at him,

84

something happens. Suddenly it's my face on the pillow. In the dim light I *know* that if I go to the bed I'll see the scar left above my eye from a tractor accident when I was five. Feeling disembodied, I re-enter the living room where I nervously light a cigarette and walk around. By the time she comes out I'm O.K. again except that the last shred of the banner of my new-found Inner Peace lies in Duffy's bedroom.

"Well, he's good for the night," she says, closing the bedroom door.

I put out the cigarette. We look at each other.

"Why do you do it to him?"

"Do what?"

"Take over. Put him down."

She gestures toward the kitchen. "Shall we finish dinner?"

"No thanks. I've had enough dandelions."

"Dance, then?"

"Not to that music."

She goes over and sorts through some cassettes.

"Roger Williams?"

"Fine."

She slips it in and a piano fills the room with something sad.

"May I slip off my shoes?"

I don't say anything. She slips them off her feet and comes over barefoot. I put my arm around her, being sure to keep a safe distance between us.

"You don't like me, do you?"

"I don't like the way you treat him."

"Let's not talk about him then."

Without shoes, she's shorter than I thought. The top of her head comes just to my mouth. Despite all her gimmicks, she wears no make-up. Her skin smells naked in a way I've forgotten, with no trace of soap or perfume to make it something else.

"David."

"What?"

"Let's make love."

"Why?"

"I want you."

I draw back a little. "You're quite a phony, aren't you?"

"Don't be difficult."

"Where's all that intellectual crap about pure consciousness and avoiding earthy entanglements? Or had you forgotten?"

She smiles. "It's hard to be spiritual all the time."

"Even with daddy in the next room?"

"He'll never know."

"I will."

"Oh, I see, you're being loyal to your friend."

"Let's just say that even if I were interested, I wouldn't go to bed with another man's wife."

"Better and better. You're not only a true friend but a moral paladin as well. A genuine idealist."

"Is that what I am? That's funny, the way you were treating me before, I was beginning to think I was a Neanderthal."

"Well, I was wrong, obviously. You're an idealist, and you've never touched another man's wife in your life. Right?"

Her eyes make me look away. "I just think that if you're married to someone—"

"Oh, you're so quick to judge. Well, let me tell you what it's been like to be married to Max for nine years. When I met him—"

"Listen, I really don't want—"

"When I met him he was a young professor at Yale who was hard at work on his first book. Everyone liked him and it was agreed he had a brilliant future. Naturally I fell madly in love with him, or shall I say was captivated by his self-effacing charm and intelligence. All the other men I knew were only boys, trying to hustle me into bed or impress me with how bright they were."

"You don't have—"

"Anyway, I married mild-mannered Clark Kent only to find that the "S" on his chest stood for Sissy. You see, bright as he was and with all the other things he had going for him, Max was what you might call a psychic hemophiliac, an emotional bleeder. If life just rubbed up against him he'd be in traction for weeks. Even a casual remark or light insult would make him brood and no matter how hard he tried, he couldn't forget it. You know the phrase, 'Get your head together'? Well, with Max it should read, 'Get your head to coagulate'."

"Didn't you ever try to help—"

"Listen, I've tried everything. I realize he has a problem, but what can I do? I've begged him to see a psychiatrist and so he goes for a while and I start to build up hope. Then a friend of mine sees him at a movie matinee and I find out he's been lying to me and skipping his appointments. And all the time he keeps losing jobs because he can't take it and going from bad to worse till we wind up here. Help him? God knows, I've listened to him cry and watched him destroy himself till I've felt as empty as he is. When he started drinking at parties I laughed and made excuses for him and drove him home, and when he stopped caring about sex..."

She stops, leaving me to listen to the haunting, indefinable melody of "Over The Rainbow." In a way it's like her sitar music, endlessly elusive and unobtainable, impossible to nail down. Never-never land, is it sad or beautiful or just a mockery of our wart-filled existences, a dream that is itself vulgar and pathetic because it's only another lie?

A bracelet rings beside my ear; she caresses the back of my neck.

As she moves closer, my eyes drift about the room, moving slowly as if I'm only now beginning to feel the effects of the ouzo. For the first time I really see the rattan, fan-back chair she sat in, and a question occurs to me: what can a woman do with such a life except try to fill it with whatever props she can?

The revelation is so sudden that I don't protest when her arms coax my head down. It's like I've broken through to a new understanding only to find out I'm about to make an irreversible mistake. I pull away.

"Don't fight it," she whispers. "You know you want me."

"No."

"Oh, yes. You want honesty? I'll give you some. When I opened the door your eyes popped right out of their sockets.

For the past hour you've wanted me every second, and we both know it."

I try to deny it but her mouth and arms mold me into her and I feel myself going under. Then like a jerk I struggle to the surface and wade to the door.

"David."

"Don't say it," I manage. "I'm a cretin and I deserve to be horsewhipped for this." I open the door and try to smile. "You know, this makes twice in two days I've walked out on a woman, and I'm getting sick of it."

"Don't do it, then."

"Sorry."

"Don't be. But you know, you surprise me. You really *are* one."

"One what?"

"An idealist."

This time I smile easily. "A lot of women would laugh at that one, honey."

"But you know, in the end it won't make a stitch of difference."

"Why's that?"

Her dark eyes pierce right through me.

"Because you're going to be back."

Ten

T HE NEXT MORNING I make two calls that seal my fate even
before I have my first cigarette. The first is long distance to *The
Enquirer,* where the name Brantley Sanford opens doors all
along the line till I'm talking to Mr. Big himself, who doesn't
waste time on amenities.

"Bryce Courtland speaking. What's this about a story on
Sanford? Who—"

"Mr. Courtland," I say, cutting him short, "my name is
David Newman, and I have solid evidence that Mr. Sanford is
engaged in illegal activities of a shocking nature. Are you
interested?"

"*What* activities?"

"I'd rather not discuss it over the phone. If you're interested,
I can be there anytime this afternoon."

"I'd prefer—"

"Mr. Courtland, this is explosive stuff and it's essential that
I see you *in person.*"

A pause. "All right. How about two o'clock?"

"Fine." I hang up and dial Hart, who I arrange to pick up at
noon along with Caroline. His cultivated voice sounds taut
with anxiety.

I shave quickly, adrenalinizing like mad. I'm a regular torpedo again and ready to go, committed all the way this time.
To hell with the consequences, FULL SPEED AHEAD! First,
though, I endure my morning class where Leroy Drummond
refers to Iago as that "B-*a-a-a*-d dude who screws Othello."

When I reach the block of Hart's address, I notice a brown
Chevy parked with three men in it. They look odd as hell just
sitting there, so I cruise around the block and pass them again.
The one at the wheel looks up at the building across the street. I

turn the corner and park on the other side, wondering if I'm becoming paranoid or a bit of a private eye.

I find Hart's name easily on the mailbox and climb to the second floor. He answers as soon as I knock, dapper and fully dressed, his vest and every hair in place. Only his eyes betray nervousness. Behind him Carol sits on a sofa. I go in, finding myself in one of those scrunched up, cooky-cutter apartments Connie thinks I should pay an arm and a leg for just so I can live in town.

"Well, kids, this is it," I say. "We've got an appointment with the managing editor of *The Enquirer* at two, so we're cracking the big leagues."

They both look surprised. "*The Enquirer?*" says Carol. "What are we supposed to do?"

She looks, if anything, more fetching than yesterday. No wonder that Hart and Sanford are both reluctant to give her up. I would be too.

"Just tell your story," I say. "Tell him everything."

"But why should he listen to us?" John says. "Or even care what we have to say?"

"Courtland has his reasons," I say, addressing Carol. "Apparently he's got a personal grudge against your father and has waited quite a while to even the score."

I move to the window to let them absorb things and also to check on the car out front. It's still there, and the three men in it are still resting peaceful. No reason they shouldn't be, of course. There's no law against it. On the other hand, if they've got any business around here, they sure don't seem in a hurry.

"John, come here a minute."

"What is it?"

"Ever see those men in that Chevy before?"

He gives a look. "I don't know, it's too far to tell. Why? You don't think —"

"I don't know," I say. "Maybe I'm just being jumpy. They're just sitting out there, and the car's the kind you might use when you *don't* want to be noticed. Anyway, where's your car parked?"

"Right out front." He points through the curtains to a place which anyone out there can watch easily.

"Hmm. Well, just to be on the safe side, we'll take my car. It's parked out back. If they are watching us, we can give them the slip."

"I can't believe my father would go so far," Carol says. "I mean, actually hire men to watch us."

"But you warned John," I point out. "And didn't you say you heard your father set it up on the phone?"

"Yes, but it's just not like my father," she says. John goes behind the sofa and places his hands on her shoulders. "I mean, he's never done anything like this before. He's always been so calm and rational."

"Love can make us do strange things," I say. "Which reminds me, John, just what did he say when he talked to you?"

She turns her head to look up at him.

"Nothing much."

"No? You said before he practically burned a cross."

"Well, he did make it plain I was a little dark for his taste and that he felt I was after her money."

"But nothing else? Didn't he try to talk you out of it?"

His hands fidget a little. "Well, at first he was very calm about it, pointing out how difficult it was for an interracial marriage to work. He seemed especially concerned with what the strain would do to Caroline."

"And that was it? Nothing else?"

He pauses. Carol notices it at once.

"What is it, John? What else did he do?"

"Nothing."

"*John.*" She's holding one of his hands now and has turned around to him. "What *else* did he do?"

He looks at her reluctantly. "Offered me some money."

"Money? He tried to *pay* you, to buy you off? How much? How much did he—"

"Now, honey, don't—"

"No, I want to know. How much?"

91

He takes a breath. "A hundred thousand."

"A hundred thousand," she says and stops. The shock and hurt register in her face, and for an instant I think she's going to cry. But she's tough. "Well," she says, "at least I know now how much I'm worth to my father. A hundred thousand." She looks up again at him. "It's a good price, John. Maybe you should have taken it."

He smiles. "Baby, I was sure tempted."

His small joke saves the moment. Even Carol manages to smile. I use the opportunity to suggest that we leave for our appointment.

We relax a little on the way to Columbia and become such fast friends that I have to remind myself to check the rearview mirror now and then for the Chevy. John and Carol keep making jokes at Big Red's expense. When their banter gets just a tad on the slanderous side, I shoot back.

"Listen, I don't know much about you kids. How'd you meet, anyway? Blind date?"

Uncomfortable as John pretends to be riding in Big Red, I notice he's managed to get an arm around Carol. She snuggles against him while he nuzzles her hair.

"Lucky guess," Carol laughs. "My roommate fixed us up."

"Not exactly a typical couple," I suggest.

"Depends how you look at it. Actually, I saw John perform at a school recital and hunted him down afterward."

"He must have been playing your tune. Tell me, how did your father find out about John?"

"Through my roommate. He went to my old place one day and she became so flustered she spilled everything. When he found out I'd been living with John and we were married, he couldn't believe it. Poor dad, he couldn't even conceive I would do such a thing. When it finally sank in, he couldn't stand to look at me. He just walked out."

"Must have been rough."

She nods. "It has been. You know, I've been—"

"What?"

"Well, I guess you could say I've been sheltered all my life, raised in what you might call the 'proper' tradition." She looks at John and blushes. "It never even occurred to me I could fall for a black man."

"Maybe you shouldn't have," John says.

"I'm not sorry," she says. "Not for one second. You're the one who's had to struggle."

"Maybe it would have been better if we had announced our marriage to begin with instead of hiding it. I should have had more courage."

"Don't be hard on yourself," I say.

He gazes out at the countryside. "You know," he says hesitantly, "Caroline and I have this much in common: we've both had it easy and never had to struggle for anything. My father's even like Sanford in a way. He's a self-made architect who was determined I'd never experience what he did."

"What's wrong with that?"

He turns away from a yard filled with black kids playing around a collapsed porch. "Everything—or nothing. It's just that what I said yesterday is true. I've never been near a ghetto, and it's been a long time since anyone called me 'nigger'—that is, until I moved down here." He looks out the window again, his fine profile troubled. "Sometimes you lose something when it's too easy," he says haltingly. "Everything's given to you so you're never tested and don't know for sure just what you are. And it takes something like Mr. Sanford calling you a nigger to wake you up and make you realize you are black even though you don't feel like it. You aren't just a white man with black skin but actually a member of a race that's survived hundreds of years of persecution."

"Forget race. It doesn't mean anything."

He shakes his head. "That's where you're wrong, Dave. I might have agreed with you before I came down from Princeton. But it means everything when you have to fight for the woman you love." He takes Carol's hand and then drops it. "Trouble is," he says, pounding the door with his fist, "I've never really been in a fight. I've never had to do it. Guess that's partly why I came here: to test myself and find out who I am by teaching kids who've never had the opportunities I've had. Looks now like I'll have a chance to find out a lot about...."

His voice fades away. He gazes out at green fields, lost in his inner battle, and it's not till we're actually in the City Room, a large expanse of cluttered desks with flourescent panels overhead, that he rejoins us. Passing a glassed-in office with City Desk stenciled on it, we stop at a wooden door. The man who has led us there raps and enters, leaving us to listen to telephones and typewriters.

"You can go in."

"Thanks." We enter and I shake hands with Courtland.

"Mr. Newman?"

"Yes. And this is Mr. and Mrs. Hart."

"How do you do. Please sit down."

He returns to his desk while we sit. "Now, how can I be of service?" he says with the brisk air of one who does not waste his time with chatter. "I believe you said on the phone that you have information regarding Mr. Sanford."

"Before we proceed," I say, "perhaps I should mention that Mrs. Hart's maiden name is Sanford."

Courtland's horn-rimmed glasses turn from John to Carol and at once he shows the quick perception and instinct of a good newsman. He goes to the door, opens it, and crooks a finger.

"Slater."

He speaks softly but almost instantly a man enters with a notepad. Courtland returns to his chair, presses a button and says, "Hold all calls." Then he smiles, gracious where before he had seemed almost impatient.

"Please go ahead."

Haltingly at first, John starts to speak, supported now and then by Carol. Occasionally Slater asks a question and writes something in his pad. Courtland just listens, giving the impression of a man who doesn't miss much. In the meantime I gaze at the gleaming newspaper award plaques on the wall behind Courtland's head and wonder why he doesn't put some distance between himself and this story by passing it on to the

City Editor. After all, Sanford could trace it back and try to prove malicious intent. Whatever Sanford did originally to make him hate him, it must have been real dirty pool.

When John's through, Courtland looks at Slater as if to ask, "What do you think?"

"Looks good, but we need confirmation. I'll check Sanford's business associates and a few of the trustees who are close to him. If it's true, I'll get it out of them."

"Good. Get on it."

Slater leaves. Courtland smiles.

"Well, that's quite a story."

"Can you print it?" I ask.

He shrugs. "Depends on what Mr. Slater finds. At the moment, it's Mr. and Mrs. Hart's word against the others that he was fired for marrying Sanford's daughter."

"What about the men he hired?" John asks.

"Unfortunately we can't prove that, Mr. Hart. The telephone conversation your wife heard is open to interpretation and the men in the car may be imaginary for all we know."

"So it doesn't look good."

"Oh, I think it does. I asked Mr. Slater in here for a reason. Believe me, if there's any proof at all, he's the one to find it."

"I see."

"Incidentally, Mr. Hart, if you're really interested in receiving satisfaction, I suggest you seek legal counsel at once."

"I don't know. I'll have to think about it."

"Are you sure? I can provide you with the name of a reputable attorney who's one of the best in the country in just these matters. And if it's the cost that concerns you—"

"No, it's not that. It's just that right now I haven't decided on what else, if anything, I'm going to do."

"I see. Well, in the event you *should* change your mind, let me give you his business card. His phone number's right on it, and I can assure you that any expense will be, let us say, quite reasonable."

I watch him hand over the card and sensing that's it, get up. Courtland escorts us to the door where he takes Carol's hands

95

in a paternalistic gesture.

"My dear," he says, "I know this has all been most unpleasant for you."

"Not at all, it's—"

"Really, you have my sympathies. I'm sure it has been very trying." He looks at John and something ugly flickers in his face. John sees it too and stiffens. "I hope you don't mind," Courtland continues, "if I commiserate with you a bit. You see, years ago I was also victimized by your father. I was involved with one of several interests seeking to buy property for industrial purposes. The bids were supposed to be sealed, but your father fraudulently—"

Christ, so that's what his hatred of Sanford comes down to: money. Carol, however, does something that raises her ten feet in my estimation. Withdrawing her hands, she cuts him off.

"If you don't mind, Mr. Courtland, I'd prefer not to hear any more criticisms of my father."

"Oh—certainly." Covering smoothly, he opens the door. "Thank you for coming."

The drive back is quiet. John returns to his private world and Carol can't get him out of it. My excitement has subsided and I'm wondering if anything will come out of this. More than that, though, I'm hung up on Sylvia Duffy. "You're going to be back," she had said. See you soon.

A block from where they live, John asks me to let him off and to take Carol to her former roommate's apartment.

"John, don't do this."

He gets out and puts his hand over hers in the car window. "Baby, I want to walk and be alone for a while."

"*Please.*"

He looks at me and I drive on. Carol sits absolutely rigid for a few blocks and then strikes the dashboard.

"Turn around."

"He said—"

"I said, turn around! Damn it, I can't take any more of this. Why do you men always have to prove how brave you are? It's like you're not even sure you exist until you've risked your lives for some stupid cause. If John doesn't stop tormenting himself, I won't lose him to my father, I'll lose him to John Hart. It's time he stopped it so we can live!"

I turn obediently and head back. When I get close I see John talking to two men outside his apartment, and even as I park I can tell it's no friendly conversation. I tell Carol to wait, for all the good that will do, and with her at my heels I cross the street, looking around for the third man.

One of the men is my size. The other is a regular monster as tall as John and maybe forty pounds heavier. He's got John backed all the way against the wall.

"Let's go inside for a minute. We want to talk to you."

"We can talk out here."

"Naw, it's not *pri-vate* enough. C'mon, be a good boy and cooperate."

"Maybe he doesn't want to," I say.

The big man turns his head and notices us. He's got heavy eyebrows that practically meet in the middle to form a single line and no one has to tell me he's one tough son of a bitch. John's face has metamorphosed into stone. He looks like someone who has come a long way to an ultimate moment.

"Well," the big one croons to his partner, "look who we've got here. Snow White and one of her dwarfs."

"Very funny," I say, hearing my voice crack. "Now, why don't you take this other goon and make yourselves scarce?"

"Yes, why don't you stop bothering us?" Carol says. "I'll pay you more than my father just to leave us alone."

"I can handle this by myself," John says. "Dave, take her to her roommate like I told you."

"Now you're getting smart," the big one croons again while the other just watches me, alert as a weasel. "C'mon, let's go."

"Like I said before, we can conduct our business out here."

"Conduct our business. Conduct our business. My, aren't we the smart nigger? Let me tell you something, boy, if you don't want your blonde gal to see her little black buck broke off, you better be more friendly." Smiling, he moves his hand with elaborate slowness and snaps a finger hard against John's fly. "Understand, boy?"

John flinches in pain and then his mouth hardens. The damn

ape's got his grinning face right up against Hart's and the other's on me like white on rice. It can't go on like this, I think. Something's got to give.

"Go to hell," John says.

"What?" The big man cups his ear in fake surprise. "I don't believe I—"

"I said, go to hell!"

"John," I say, "let's shake it," and throw a right at the one before me. I do it as fast as I can, but even so I barely get a piece of his cheekbone while he digs a fist into my ribs. From then on it's cover-up time for a while with me folding against the wall as he tries to neuter me with his knee. I manage to catch it on my thigh and block a shot to the head. His knee comes up again and I grab it and jerk him down. Carol's screaming and behind me I hear some heavy blows, but I'm too busy to see what's happening. The guy's on top and chops down. My head explodes; I feel myself going under. I try to kick him off and partly succeed, only to have him connect with a left that rips my cheek like a scalpel. Damn bastard's wearing a ring. I struggle up and as he moves toward me I throw my last punch. The timing's just right. I nail him just as he comes in and about thirty phalanges go in my hand. The impact travels all the way to my shoulder, and he drops to the sidewalk and stays put.

Swaying dizzily, I wonder if I'm going to join him. When my vision clears, I see that John has squared off against the other man, and as I watch, he removes his coat with almost a theatrical gesture and casts it behind him.

I'm so surprised he's still standing that I forget his opponent. Then I notice there are streaks of blood streaming from the big man's nose and mouth. John, in contrast, looks magnificent. Poised on his feet, he has his hair mussed for probably the first time in his life, and his snug vest accentuates the powerful build of his chest and shoulders.

"You fuckin' coon, I'm gonna kill you!"

The man charges in and hurls an enormous roundhouse right. John slips it and moving like Ali, shoots three straight left jabs. Wap! Wap! Wap! Each one connects, the man's head snapping back as if hit by a drill. I watch in amazement. Moving gracefully like he's been doing it all his life, like he learned it at his mother's knee, he outflanks the man again and again, pumping lefts and rights into his face and belly. Then as John slips between him and the wall, the man lunges forward and manages to grab him around the waist. He lifts John against the wall, trying to crush him, and for what seems an hour they struggle there. At last John gets the heel of his hand under the other's nose and slowly forces his head back, and when the man drops him John starts to hit him with everything but the corner lamppost. A left, a right, a left... Overwhelmed, the man tries to cover up and then desperately lunges forward again, and when he does, John shifts his feet and finally throws it. It's a beautiful combination, a short right followed by a left hook, and it lands where all the marbles are. The man grunts, staggers away, and goes down like a sack of shit.

For a moment we're all stunned. Then Carol runs and embraces him. He holds her close and blinks at the man on the sidewalk, trying to believe it. I feel the laughter coming from a long way down and stagger toward him.

"John!"

"What?"

"Man—you is—one tough nigguh!"

He stares back and then slowly grins.

"Honky, you ain't no slouch yourself!"

By now Carol's laughing and crying at the same time and we're laughing and slap hands like brothers. Suddenly it feels so damn good.

The guys on the sidewalk, though, don't quite share our enthusiasm. John retrieves his coat and we get them up. One arm around Carol, he prods them across the street toward a car I had overlooked, which turns out to be the brown Chevy. The big man's silent and sullen, and a couple of times John has to push him ahead, snapping his orders in a voice that has in it the best stuff I've heard from him. When we reach the car the men get in and John goes to the back where a distinguished looking man with silver hair glances at him with a feral hatred similar to Courtland's before riveting his gaze to the front. The third man.

"Mr. Sanford," John says softly, leaning his head down, "I'm only going to say this once, so you better listen. You can't buy me off, scare me off, or shoot me off, so get used now to the fact that I'm going to be married to your daughter for a long long time. And one more thing, if you ever try to intimidate me and my wife again, you better be prepared, because I won't be going to the police, I'll be coming for you."

Sanford stares straight ahead, expressionless and implacable. John steps back and just as Solomon Wise did for me, he presses the button down on the door to lock it. The Chevy pulls away, and as it gains speed it occurs to me that this time *I'm* a reflection in a rearview mirror. A phrase enters my head. *Polarities of existence.* Wonder if it means anything? But before I can decide, the car's three blocks off and going away fast.

Eleven

For three days I check *The Enquirer,* hoping to find that they've published the story. Then on the fourth I'm sitting in McDonald's with the newspaper before me, when I happen to glance up and see Sylvia come out of Piggly Wiggly with some groceries. For a minute I just sit there as she turns left past Bankers Trust in a wood-paneled station wagon and disappears. The paper crinkles in my hand. A fat woman sausaged into toreador pants waddles past.

Then I'm skitterfooting to Big Red like a character in a Keystone Cop comedy and sweating over the ignition which gargles over and over, trying to clear its throat. The woman in toreador pants comes back, lured by the music. By now, I tell myself, she could be in the next county if she made every light. And even if she didn't, it would take a pack of bloodhounds to track her down. Come to think of it, what am I doing this for? Why don't I just go back and scan the rest of the late edition?

The engine catches. Missing Toreador's tush by inches, Big Red lunges onto the street and follows the cold scent of the station wagon. Turning at the bank, I race to the light where I glance left right. Nothing. It's a toss-up. Since it's legal in S.C. to turn right on red, I head that way. A light turns red. I roar through, forcing an old lady to jump back to the curb. Any second now they're going to stick a siren in my ear. Then far up the street I spot the station wagon. I whip around a pickup truck and pass two cars. Somebody blasts his horn. I run another light and catch her entering a parking lot outside another supermarket. Slowing, I turn over to the curb and slip the gearshift into neutral.

As I light a cigarette some drops spatter the window. Pit pat. Pit pat. In a minute it's raining lightly and steam begins to rise

from the hot street. I consider the Pepsodent front of Red &
White. Which door will she come out of? Five Georges says it's
the left. Will she have one bag or two? Ten says it's two. What
about her umbrella? Will she open it inside or outside the
store? In my mind I see her struggling in the parking lot to open
it. A gust of wind comes along and rakes it inside out, snapping
its metal ribs. Twenty big ones says she opens her umbrella in
the parking lot and almost drops a bag of eggplants.

When she comes out of the left door with one bag and no
umbrella, I pay myself twenty-five dollars and watch her hurry
to her car where she searches for her keys. She does it all
wrong. Instead of setting the bag on top of the car, she tries to
hold it and get her purse open at the same time. To do this she
must tuck the bag up under her chin and lift her knee slightly to
support her purse. The pose is so feminine that I'm amazed; it
links her despite her quirks to that Great and Imperial Time-
less Order of Women. Dry and comfortable, I feel protective
toward her in a way you can only when you are watching
someone without their knowing.

Finally she finds her keys and we hit the road again.

The chase now takes me clear across town and down some
of Green Town's most beautiful streets. I pass white colonial
mansions with stately colonnades and ranch-style homes with
walls carpeted by ivy. Above, trees arch to form a natural
canopy and in the rich semi-gloom the contrasting colors har-
monize perfectly. Spanish moss hangs down like brown beards
from leaves of a million different greens, some dark, some so
light as to be translucent. Here and there sunlight lances down.
The rain, a mere drizzle now, floats in these patches in a glittering gauze and I can smell the air's freshness.

So caught up am I by the scenery that I do a dumb thing. I let
a Sting Ray butt in between me and the station wagon, and
when it turns off and I get to the corner she's gone.

For a moment I just sit, refusing to believe it. It's such a long
way to the next turn that she could never have made it before I
reached the corner. Flooring the pedal I race to the corner and
check in both directions. Zilch.

Asshole! How could you do it? As I start combing the streets, the absurdity of it burns me like a chancre. First, like a miracle, I find her all the way across town, and now practically filling her rearview mirror, I lose her. And why am I doing all this, making a fuss and risking a ticket over a woman I just met? My search takes me further and further, ranging down streets where tin shacks sit on blocks and black folks watch me streak by. At one corner I damn near bag my first chicken, which squawks to safety before my bumper. Hopeless, I double back, tires screeching as I run stop signs and plunge around turns. Then out of nowhere I'm on Main Street, which in Green Town is a Shit Strip cluttered with Hardies and McDonalds signs. The bird has flown the coop, and I have as much chance of finding her as I do of being nominated by Bledsoe for Teacher of the Year. Still, I cruise along, for no other reason than it seems better than doing nothing, and am rewarded by the sight of the station wagon parked in front of one of those roadside markets they have around town.

I pull over. She's standing near a sign marked PECANS, fondling what looks like an avocado. I watch her move from table to table, squeezing here, probing there, picking this up, putting that back. When she finally finishes I'm ready, edging out into traffic so as not to get separated again. But this time there's no need to worry. She hangs a left in front of a Winn Dixie Mr. Magoo could follow and I take a gamble and turn a block before she does into the parking lot *behind* the store.

Now it's a race to the turnip patch, pure and simple. All I have to do is open the door and leap out and jump puddle and sprain my ankle and hop on my one good leg to the rear door and enter and hop to vegetables on left side of store and rip off plastic bag and look busy. Success! She's not even in sight and all I've had to pay for my victory is a throbbing ankle.

Unless, that is, my latest stunt has clinched the Schmuck of the Year Award. After all, how do I know she has turned into the lot in front of the store and entered it? How do I know she hasn't simply slipped the juice to those 350 horses and galloped for home, leaving me standing here like a prize goose?

O.K. O.K. Cool it.

I pick up a tomato and drop it in my bag, aware that I'm nervous and short of breath. My shirt feels too tight. I start loving up another tomato the way I've seen housewives do, checking it for ruptures and midriff bulge.

Footsteps.

Coming my way.

I turn the tomato over and massage the other side, examining its muscle tone and looking absorbed in what I'm doing. The footsteps stop and I casually look up.

Into the face of a plump black woman.

So I guessed wrong. She didn't stop. The woman leaves and I move down by the cantaloupes and glumly paw a few. What the hell, I'm wasting my talents here. She's had all the time in the world to show up. Disgusted, I turn to leave just in time to see Sylvia Duffy coming my way.

"Mr. Newman."

"Hi, it's a small world."

What an original, super hip conversation opener! Tomatoes in hand, I resist the urge to swallow, afraid of showing how nervous I am. I can't think of a damn thing more to say. Sylvia saves it, though. Looping an arm through mine, she escorts me spiritedly over to the lettuce where she recruits me in her search for a small head. "And remember, I want it crisp and tender too."

I pitch in but she immediately outdistances me. Her hands move quickly, expertly, like those of a peasant woman long schooled in the ways of the market place. As a matter of fact, she wears what looks like a peasant dress, something plaid and high-waisted with long white ruffled sleeves. The thing's at least five years too young for her.

"Voilà!"

She holds up a small head of lettuce.

"Congratulations."

"Go ahead, feel it."

I comply. "Vintage."

"You bet it is. Do you know, I've been to half a dozen stores looking for a head like this? I'm trying out a new recipe."

"What is it?"

"Aguacate Con Chirmol."

"Come again?"

"Avocado with fresh tomato relish."

"Oh."

"And what's that?"

"This?" I hoist the bag. "Tomatoes."

"I can see that. What are they for?"

"Chili. I was thinking of mixing myself a batch."

"Chili?" We look at each other and then break out laughing. A kid stamping cans turns to look at us. Suddenly everything's all right.

"Hello, Sylvia."

"Hello, David."

I stand there, aching to touch her. Surprisingly, drops of rain still glisten in her hair.

"Well, aren't you going to offer me some?"

"Some what?"

"Chili."

"Are you serious? I thought you were a princess of high cuisine, not to mention a vegetarian."

"Well, I've been known to slum occasionally."

"Then I'm your man, milady. And if chili's your dish, the Greasy Spoon next door should be just your cup of tea."

Next door we inherit a booth from an old friend, Solomon Wise, who has just finished.

"David, who is that boy?"

"What boy?"

"The tall black one we took the table from. He acted like he knew you."

I glance over at the cash register where Solomon stands, his eyes seeming to reach deep inside me. I look away.

"Just a student."

"Oh. By the way, how did you get that cut?"

"This?" I touch my cheek where Sanford's thug marked me with his ring. "It's nothing. Just a shaving accident. Incidentally, how's Duff?"

"Why ask?"

"Well, I haven't seen him since your place. I get the feeling he's ducking me."

"Could be. He's pretty embarrassed, you know. And when Max gets that way, he hides from *everybody*."

"Yes, but—"

"He still bothers you, doesn't he? Just because you desire me."

Desire. How quaint. Damn it, why does she have to put things so plainly?

"What makes you think I want you?"

She takes my hand. "Forget Max, this has nothing to do with him."

"I don't—"

"Don't you?" She smiles like she's cornered a mouse. "Well, if you're not interested, why were you pursuing me a while ago?"

"Pursuing?"

"Yes." She brings her other hand over and pets my fingers. "Poor David, you really ought to take a course in Trailing and Tracking."

Red faced, I consider bluffing but give it up.

"Was I really that bad?"

She laughs. "Oh, David, I've never seen anything like it. In that red station wagon you glowed like a neon sign, and I couldn't believe it when you started crashing those lights and screeching your tires behind me. Didn't you hear all those drivers honking at you?"

I look away. "Well, James Bond I'm not."

"No, but you're persistent, though you managed to lose me a couple times. Once I even stopped and waited, hoping you'd find me again."

"Looks like you succeeded."

"I'm not so sure. Somehow, I think there was a Comstock lode of luck in the whole thing, like when you guessed I'd be stopping at Winn Dixie and arrived there first. David?"

"Yes?"

"Do you think we're destined to be lovers?"

"Destined? Like in the stars?"

"Hmm."

"Like maybe Venus is hot on us making it together?"

"Something like that. Do you?"

"I don't know, Sylvia. To tell the truth, I think she's got better things to do than run a mating service."

"Still, it would account for one thing, wouldn't it?"

"What's that?"

"Why you can't resist me."

"Honey, there's been a hundred women I couldn't resist, and I don't think Venus had anything to do with them. Not unless she's a switchboard operator who can plug 'em quick as I do."

She lifts my hand and moves her cheek against it.

"Shhh, don't fight it so much. Just let yourself go."

At this point the waitress comes and I hear my voice order chili and cokes. My hand remains incarcerated against her cheek with the lock of entrapment being my confusion. Who *is* she, anyway? Sophisticated one minute, the next she throws a word like destiny around with all the ingenuousness of my students who make a pop religion out of astrology. Christ, does she believe in such junk or is she just playing? Maybe a little of both. And maybe she's right. Maybe Pluto has zapped me with a triple whammy and that's why I'm chasing her like Bozo the Clown.

Whatever the case, she's got my hand, and it's not till the chili comes that she releases it. Freedom, though, proves not to be worth it. The stuff tastes like Pampas grass and I can see from her face it isn't scoring any points.

"Sorry about the chili."

"It's not bad, really."

"You ought to try it the way I make it, Chili à la Newman. Lean hamburger, beans, tomatoes, onions, plus my own special blend of herbs and spices aged and simmered to a turn. An exquisite gustatory delight, guaranteed to make your taste buds snap to attention and salute."

"I'll tell you what I'd *really* like right now."

"What?"

She smiles wickedly. "Mr. Newman, now that you've shattered my resistance with haute cuisine, don't you think it's time you invited me into your bed?"

I swallow and glance out the window where it's started to rain again.

"O.K.," I say after a moment. " Just remember to follow the idealist in the neon sign with the loud tires."

Twelve

So now *she* follows *me,* and every five seconds I check the mirror to see she doesn't get more than fifty feet behind.

The Pee Dee River is jet black. Peppered by rain, it flows past a bamboo brake, azaleas, dogwoods, palmettos, and finally down a corridor of cypress trees festooned with Spanish moss toward a wooden water wheel soft with mossy decay. Climbing a hill, I look briefly down upon a group of black swimmers. The males are lean and sinewy as few whites are, the women softer, some swollen and grotesque from Colonel Sanders and too many sweets, others succulent as mangos with melon breasts and the extra high firm buttocks they often have. Children squeal, splash, catch minnows, and dive from a pier into water that has almost never known a white swimmer.

Leaving the river, I turn onto the Shit Strip again, heading the opposite way from which I followed her earlier. My brain's like Grand Central Station. Duffy's there along with a throbbing conscience, not to mention Courtland and Sanford, John and Carol, and the mugs we whipped on the sidewalk. When I come out of it, we're in my pad and she's stashing our groceries in the fridge. Closing the door, she takes my hand and draws me to the bed where the Sunday funnies lie scattered.

"Make me naked," she whispers.

I go for the zipper in back but my fingers are not only numb but shaking, which makes my task comparable to peeling a pea with a catcher's mitt.

"I thought you had done this before."

"I have, nine thousand times."

"You're not a virgin, are you?"

"Don't be mean."

"Shhh, just take your time."

Finally I get the thing down but stop like I've forgotten everything I've ever learned. I'm twelve years old again, fumbling with an older girl in a wheat field. Like her, Sylvia has to take the lead. Her dress cascades onto the floor and in a few seconds she's more naked than I've ever seen anyone before, a continent of skin waiting for exploration. Bold pioneer that I am, I swallow loudly in the silence.

"Come here."

I obey and don't protest as her fingers busy themselves at my shirt. When she gets it off she sits down on the edge of the bed. I feel her fingers flit from button to button like bees, touching lightly and extracting honey from each moment. In the semi-darkness her face wears a peaceful, pensive look like that of a mother undressing her child. When she gets my pants and jockies down I obediently raise each leg so she can free them. Then she's removing my shoes and socks as if she's progressing from step to step of a ritual. Calmer now, I submit as her hands caress my calves and thighs and rise to the proud pole of my manhood. Her touch there is a form of praise, an acknowledgment, and quickly I urge her back and take command. She acquiesces with a smile that seems both maternal and wanton, and as I melt into her I lose pieces of myself all the way down, falling and falling until I open and come out the other side. Then I'm there, splendidly there, and the surging of my seed is answered by her contractions about my core.

Afterwards she holds me tightly while I listen to the rain on the roof.

"David."

"What?"

"Do you know what 'David' means?"

"Tell me."

She puts her mouth against my ear. "Beloved."

"Oh."

"David?"

"Yes."

"What are you thinking about?"

Above, the rain strums a delicate riff, and I recall how it had also been raining that first time in the wheat field. Only this time it had been better. Snuggling close, I inhale the perfect wheat smell of her.

"You."

She squeezes me again.

Watch it, bud. Already she's showing the kind of possessiveness that an old artful dodger like you should recognize on sight. Better bail out now. Besides, she's Duffy's woman.

Suddenly I leave her and sit up.

"David?"

"What."

"Why are you still pushing me away?"

"I don't know what you mean."

"Don't you? Look at me."

"O.K., now what?"

She takes my hand. "Am I coming on too strong? Is that it?"

"Don't be—"

"Oh, I know what you must think. God, it's practically a cliché: 'Bored neurotic woman married to Walter Mitty type pounces on first man that comes her way.'" She pauses. "I suppose you hear talk all the time at work about how easy I—"

I touch her. "Don't."

"All right. I just want you to know I'm not trying to trap you. Being married to Max isn't easy, but I'm tough and don't want any pity. And I don't make alibis for anything I've done, either."

This time I stop her with a kiss. When I finally pull away I'm so confused I jerk my pants on and go to the window.

"Do you know one reason I'm drawn to you?" she says.

I turn around. She's half-kneeling in bed with her weight resting back against her ankles so that the smooth muscular contours of her thighs are accentuated. A loop of dark hair falls across her cheek and she brushes it back.

"It's because ever since I met you, I've been receiving waves or psychic emanations which suggest that you're searching for yourself, that you're trying to find out who you are."

I shrug. "Most people are like that a little."

"Oh, no they're not. Whether they admit it or not, most people decide early who they are and don't change." Her eyes turn inward. "Or else they have it decided for them, make a commitment of some kind that determines everything."

"You could always leave him," I say, the words out of my mouth before I know it.

She colors. "It's not just Max. It's *me*. Oh, David, people get molded and freeze up so quickly. And once they do, there's no going back. Leaving a husband or finding a new job won't do it because it doesn't change *them*. Take me, for instance. I can't simply go back to college and major in Business Administration, which was what I was doing when I met Max. It's too late for that."

"You majored in Bus Ad? That's hard to—"

"Listen, originally I wanted to have my own boutique and sell exotic objects from all over the world. Art, jewelry, incense, clothes. I'd call it Sylvia's Curiosity Shoppe—that's 'Shoppe' with two 'p's' and an 'e'—and after a while I'd branch out into other shoppes all under my name. I wanted to own and run things, be a success."

Which explains why you still want to dominate and control, I think. Not to mention your arty lifestyle. So your wacky apartment's the boutique you never had, the remnant of a dream. I shake my head, amazed at how I've misjudged people lately. First Connie with her radical past and now Sylvia, a merchant turned mystic. Does any of it add up or make sense? Yes, it must. But how and why we end up the way we do is beyond me.

"I'm not sure I buy what you say," I venture. "If it's true, we're pretty damn rigid and can't do much of anything about our lives."

"And so we can't. But with you there's the aura somehow of malleability, as if your life force is still in flux and the big decision or shaping event in your life is yet to come. And when it does, I want to be there to see it." She gets up and comes over to me. "Do you understand what I mean?"

I put my arms around her, thinking of how much I want her and of the indirect role she played in making me go see Courtland. If she hadn't kept irritating me by her behavior and by putting Max down, I would never have mentioned Hart's troubles to him in the first place.

"In a way I do," I say. "Like the other day I tried to stop taking things so seriously all the time and trying to make them better. But it didn't work out."

"Why not?"

"I met you."

She rubs herself against me, so pleased she almost purrs. "Well, that's a change, isn't it? The Redcross Knight gets himself *involved*. The idealist comes down to earth."

I shake my head, getting sick of all this talk because it's only getting me more confused. Looking at her, I feel suddenly both better and worse than I've ever felt in my whole life, and plaster a big phony grin on my face.

"So you're the big change, huh?" I lower my head and nuzzle her breast.

"Maybe I am, a little. But somehow I think it goes much deeper than that." Slipping my grasp, she goes back to the bed and starts getting dressed. "And when the big moment does come, we'll both know it."

Speaking of big moments, there's a nice little crowd pleaser coming our way, and it doesn't take the *Bhagavad-gītā* or Sylvia's mystic brand of ESP to predict it. The sound of a car door slamming reminds me of what I would have remembered if she hadn't bewitched me. Idiot, how could you forget? In the five seconds left to contemplate my sin and do penance, I only have time to stick a mental boot up my ass before the door opens and Connie walks in.

Naturally she's got a laundry bag, and just as naturally, she takes the whole scene in at once without a flicker. There's Sylvia with only her slip on, and here's me with just my pants. Do I at least have my fly buttoned? A flash of reflection informs me that when I jumped into my denims I skipped over that nicety. Talk about lousy etiquette: you expect your mistress and when she shows, you're shacking up with someone else with your cock hanging out.

Luckily, though, I'm not the kind who gets tongue-tied in a crisis.

"Hello, Connie, I'd like you to meet—"

"I'm Sylvia Duffy," says Sylvia, walking half naked over to her and shaking her hand.

"Connie Weston."

"Well, I'm so glad to meet you. It's been quite a drizzly day, hasn't it? Hope it doesn't last." Still talking, she goes back to the bed where she slips into her dress and sits down. Briskly she straps on her shoes. "You know," she says, not even looking at me, "it's odd David never mentioned you. I thought I knew all his friends."

"Really? I don't find it odd at all. He never mentioned you either."

Sylvia smiles. "Well, now you know, don't you?"

Sylvia's bitchiness plus being discussed in the third person are beginning to make me burn. But before I can say anything she's up again like a dynamo.

"Honey, do me in back, won't you?"

"Sure." Feeling like a clod, I work the zipper up.

"Thank you, dear." She turns and gives me a proprietary peck. "Oh, my groceries. Guess I'll just leave them here in the refrigerator. See you tomorrow, huh? I'll cook lunch."

"Well..."

"Fine." Snapping up her purse, she smiles again at Connie. "It's been nice meeting you, really."

"Same here."

"Hmm. Well, wish I had the time to chat but I've got to rush." Breezing past her, she disappears. The screen door bangs.

Connie looks at me. I clear my throat.

"Sorry."

"What for?"

"For dumping on you like that. I just forgot you were coming. And Sylvia—I don't know why she treated you that way."

She gives a brittle smile. "She obviously felt she had a right to."

"Well, she didn't."

"No? I'm not too sure. After all, she *is* my replacement."

"That's ridiculous." I go over and touch her shoulder.

"She's just a woman I met."

Connie shakes her head and moves toward the window, through which I can see the rain. "I'm a sensible, old-fashioned girl," she says. "Pre-Womens Lib. And I've learned that one of the surest signs it's over is when someone else starts leaving groceries in your man's refrigerator."

"That's a lot of—"

"Look." She stands neatly efficient in her starched uniform, every hair, unlike Sylvia's, crisply in place. "I first got the feeling things were different last week when I cooked you veal scaloppini for dinner. I guess I should have known then, especially when your mind seemed to be elsewhere in bed. But I just didn't want to admit it." She folds the laundry bag and gives it a pat. "Well, that's that."

Again I go over, only this time I put my arms around her. "Aw, honey, don't talk like that. Nothing's changed. We can go on just—"

"Why do you keep denying it? Don't you know what's happened?"

"Happened? What's happened?"

She starts to answer but stops. For a moment she studies me in surprise and then touches my cheek.

"Poor baby," she says, her voice suddenly soft. "You really don't know, do you? But of course you don't. You've been alone so long you haven't learned to understand or handle it yet."

"For God's sake, what the hell are you talking about?"

"Funny, I always thought when it came to someone he was supposed to know it. But I guess I was wrong. Some people need more time." She strokes my cheek and smiles slightly. "But it's good for you, honey. It'll be rocky, especially for you, but when you think about all the people it never happens to at all—well, it's the only thing in life that counts. Good or bad, without it there's nothing."

Dropping her hand, she goes to the door. "Damn it," she says after a few seconds, "I would have been better for you. I would have cared. This one will only bleed you if you don't

115

stop her." She pauses. "But I guess that's part of it, isn't it? All of those new things you have to learn." She opens the door and closes it from the other side. "Good-by."

At the window, I light a cigarette and part the curtains she picked for the place. On the pond in back, I can see ducks glide in clusters. The wind blows, scattering leaves over the water. A tall figure's standing beyond the pond, his eyes probing mine, and in the instant before recognition I feel a nerve rip through my body. Wise.

I drop the curtains and step hurriedly back. Solomon Wise. What the hell is he doing there? Must be seeing things. Nervously I separate the curtains again and look out. The ducks and pond are still there but he's gone. I scan the area, my eyes so sharp I even spot a fallen branch lying in the water near the far bank, but it's not for some time that I notice the wind has died and it has stopped raining.

Thirteen

At the fairgrounds there's a large brown tent staked up. Beside it, parked so that it can be seen by anyone passing on the road, a gray-white tin trailer fifty feet long makes its carnival pitch:

Known As
Divine
Heart

SHOWERS OF LOVE
REVIVALS INC.

THE HONORABLE
DR. MARTIN LUTHER EAGLEHART
"THE PROPHET WHO NEVER DOUBTS GOD"

Blind See   Lame Walk   Deaf Hear   Dumb Talk

Hallelujah, Brother! Step right in and get your soul picked clean by Jee-zus. If there's a dime in your dungarees anywhere, He'll ferret it out and Save you from the Temptation of spending it. So Repent ye of worldly things and open your wallet to Jee-zus. Amen, Brother, Amen.

Leaving Dr. Eaglehart behind, I beat Engine Jack to the tracks and turn into the school where the walls have acquired the power of speech. Contract Time! Contract Time! The President has met with the Board of Trustees so it could be Any Day Now. In the Ad Building the Munchkins squeak and whisper. *Contracts. Could be today. Benson said he saw a stack of envelopes on The President's Desk. Said he heard Him Typing. (The President fills in the Contracts personally, you know.)* Everywhere, human mice scurry on tiny feet spreading rumors while I glance about, afraid of running into Duffy again.

I saw him just two days ago, and I felt so guilty I barely managed to tell him about going to *The Enquirer* last week with John and Carol. Surprisingly he didn't seem interested, even though it had been his idea in the first place.

"Dave, I think she's seeing someone again."

"She? Who—?"

"Oh, come on. You've heard the talk around this place. I think Sylvia's seeing some man again."

"I see. How—that is, how do you know? Did she say something?"

"No, and she didn't have to. I've been through this so many times I recognize the signs. Damn it, Dave, I'm not going to take it anymore. I've had it."

"What are you going to do?"

"Do? I'll tell you what I'm going to do. I'm going to kill the bastard, that's what I'm going to do. Whoever it is, he's going to be sorry."

Shocked, I had stared back at him. Meek, mild Duffy. Look what I've done to him. Yet I had been split, half of me flooding with that sense of brotherhood I had felt for him in his bedroom, the other half aching with a different need. *Sylvia. Haven't seen you in three days. Why haven't you called? When will I see you again? When?*

The look on his face had changed then and he had sounded suddenly less assured, more like his old self.

"Dave, I don't know what I'm going to do."

"It'll work out."

"I don't know. She's all I've got. Damn it, Dave, everything's falling apart on me right now. The students are on my back and I don't know what to do."

"The students? What do they want?"

"What they always want. Good grades."

"I don't get you."

"It just got out of hand, that's all. I lost control. I wanted to motivate them, get them interested. So I told a few of my worst students from last semester that if they came to my office to go over their work, I'd raise their grades."

"So what happened?"

But he had just shaken his head desperately and walked away, leaving me there....

"Doug! How have you been? Listen, can I interest you in a cup of coffee?"

My sphincter turns to ice as Happy Ray's jolly voice booms out like thunder. Ray. That's one bastard who always speaks like he's parting the Red Sea, even if he's asking you for toilet paper from the next stall. Happy Ray. Happy Happy Happy Ray. See him charge across campus, jaws jutting, shoulders squared, hands gripping the thermos of coffee and stacks of styrofoam cups sealed in cellophane he was apparently born with which constitute his badge and ticket of admission into any office on campus. Once I went into cardiac arrest when he burst into my building and inflicted himself on the first person he saw. HELLO THERE! HOW ARE YOU? SAY, I DON'T OFTEN SEE YOU FOLKS OVER HERE IN MASON! LISTEN, CAN I INTEREST YOU IN A CUP OF COFFEE?

Un unh. Not this time. I say later and shoot to the Science Building to see Duffy, where, talk about guilt, I can't even bring myself to knock on his door. What will I do if he finds out I'm the one? Probably I should just barge right in and blow us both to a fancy lunch. It's the least I can do. Instead of avoiding him, I ought to show him a good time.

Giving up I head back to my office, decide to check my mail and re-enter the Ad Building where I'm just in time to catch the end of Ray's act.

I'll tell you true: whenever I cross Ray's scent I'm a deer ready to spring. Sometimes I see us as enemies in a morality play. Chairman of the Education Division, Ray's the complete politician, a grinning phony who will suck your hand like a teat and crucify you as soon as you're out the door. Farnsworth sniffs after him like a bitch in heat and together they control half the faculty committees. To get blacklisted, just tell Ray something's rotten in Denmark. Criticism he takes as a personal insult, for as Ashland's Reigning Spirit he knows everything's perfect. Are our students unable to read or write beyond the seventh grade level? Don't worry. After all, passing them automatically whether or not they can read or write keeps the system rolling—even if it is downhill.

Visit the Ad Building sometime. If you suddenly find air pollution reaching dangerous levels, then you are in the presence of Oz, the Great and Terrible. Like Dr. Martin Luther Eaglehart's trailer, Ray speaks in BLOCK LETTERS: AND SO, LADIES AND GENTLEMEN, WE SEE THAT A COMPETENCY BASED CURRICULUM MAXIMIZES THE POTENTIALITIES INHERENT IN THE CLASSROOM SITUATION BY EMPHASIZING BEHAVIORAL OBJECTIVES DESIGNED TO DETERMINE THE EXTENT TO WHICH CERTAIN LEARNING-BASED SKILLS HAVE BEEN INCULCATED...

When you get the chance, take a look through Ray's door and catch the Teacher of the Year in action. If you can tear your rapt gaze away, scan the cows that stare back at him as if stunned by a sledgehammer, students who have never learned to speak whom the educational system, thanks to Ray, is failing now for the last time. For it is an axiom in his classes that students don't speak. Never. Although he always proclaims his concern for their needs, not once have I heard a voice other than his raised in class. Once, in those moments of candor he's remarkable for, he confided to me that he's only interested in stroking and sweet-talking the black brass. Ashland, he said, "exists for the teachers," and he didn't "give a damn about the students."

For some reason he seems to feel that anyone who enters the building comes to see *him,* and so he'll thank you for dropping by even though he was the one who muscled you into his office in the first place. Right now Doug Winston's getting the treatment with a farewell pat on the shoulder. Ray turns away beaming, looking for another fish to fry.

"Dave, how have you been?"

Uh oh. Shark-infested waters.

"Not bad."

"Great! Say, care to join me in some coffee? I've got a juicy piece of gossip for you."

Actually, being in the same room with him doesn't make a lick of sense. Even at a party when I'm drunk and inclined to love everybody, I'm not exactly what you'd call Ray's kind of person. In various ways, some subtle, some less so, I've let him know I'm not ripe for a romance, and he has reciprocated by grinning when we meet and commenting behind my back how I'm not Ashland material and the sooner I get wasted, the better. Now, like a flunky, I follow his bald red head into his office and watch him extract a styrofoam cup from a stack of other styrofoam cups.

"Say whoa."

"Whoa."

Affably, he offers it to me and rescrews the thermos, which is red white and blue and has the American flag on it. I hook a chair with my foot and sit down, looking around at Ray's shoebox office with its piles of books and papers scattered everywhere. Once a cloakroom, it's about five by twenty with clothes hooks on the wall and naked water pipes running from floor to ceiling. Christ, it's like a straitjacket in here. You can't even get an erection. Not to mention the fact that there's always the risk of plaster dumping on your head. Still, it's the most popular place around and someone's always dropping in.

"The word is," says Ray, "that Max Duffy won't be back next year."

"Really?"

"That's right, he had a real run-in with the Dean yesterday. Here, let me get that for you."

A lighter materializes and he leans forward to torch me up.

"Thanks."

"My pleasure. How about an ashtray?"

"Thanks. You were saying about..."

"Duffy. Well, he and the Dean had an argument about grades."

"What kind of argument?"

"A real donnybrook. Bledsoe...why Hello, come right in!"

"I'm not disturbing anything?"

"Not at all. I was just filling in Dave here on a bit of scuttlebutt. Say, have you two met?"

"I don't believe so."

"No," I say, barely looking at him.

"Well, let me get you two gents together. Dave Newman — Sherman Oldcastle. Sherman's new in Education this year and doing a bang-up job for us."

"That a fact?" I nod at him, seeing a neat suit and styled hair the guy probably spends half the day with. "You were telling me about Duffy," I say, trying to steer Ray back to the subject.

"Oh, yes. Well, it seems—say, can I interest you in a cup of coffee?"

"Sounds great to me."

"Fine."

I watch him extract another cup and unscrew the American flag again.

"Well," says Ray, when the tools of his trade are at rest again, "it seems that next year we'll be having a new chairman of the Math Department."

"Oh, is Duffy leaving?"

"Evidently. And under a cloud too. The way I heard it...Hello, come right in!"

At the door two more heads appear: Farnsworth's and Brewster's. According to the grapevine, Brewster swings from both sides of the bed with the ease of a trapeze artist. He's accomplished in one year what wags refer to as Ashland's version of the hat trick and is a shoo-in for this year's Rookie of the Year. Since joining the Chemistry Department last August, he has managed (1) to ram bam the Director of Student Personnel, (2) plow the President's secretary, and (3) bounce students of both sexes like tennis balls. Ordinarily, for a white dude to sample the local color at all is grounds for the black KKK at the helm to conduct a ritual lynching, but in Brewster's case the picture's crowded by the scandal that could develop if he talked. But if there's anyone here on thinner ice than I am, it's this charmer in a canary sports jacket who wears shirts with ruffles at the wrists. What Farnsworth's doing palling around with him is anyone's guess.

The place is Standing Room Only, and I have to jam myself in to let them enter. Damn it, when am I going to hear about Duffy? If this immigration continues, Ray will never rake his muck and I'll end up perched on his knee. Naturally I have to watch him go through his coffee routine again.

Amenities performed, we lift our styrofoam cups while Ray savors his coffee like it's a fine wine. "Gents," he says, mischievously lowering his voice, "I have a *real* piece of news to share with you."

Few people can bring this sort of thing off as well as Ray, who triumphs like a master. His impish intonation creates just the right relaxation of standards, a kind of Boys-Will-Be-Boys climate in which we can bask and huddle like conspirators. As if on cue, Farnsworth lights his pipe.

"The way I heard it," Ray says, "Max Duffy's been going over every couple days and raising his students' grades from last semester. Just hiking them en masse. And apparently the Registrar got wind of it and brought it to the Dean's attention."

"Why'd Duffy do a thing like that?" says Oldcastle.

Ray shrugs. "Guess they got to him, that's all. And around here, you know, once they find they can do that, you've had it. Anyway, word got out and they just *swarmed* in. Mrs. Sharp said they were lined up outside his office like there was a party going on in there."

"Well, how many grades did he change?"

"About thirty."

"Thirty? Jesus, that's just asking for it."

"Max is soft," says Farnsworth. "Lets everyone—"

"Anyway," says Brewster, "what did Bledsoe do when he found out?"

"Called him in and threw thunderbolts. I happened to be outside his office yesterday talking to Mrs. Sharp, and believe me the place started to emit sparks and smell like sulfur. Even with the door closed I could hear him shouting. 'What do you *mean* changing all their grades? Do you have any idea of the *mess* you've caused? What's wrong with you?' He just went on and on like that, louder and louder without even once coming up for air. Half the time I couldn't make out what he was saying, but whatever it was, he sure wasn't happy." Ray shakes his head.

Farnsworth removes his pipe. "Well, you know how Bledsoe scuttles him at meetings."

"Sure do. You know, it gets downright gory at times, huh, Dave?"

"Uh huh. Remember the time he ripped into his course descriptions?"

"Oh, yeah. Ha ha ha."

"Ha ha ha ha ha."

"That was murder, all right. Max kept shriveling up, poor guy, till I thought he'd disappear under the table. But I'm surprised I scooped you on this one, Dave. Usually you get the news first and pass it on to me. Especially—the *real goods*."

"Real goods?" Farnsworth's overbite comes out and takes hold of his pipe stem.

"Yes." Ray takes a long sip of his coffee, savoring it. "Duffy's been—canned."

Farnsworth's pipe comes out of his mouth, which opens wider and wider. "Ah."

Ray grins, gloating. "Thought you'd be interested. You see, after a while it wasn't just the Dean's voice coming through that door. Toward the end it was Duffy's, answering him blast for blast."

"You're kidding."

"Duffy?" says Oldcastle.

Brewster puts his hand on Farnsworth's shoulder. "I don't believe it. Not Duffy. Not that little—"

"Well, you're wrong. Course, it didn't do any good, since Bledsoe fired him on the spot. Whereupon Max told him to— now get this—told him to stick his job where the sun never shines."

"Whooo-ooo!" says Oldcastle. "He said *that*?"

"Sure did, which puts him one up on a lot of folks who've never even *tried* to tell him off. Anyway, Bledsoe's got him out now, which is something he's wanted for a long time." He pauses for a moment. "I saw Max clearing out his office this morning."

On Farnsworth's shoulder, Brewster's fingers commence a quick drumbeat. Then there's a knock on the door and suddenly everything dissolves. Brewster removes his fingers and turns, his eyes sliding up my thighs as Farnsworth and Oldcastle exchange glances. After a moment Oldcastle goes to the door and opens it.

"Excuse me, sir, you got a minute?"

"I certainly do, Mr. Chambers," says Ray, his voice loud and public again. Funny I've never noticed his politeness before in calling them "Mr." and "Miss." No one else does it. Not even teachers who respect them.

Oldcastle's already out the door, followed by Brewster who says something about a report he has to write. Farnsworth lingers a second, saying something behind his hand to Ray before following the others. That leaves me. Rising, I leave the office without looking back.

"Dave."

I turn to find Ray coming after me. He comes all the way to where I've stopped by the stairway banister and lays his hand on my shoulder.

"Listen, I just want to thank you for dropping by."

My voice works around the catch in my throat. "But I didn't drop by, Ray. You asked me in."

"Oh, well, I just—"

I start to leave and then turn back, wondering if I'm going to hit him first with my left fist or my right and whether I'm going to bring my knee up into his groin or under his chin as he topples over. Instead I shove my face within an inch of his so that I can smell the coffee on his breath, and say something. I don't even know what it is, but his smile lurches and his head snaps back like it's been flicked by a jab, and I watch as he tries to bring things under control. It takes some doing but he manages, and as I continue, the head steadies and the smile reassembles itself. How long I work on him, I don't know. Could be one minute or ten. But before I leave, there's enough hate in his eyes to burn me alive and put me on his blacklist forever.

Fourteen

TELLING RAY HOW much I love him makes me feel good for about ten seconds, as if I've purged my gut of something that's bothered me for a long time. Then my balloon pops and I crash to earth. Duffy, poor bastard, look what he's done to himself, not to mention what *I've* done to him. Sylvia: I see her again as she was when we made love, her dark eyes and body like a field waiting to be planted and even better than that first time on the farm. God I want you why haven't you called I've never felt this way never.

Can't believe how I feel. Ten feet tall and fat with guilt. A king and a clown at the same time. Hey, everybody, look what's happened to Newman. He walks, he talks, he babbles, he tells one of the most important men around he's a schmuck and dumps a sweet woman for one he can't even understand.

Come to think of it, I'm getting in over my head in just about everything these days. Besides Sylvia and Duffy and Ray, there's the little matter of the Harts. Wonder if Courtland ever will publish their story? From the way he acted, I would have sworn he'd do just about anything to nail Sanford. But it's been nine days now and nothing. Well, maybe it's better this way. If the shit ever does hit the fan and they find out I'm the one who turned it on, it will probably be my job and a one-way ticket back to the farm.

Soaked in May sunshine, the Plantation's really jumping. On the commons, natives shake it to a primal beat. Can't speak or write but bang them drums and watch 'em strut! Laughter is everywhere. Girls lean out of windows, some of which are broken, and jive with friends on the cracked sidewalks. Their voices are liquid, high-pitched, and off-key musical, flowing so fast they melt into each other. Even after two

years their words skip across my ears. Hey, Beulah, still seein'
Billy? What yo' somethin' somethin'. That dude? I sho' some-
thin' somethin'. Don' you like 'im no moah? Naw, he poisin.
He somethin' somethin' somethin'.

Passing the Fine Arts Center, I watch Rinehart cruise by in
his sleek red Mark VI like a monarch going to his coronation,
and cross the street to watch the kids freak out on the grass.
Dudes are in one line, gals in the other. The boys, especially,
are sinuous and snap like whips. Wearing tank shirts or shirts
open to the waist, they pump their loins toward the girls who
thrust to receive them, making those rock n' roll puberty rites I
grew up with seem virginal in comparison.

Thinking of high school reminds me of my birthday. Jesus,
in a week I'll be thirty-nine. How did I ever wind up here in
S.C. watching kids grind away in the sun? The thought,
magnified by a set of blaring speakers, swings me around so
that I'm staring into the eyes of Solomon Wise. Thirty feet
away, he gazes back like a sphinx, seeming to look right into
me.

Feeling uneasy, I cross the street again where I notice that
two black painters have run a forty foot ladder all the way up
the rear end of the Fountainbleu. The guy at the top looks like
a leaf in the wind. Personally, I've always supported urban
renewal. After all, paint can work wonders for a condemned
building when it's slapped onto boards that have been nailed
over broken windows.

Inside I dial Sylvia's number. Pause. Click. Then, finally,
ring…ring…ring…five, eight, a dozen times. I let it ring on,
twisting the cord. Fifteen times, eighteen…

"Mr. Newman?"

I slam the receiver down, finding myself in Rev. Lester Godwin's benign presence.

"What?"

"May I see you for a moment?"

Suppressing a swear word, I head down the hall.

"This way."

Make no mistake about this boy, he's a comer. Plump and

baby-faced, he was born stuffed into a black suit, vest, and tie, and reminds me of an aggressive panda bear. Like Rinehart, he's an American success story in the making. Not only is he the President of the Student Body but an occasional chaplin at faculty meetings where he recites benedictions in a rousing, precise voice. At least once a month you'll see his picture in the paper, usually shaking the President's hand. If you get him in class, you might think yourself blessed, only to find that like other student ministers, he may "Deliver the Word" but he sure can't spell it, or explain it either for that matter.

One thing he can do, though, is jerk you off with one of those big, phony, Abraham Lincoln voices that makes you feel like a crud. Talk about sincerity and conviction, this joker can talk you out of your pants and not even let you feel the cold.

"Mr. Newman," he intones, his test paper in Introduction to Literature appearing from nowhere like an injured wing, "surely this *must* be some kind of mistake."

Desecration and blasphemy. As I reach for it, the wing curls away as if singed by sacrilege.

"May I?"

With infinite dignity, he looks at my fingers and reluctantly surrenders it. I receive the pages like they're Holy Writ, awed by the beautiful handwriting and already ashamed of the big red D scrawled at the top. Reverently, I start to examine it.

After all, a guy can always make a mistake. Maybe I was irritated at the time or had just read an A paper. Let me see. Well, my grading on the short answers checks out. Now for the forty point essay on Pound's "Ballad of the Goodly Fere."

> In Pound poem he tell how Christ die for us
> on the Cross Jesus disciple the Goodly Fere say
> Christ save us from Sin and Temptation and
> the Devil...

I flip the pages over and hand it back to him.

"Sorry, Rev."

"Oh, come now, you can't be *serious*."

"I assure you, I am."

"Mr. Newman!" he says incredulously. He presses close and turns the pages. Tapping the last one, he starts instructing me like I'm a nitwit.

"Sir," he says, rubbing my nose in the word like it's a turd, "look what I say here. How through Jesus Christ we are BORN AGAIN, MADE NEW. Saved from hell and filled with his divine love."

"Yes, but—"

"And surely the poem is about THAT, sir, about what Jesus has brought to US. Yet you give me only FIVE points for my answer. Why, if you give me just half-credit I'll have a B."

J.C. on a bicycle, he's speaking in block letters like you-know-who. Patronizing bastard treats me like a nincompoop. I better put a stop to this now.

Twice more I try to interrupt, but he rolls on like Bledsoe with his unctuous voice. Keep your eyes on this boy. Ten years from now he will have improved his English and smoothed out the rough spots. Then he'll be about as easy to stop as a Mack truck. As for now, he's still a bit green behind his gospel, and I move to head him off at the pass.

"Reverend Godwin."

"…and if you check what other students wrote, you'll find they didn't write HALF as much—"

"Godwin!"

That pulls his plug. "Sir?"

"The point is not how much you've written but the quality of it. And in addition to the poor grammar and the numerous mechanical mistakes, I get the feeling that you never read the poem or if you did read it, failed to understand it."

"That's ridi—"

"What you've done here is simply spout a sermon about how Jesus died to save us and spiced it up with a little 'Born Again' Christian jazz. But the poem is only incidentally about that. What it—"

"But that's the way I—"

"…is mostly about is the fact that Jesus is not the aloof chicken 'priest' we always see him as, but one of the gang, a man among men, a brave and joyous comrade who loved life and lived it up. Besides that, you also make a critical error. It's not Simon, the disciple, who's the "goodly fere" or brother, it's Christ. That's the point of the poem."

Service ace. At least you would think so. But with high style he just smacks it back at me.

"Surely, sir, you're not saying it's impossible to have another point of view? I can show you right in my notes where you said poetry was open to interpretation. What I've done is express what the poem means to *me*. I don't think it's fair you should penalize me for stating my opinion."

This is good stuff. He not only gets the ball back, but deep near the base line and to my backhand. I watch it streak over, marveling at his natural flair. You just *can't* teach this sort of thing. It's not just what he says but how he says it, the way he makes you feel like a creep for standing by what you know is right. Still, Pound's poem won't sustain what he's done to it, and like the old pro I am, I get set to smash it down his throat.

Then I stop, overwhelmed by a sense of fatigue and futility. After all, what's the use? Consider the system: brutal, dishonest, built to reward the massive lie and the large-scale rip-off. And here, in a dingy little office in a sleazy little town, Sir Galahad defends intellectual honesty against a black Nixon of the future. I mean, what's the point? My act's not only silly, but stupid and irrelevant. Shit, give him what he wants, give him an A. Give him ten A's. Sell them to him for a dollar apiece. Nothing I do will make a scintilla of difference anyway. With me or without me, he'll end up as Chairman of the Board.

Then I think of Duffy again. Duffy in his office. Duffy surrounded by students. Duffy pulled this way and that like taffy in their hands. Who knows, maybe it was even the Reverend himself who initiated his fall from grace. Christ, if so he would never have had a chance. The thought, fed by frustration, makes my mind turn red and suddenly he's Happy Ray all over again. Almost viciously, I yank the textbook off a shelf and slam it on the desk.

"Look," I say, opening it to the poem. "Right from the beginning Pound echoes what we established in class. Christ is a 'lover...of brawny men,/O' ships and the open sea.' He's no chickenshit 'capon priest', no Bible-thumping phony or 'mouse of the scrolls' who enters God's house to plunder its 'pawn and treasury', but—"

Godwin waves his hand. "I'm not interested in that stuff."

"No?"

"No. Do you know what I was thinking?"

I don't answer.

His tongue comes out, large and red as it gives a healthy swipe to his soft underlip. For some reason I can *sense* him assaying my earlier hesitation and reading it as—weakness. Yes sirree. Baby Face Nelson is going to gamble and take some kind of plunge.

"I was thinking," he says, "how someone else might take a different view of the matter."

"Oh?"

"Yes, and how someone else might be inclined not only to question your judgment..."

"Go on."

"...but decide that *now*, especially since faculty contracts are about to come out, doubts concerning your fitness to remain as a teacher here at Ashland can no longer be ignored. I was also thinking that this person would be inclined to act on these doubts if he were not only shown this test but also informed of the disturbance you caused recently in The Rainbow."

Wow. For a moment, precocious as he is, he has to struggle to master his audacity. But he succeeds. I watch his wrinkleless face settle into smugness. Looking like Buddha, he waits calmly to receive the fruits of his labors while I pick up his test and make a lame show of examining it. No doubt about it, he's got me by the jewels. The only sensible thing to do now is punt. Quietly, I read a sentence here, a paragraph there. The test comes down, and I watch my pen slash out the D and scrawl a big red F beside it. I hand it back.

"There you are. You may take it to Dean Bledsoe and tell him that after careful consideration, I've decided to lower your grade."

Revelation's slow in coming. "You mean...you're *failing* me?"

"That's right. You're good, kid, but you've still got a lot to learn."

"But...but..." Disbelief struggles with horror for supremacy. Then his face goes to pieces. I watch him, surprised that I flunked him and tasting the slime of joy on my tongue. You bastard, you're gonna remember me. No matter how high you climb, you ain't gonna forget this. Funny, I guess when you get down to it, the reason I never got into religion much is the people who preach it. Always seemed they should be better than other folks because the special blessing they had received should *make* them better. But if the best way to judge a product is by those who sell it, then religion falls in somewhere midway between sheep dip and snake oil.

"Sir, please, won't you reconsider?"

"Sorry."

"But...but...if I fail your course, sir, I'll be on probation, and I won't be permitted to offici—to officiate at college events."

Suddenly his practiced diction begins to crumble, and he's a penitent about to kneel at my feet. He touches my shoulder.

"Sir, *please* won't you reconsider? If I fail—"

Nice going, Dave. First Ray, now the Lord's annointed. Self-recrimination fills me. Then I think of Duffy again and repent. Yeah, guess *I'm* weak too. The only way to hold your own against these birds is to be as hard as they are. Compassion they see as weakness, as a chance to cut your throat. To soften you up, they're not above licking your boots like Godwin, who does it as expertly as he does everything else. After all, self-debasement is just another weapon, for the only thing they really believe in is success.

I brush his hand away. "Scratch it, Godwin. You've still got the Final. Study hard and you can still get a C for my course."

133

"Do you mean it, sir? Can I still get a C?"

"I just said you could."

"And you'll overlook—"

"If you don't mind, I've got work to do."

"Oh, *certainly*." He goes to the door and turns with a smile. "Would you mind shaking hands, sir?"

"WHAT?"

"I said, would you—"

"Oh, Shit." Now we're buddy-buddy and he never even thought of gutting me. Talk about chutzpah. If I don't watch it, in a minute we'll be dancing cheek to cheek. Tempted to tell him where he can put his hand, I use my own instead to give him the bum's rush, right into the path of the Harts who greet me like a long lost friend.

Fifteen

"Dave! WHERE HAVE you been? We've been looking All Over for you!"

"Yes," laughs Carol, her arm linked with John's, "we've buzzed your home and even called Missing Persons. What's the matter? Trying to avoid us? Ashamed of your old friends?"

I try to answer, but they're so hopped up it's hopeless. For a minute all I get is jokes at my expense. Carol hangs and swings on John's arm and then snags my hand.

"What do you think?" she winks. "Should we ask him?"

"Whatever you prefer, my dear. But first—a toast!"

Magically, he produces a bottle of André and three champagne glasses, which he passes around. I watch him strip away the gold wrapping and pop the cork, which ricochets about my office. Critically he examines the label before pouring us all a healthy shot.

"Hardly your nectar of kings, but I think you'll be alive to its aspirations."

"I assume," I say, "that all this is taking us somewhere."

"Mais oui, monsieur. To our toast, then." He holds his glass up. "To May 12: The Day The North Finally Wins The Civil War."

We all take a sip and then John solemns up.

"Dave, we'd both consider it an honor if you'd announce our marriage for us."

I look at both of them. "Why, sure! Where? When?"

"Here. Now. At the faculty meeting in the Fine Arts Center." He checks his watch. "It should be starting in about five minutes."

Shock and amazement pour through me.

"Wow. Nothing like charging into the teeth of the enemy!"

"Ah! As to that, my friend, let me reveal our secret weapon, our pièce de résistance." He reaches inside his coat and pulls out a folded piece of paper, which he snaps open.

"It's out!"

"What is?"

"Our story! They ran it!"

"But I checked the paper. It's not—"

Carol shakes her head. "This is a page from *tomorrow's* paper, Dave. Apparently Mr. Courtland wanted me to have it so much he sent it by special messenger."

"It's dynamite!" John says. "Courtland gave us a complete sendoff with all the trimmings. Three columns on the bottom of page 1. If this doesn't frizzle their hair, nothing will."

Hands shaking, I read it quickly.

ASHLAND COLLEGE CHARGED WITH RACISM

An interracial couple charged last week that Ashland College has practiced racism in its employment procedures.

According to Mr. and Mrs. John Hart, Mr. Hart, an Associate Professor of Music Education at the school, had his employment terminated because he married a white woman. The action was allegedly ordered by Mr. Brantley Sanford, the woman's father, who is Chairman of the college's Board of Trustees…

There's more. Slater has done his work well. Two trustees close to Sanford confirm the Hart's testimony and spokesmen for the college decline to comment. Well well. Unless I miss my guess, Courtland has evened the score. It's all here: abuse of power, corruption, plus more than enough red faces to go around.

I hand it back. "Looks like we got what we wanted."

"Yes, and that's why I want you to be there, Dave. We started it together, and I want us to finish it the same way." He places his hand on my shoulder. "Thanks, Dave."

"Forget it. I'm just glad the truth's out."

"I don't mean that so much," he says while Carol touches me too and kisses my cheek. "I mean, thank you for *everything*."

"Oh." Awkwardly I take another sip, which barely gets past the lump in my throat.

"Incidentally," he says, "after you make the announcement, Carol and I are going down front to gather the kudos." He pats his coat over his inside pocket where the page is. "Thought I'd wave *this* in their faces a little."

Suddenly I think of what these new developments mean to my job.

"Do you think that's wise, John? I mean, to rub their faces in it that way."

His face toughens. "I'm talking about dignity, Dave. Our dignity. Why so cautious all of a sudden? If I've learned anything from you, it's that somebody has to stand up for the truth and have the guts to tell it."

"O.K.," I say, "let's go tell it then."

Outside they make a handsome couple as they stroll hand-in-hand across campus. John, as always, is dressed to the teeth, and Carol's wearing a soft print of spring colors. She moves gracefully, long hair flowing about her shoulders.

Funny. Sylvia said people don't usually change much. But John has. In less than two weeks he has grown up into himself. He's a tough customer now, maybe even an earth shaker of the future. Guess all he really needed was a chance to show his stuff. Something that would test him.

The meeting has already started by the time we get there. The Director of Student Personnel is leading the two hundredth pointless discussion on class attendance, and as we enter, heads start turning everywhere. Murmur sweeps the room like wildfire. In front, Bledsoe turns to see what the fuss is and stiffens. *They know!* I think, a sentence from the paper leaping through my mind. *College officials declined to comment.* Of course: Slater snooped around, so the boys at the top know something's about to break.

Holding hands, the Harts stand there, surveying the room

while the Director tries to maintain order. I spot three empty seats in back and we sit down, me on the aisle. The Director does his best, but our presence undermines the proceedings. The debate peters out much earlier than usual, and he's forced to ask if anyone has any announcements.

That's my cue. "Yes!" I say, and as I move down the wide carpeted steps to the podium, the mood tenses. I can feel it: it's like a vast intake of breath at the top of a roller coaster. The whole room's going over the edge. Half of them think they know what's going to happen, and all it takes is me to make it real, to bring it out of that twilight world where things aren't quite true because no one has dared to express them. Reaching the stand I look out at their faces, caught in some kind of a feverish dream. I've been here before, or someplace very much like it. Then I remember. I'm in The Rainbow again, standing on the pool table. Only now the multitude I'm addressing are my colleagues, and Reggie and his friend are Bledsoe and the President. Holding the stand firmly in both hands, I look down at Bledsoe, daring him to pull his switchblade.

"Ladies and gentlemen," I say, and for once you *can* hear a pin drop, "it gives me great pleasure to announce the marriage of one of our colleagues. Two months ago, in Myrtle Beach, Mr. John Hart married Miss Caroline Sanford, the beautiful daughter of Mr. Sanford, Chairman of our Board of Trustees."

Somewhere in the room, someone starts to clap, realizes his mistake, and stops. In the silence John escorts Carol down to the podium while I return to the back where I can see everything. They look damn good down there and it gives me a deep sense of satisfaction to have been a part of it, to watch now as John removes his arm from his wife's waist and approaches the microphone.

"Ladies and gentlemen," he says, "I'd like you to meet my wife, Caroline."

The room stares back at him. After a long moment, he continues.

"Having done that," he says, "permit me next to apologize

for failing to inform you earlier of my marriage. You see, while my wife is a courageous lady, I was not equal to her. She wanted to announce it at once, but I was afraid of what others might think. I had not yet learned that the only opinion that ultimately means anything is your own."

He pauses. Briefly, our eyes meet.

"So I'm making amends now, and to do that it is necessary to share with you a truth. Some of you may have heard that my relationship with this school was severed recently because of unauthorized trips I had made with my classes. However, that is *not* the case, as tomorrow's *Enquirer* will reveal." He reaches in his pocket to get the sheet. "The truth is—"

Suddenly, Bledsoe's on his feet. "MISTER Hart, I hardly think—"

"The truth is—"

"You're out of order! Please return to your—"

"What's the matter? Don't you *want* them to know the truth?"

"I repeat, 'You're out of order!' " Bledsoe says, making his way toward the stand. "If you don't stop immediately it will be necessary—"

"Let him speak!" someone says.

"Yes, let him go on."

Bledsoe stops. Incredibly, John is winning support. At the stand he stares steel-eyed at Bledsoe, who has halted barely ten feet away and is now reconsidering matters. To force John to leave is to run the risk of worsening an already bad situation. Besides, what if he can't do it? Hesitantly he sizes Hart up and decides to err on the side of discretion.

John chooses to summarize.

"Perhaps Dean Bledsoe is right. This is neither the time nor the place for a speech." Unfolding the newspaper, he holds it up before them. "So let me simply urge you to read tomorrow's *Enquirer*, for it makes clear that I was fired not for the reason given but solely because I exercised my God-given right to marry the woman of my choice, who stands here now beside me."

"And one more thing!" he says, pounding the stand with his fist. "I came here to Ashland because I wanted to teach black kids, because I wanted to share with them some of the benefits I had received. And in my innocence I naively believed that my desire would be enough. I have since learned that it is not, because there are various forces that must be fought if I wish to pursue my goal. So I want to make it clear *now* that I'm not going to give up, that I will do *anything* from using the law to consulting the American Civil Rights Union, to remain!"

He steps back from the stand and fires a last look at Bledsoe, who confronts him like a block of granite. I leave them that way, suspended in silent combat before the entire room, and pass out into the sunlight where everything's harmony and the sound of pigeons. Like the scene behind me, I'm also suspended, my feelings frozen in some kind of limbo. I don't even know where I'm headed.

Somewhere a phone rings.

My legs move and I break into a run without even knowing what I'm after. Then I remember and stop. Is it the right phone? Listen. Yes! I break into a run again, forcing my legs to move faster and faster, just as fast as I can make them. Hurry! It must have rung a thousand times by now! Leaping a chain, I cross the grass, ankles breaking knees snapping, and dash inside Mason where I snatch the phone off the wall.

"Hello!"

"Hello, may I—"

"Sylvia?"

"Yes. Dave—is that you?"

"Yes." God Almighty, yes! Heart pounding, I race again to get my next words out. "Where—"

"The Green Town Country Club."

"Country Club? What are you doing *there*?"

Her voice sounds sensuous, intimate, close as a kiss. "Well, right now, I'm talking to you from a table beside the pool. Please come?"

"Of course. Duffy?"

"Yes. You've heard?"

"Yeah, it's just getting around."

"Well, I don't want to discuss it over the phone. Anyway, there's more."

"What do you mean?"

Faintly, I can hear ice cubes clink in a glass.

"It's Max," she says. "But I'm not going to tell you anything more till you get here."

Sixteen

On the way over I keep trying to figure what Sylvia is doing at the Country Club and what she wouldn't tell me about Duffy over the phone. Christ, hope he hasn't gone bananas. More often than not, it's the quiet ones you wouldn't look at twice who blow their brains out or go on shooting sprees.

I only saw the Country Club once, and that was months ago when I drove by. However, it doesn't take a bloodhound to sniff it out. Just follow the smell of money, and when you come to homes that make Xanadu look like an efficiency, you're starting to get warm. When I get to the place, it looks just as unreal as it did from the road, a kind of Sunny Acres for the rich and those born without alimentary canals.

Ahead, as I enter the parking lot, there's a ranch-style clubhouse that's big enough to hold a dozen pro shops and banquet rooms. To my left, tennis courts in tiptop condition gleam in the sun. Men in white shirts, white shorts, white shoes, and white socks spank yellow tennis balls back and forth. To my right, a lush, manicured, impossibly green golf course adds to the fantasy.

Parking Big Red next to a Mercedes, I get out conscious of my rumpled pants and feeling like a sweathog among the thoroughbreds. I'm half-tempted to run out to the street to see if there's a No Trespassing sign I missed. The excitement of seeing Sylvia, though, blows down my nervousness, and I cross the parking lot like a jumping bean and follow the flagstone walk around the clubhouse. Let's see, she said out by the pool in back. Turning the corner, I'm just in time to run into an attractive blonde in a bathing suit. She bounces back with a squeal and goes down. Something wet hits my face.

"Hey, I'm sorry. Here, let me."

"No, that's all right. I'm—"

I stoop to help her up. In doing so, our faces touch and for a moment we're in a loose embrace.

"You all right?"

"Yes, quite. Everything seems to be working." Her hand touches my face. "Oh, I'm sorry, looks like I spilled my drink all over you."

"Forget it. Should have been—"

Suddenly I spot Sylvia sitting by the pool and everything else goes out the window. It's just like when we make love, only now we're not even in bed. Moving toward her, I lose pieces of myself all the way down.

"Hi."

"Hi, there. That was quite an entrance you just made. Do women usually fall so hard for you?"

"It's this fatal charm I have."

"Well, it's obviously potent. She's been watching you ever since you left her."

I sit down shyly, surprised to see her in a conservative pants suit.

"How's David?"

"Just fine. How's Sylvia?"

"Not so good."

"Tell me."

She shakes her head and motions at someone behind me. "Let's have a drink first. Something tall and cool."

A black man in a white uniform appears at my side.

"Sir?"

"Uh, what would you like, Sylvia?"

"I'll have another Collins, please."

"Thank you. And you, Sir?"

"Budweiser."

"Oh, try a Tom Collins, Dave. They're awfully good here."

"O.K. Make that two."

He leaves, and I watch her brush back a lock of dark hair. I look away with an effort, taking in the sparkling blue water of the pool and the patio tables arranged here and there on the turquoise tiles. Off to our left, two men briskly stroke a tennis ball. I watch them finish a volley before turning back.

"I've missed you."

She smiles. "So have I."

"I've been waiting for you to call like you said you would. I was beginning—that is, I was begin..."

At that moment the waiter returns and covers my fumbling by placing napkins beside us. With graceful, surgical neatness he deposits drinks in their centers and disappears.

"Here's looking at you, kid."

"Skõal."

We take a sip.

"Like it?"

"Hits the spot. You know, I don't usually go for these sweet jobs, but I could learn to change." I take another chug of the drink, which is really excellent, and find myself grinning.

"What's so funny?"

I lean back and stretch out my legs, basking like a lizard in the sun as a woman with middle-age spread walks gingerly out onto the board and dives in. Just before entering the water she bends her knees, causing a splash.

"Oh, nothing," I say. "It's just this whole scene."

"What about it?"

"Well, it's exactly what I always imagined these places would be like. All the stereotypes are true. The idle rich. Tennis in the sun. Uncle Tom Collinses served beside the pool. My God, the waiter even looks like he stepped off a box of Uncle Ben's Converted Rice. You'd think this was the Old South and the twentieth century hadn't arrived here yet."

"In some ways it hasn't."

"There are no negro members, of course."

"Of course."

"Jews?"

"A few."

"Well, that's something. They're liberal as hell. Wonder if any teacher at Ashland could get in here."

"I know one who did."

"Who?"

"Max."

"He's a member?" This brings up the question again of Duffy and what we're both doing here, but before I can ask anything she nods at the pool.

"Watch carefully. This is for your benefit."

"What's that?"

"The act on the high board. She's been strutting her stuff for a minute up there hoping you'd notice."

I look up and catch her looking away. It's the blonde again. She's got a dynamite figure and about enough of a suit to serve a drink on. Gracefully, shoulders back, breasts forward, she walks to the end of the board and returns. As she turns to face the water again, she glances at me. Then she raises her arms parallel to the board, lowers them, and striding queenlike to the end of the board, executes the prettiest one-and-a-half I've ever seen, entering the water with scarcely a ripple. Even the board barely seems to vibrate.

"Looks like you've made a conquest," Sylvia says.

I shrug and scrounge around for a smoke. Finding a crumbled pack, I finger one out and light it.

"I suspect you've had quite a bit of luck with women," she says.

"Well, you know, when you've got it—"

"Oh, you're smug. But you know, from where I sit it looks like you've been especially fortunate with *married* women."

Together, we watch the blonde climb up to the high board and glance at me again. This time she goes to the end and turns, positioning herself on her toes with her heels extending out over the water. Her thighs are slender and lithe, and I find myself wondering how they would feel wrapped around me. Slowly, she raises her arms to shoulder level, her toes still feeling for balance, the right hold, and then lowers them. Again she raises them, again lowers. Then there is that moment when time stops and she communes with some counselor within her. Sun glitters on her skin, the water, the umbrellas at the tops of the patio tables. My drink freezes in my hand.

145

Suddenly her weight comes down, her arms rise, and she archs upward and back so gracefully I can't quite believe it when she falls like an arrow and splits the water. From somewhere inside the clubhouse there comes the sound of clapping.

Smiling, Sylvia leans forward and kicks me under the table.

"Hey! What did you do that for?"

"For what you're thinking."

I rub my shin, which hurts like a bastard. "I wasn't thinking anything."

"Yes, you were."

"Well, what's—"

"Look, you're spoken for, so don't let me ever hear you thinking of straying. And if I catch anyone making eyes at you, I'll cut her heart out and serve it to her on a platter."

"Like you did with Connie? That really wasn't very nice what you did to her, you know."

She smiles. "In some ways, I'm not a very nice person."

I take a belt of the Collins and consider the matter. Despite her tone, she's only half serious. Still, I've just had the riot act read to me, and a couple of weeks ago, if any girl had tried to hamstring me like this one, I'd have dumped her on the spot. But I'm long past the point where I want to leave her, and in a masochistic way I even like getting kicked. After all, it proves she cares.

However, there's a rival, and I remind her the sword cuts both ways.

"Max? You don't have to worry about *him*. Besides, he's left me again."

"Left?"

"Hmm-hmm. After his little session with the Dean he came home half-drunk and told me he was moving out."

"I don't believe it."

"Oh, it's true. He's done this sort of thing before, but he always comes back." She shakes her head, her voice taking on a tone of contempt mingled with pity. "Poor Max. This isn't the first time he's come home from one of his little crises and told me he's striking out on his own to find himself and said it would be best for both of us to start over. I've seen him slap up whiskey for courage lots of times and throw clothes into a suitcase like he was launching the Queen Mary." She sighs. "But he always comes back. Usually in just a day or two."

"Did he tell you what happened?"

She looks down at her glass and drains it. "Only that he got fired for changing too many grades."

"Did he also tell you what he said to Bledsoe?"

"No."

"He told him to take his job and stick it."

"Oh, come on!"

"No, it's true. There was a witness."

"As a matter of fact, he did say something about telling him off." She shakes her head. "But I don't believe it. Max just doesn't have it in him. Besides, whatever he said, he's still running true to form."

"What do you mean?"

"Well, yesterday he said he was leaving for good, and today he's already called me on the phone."

"Yeah, what about?"

She pauses. "He wanted me to call you and arrange it so he could meet us both here at two o'clock."

Time stops again. Up in the sky, so far up it's a speck against the blue, a bird hangs motionless.

"He knows."

"I'd say that's obvious."

I get up and walk past the pool to the tennis courts where I light my last cigarette. Behind the fence, a war is going on. One man is six and a half feet tall and serves with such power that the much shorter man on the other side is forced to stand all the way back against the fence and hold up his racket in self-defense. But it works. Again and again I watch the ball boom over like a rocket only to come sailing back in slow motion. From that point, the shorter man leads him a merry chase, neutralizing the other's powerful ground strokes with tricky little chop shots and superior placement. Finally, after one long volley in which he runs himself ragged after a half-dozen shots only to lose the point on a dinky little return with a wicked backspin, the taller man swears in frustration and tells him to perform an anatomical impossibility. The shorter man laughs and spins his racket in delight.

Flicking my butt away, I go back to the table, getting there just in time to see Uncle Ben disappear with his tray.

"Thought we could use another drink,"she says.

The sun is warm, the smell of clipped grass languorous. I take a deep pull from my glass, finding it as cold and delicious as the first, and let her take my hand between her own.

"Oh, shit."

"It'll be all right."

"I didn't want him to know."

"I know. But he had to find out sometime, didn't he?"

I don't answer. The place is so beautiful it seems inconceivable that problems could get at you here. On a sunny day especially, without even a cloud in the sky, you'd think you could come to a playland like this and escape all the sordid complexities of the world. After all, what's the point of fancy dues and $2.00 a drink prices if they don't buy you a little peace? Just lay your money down, and get your personal No Trespassing sign. NO CARES OF THIS WORLD ALLOWED. ANXIETIES WILL BE SHOT. But it doesn't work that way. It never does.

Sylvia seems to read my thoughts. "It's hard to believe such things could touch us here," she says.

"What do you mean?"

"Oh, the club. It's so lovely, so peaceful. Do you know, in a way I can understand Max. I think he only joined the club so he could use it as a refuge. When things get bad, he often runs here and tries drinking his problems away."

"Let's not talk about him."

"Oh, David, if you could just have heard the way he sounded on the phone when he told me to call you."

"Stop it, I don't want—"

Suddenly, unbelievably, her eyes are full of tears. "Poor Max, what's he going to do now? It's the end of the line for him. He has no place left to go."

Her crying tears me to pieces. I've never felt this badly for anyone before. What's happened inside me in the last couple of weeks has completely switched me around. It's unthinkable that I could care so much for anyone, let anyone get to me this way. Impulsively I pull my chair around so that I'm practically sitting on her lap, and before I know it I'm kissing her everywhere, on her face, her lips, her ears, trying to soothe her, stop her from crying. In the meantime she keeps going on about Duffy, crying about how she's let him down, and it's not until she comes up for air that I can edge a word in.

"Look, Syl, don't blame yourself. You've tried your best with him."

"Oh, that's not true. I've ridiculed him and turned away when he's needed me."

"Look," I say, ignoring the stares we're getting, "you've tried and I know it hasn't been easy. Besides, he's done it to himself. I don't like to say this, but he didn't *have* to get fired. Syl, look, listen to me, the thing is, we've *got* to start thinking about ourselves. Just you and me. We've got our own lives to live. *Together*."

Sobbing, she reaches down and lifts a mammoth bag purse which she starts to rummage through on the table. It's a regular monster, one of those Bohemian jobs that flops all over creation. In a way I'm glad to see it. The natty pants suit she wears isn't her style at all, but the bag seem custom-made for her. It's exactly right, and no society bitch would be caught dead with it.

Finally, she excavates a handkerchief and goes to work with it. I straighten up and then put my arm around her again, gently stroking her cheek with my forefinger. "Listen," I say as softly as possible, "do you know what you've done for me?"

She shakes her head into her handkerchief. I pause and plunge on.

"Before I met you," I continue, "I was nothing. Just a drifter. For a long time, I guess for twenty years ever since I left my father's farm, I just floated from place to place and from woman to woman. I couldn't seem to catch on anywhere. Why it was that way, I don't know. Maybe there's something lacking in anyone to begin with who leaves home to find something and is never satisfied. Maybe it was the kids I saw getting killed at Kent State University when I was in graduate school. Like the one who looked at me before he died as if begging me to make it right. Well, I could never make it right, Sylvia, could never bring him back or remove the horror from his eyes, or beat the system that did it to him. Anyway, I've had more jobs than I can remember and after a while the places just started to run together in my mind. And none of them were any good." I pause. "Do you know what I mean?"

She's nearly stopped crying now and nods her head. I clear my throat. Now comes the hard part.

"It got so bad that sometimes, Syl, I took stupid chances and maybe even—tried to kill myself. It was just that I felt so empty and burned out, I didn't care anymore. I'd seen too many places and the women—well, it just got to be like bowling. Set 'em up and knock 'em down, set 'em up and knock 'em down. You see, none of them meant anything until..."

"Until what?"

"Until I met you."

I've said the right thing. She leans toward me and we embrace. Her lips are salty-sweet, warm and open in the sun. I hold her close.

"Well, what a tender, touching scene we have here!"

I pull away. Coming toward us with a straw hat tilted at a jaunty angle, Duffy gives us both a grin. "David, the giant killer," he winks. "How's it go, old man?"

I open my mouth. Sylvia's quicker.

"Max—how long have you been watching us?"

"Quite some time, my dear, quite some time." He goes to a nearby table and returns with a chair, which he turns with its back to us and then straddles. Dropping a large envelope next to Sylvia's bag, he thumbs his hat back. "Yes, sirree," he grins, "I've been sitting at the bar inside for some time now, observing this moving little drama. Just sitting there watching the human condition unfold out here in the sun as you good folks sip away and work yourselves up into a dandy little clinch. And let me tell you, it was well worth the—"

"You bastard. You set it all up."

"Correct, my dear. Cor-rect. But you needn't get so huffy about it. Seems to me you have things turned around a bit. I'm the injured party, *remember*? The one with horns. If anyone has a right to complain, it's me, especially since you chose to involve my only friend who, I might add, is far from being the first." Picking up my drink like I'm not even here, he salutes her with it before taking a sip. "Oh, yes, I'm not completely stupid, you know. I've heard the whispers. It's not easy keeping a straight face at work when everyone knows your wife's a tramp."

"How did you find out?" I ask. "Did someone see us?"

"No." He taps his forehead, smiling with pride. "It was the old shit detector again, Dave. When I saw you a couple days ago, I told you I could always sense when she was up to something. Besides that, there was the look on your face when you asked if she'd said anything. You know, Dave, you'd make a poor crook. You're just not the kind who can disguise his feelings. Later, when I got to thinking about it, I just put two and two together and played a hunch."

"And what do you hope to prove by sneaking around like a mouse and acting like some pathetic little tough guy?"

Her cruelty surprises me. Still smiling, he twirls my glass.

"Wellllll—let's just say even a mouse likes to be a man now and then. You know, dear, you may not understand this, but I've been pushed around all my life, and I thought it might be nice to tinker with others for a change. Besides, there's poetic justice in this. Tell me, how does it feel to have someone sneak around *your* back and not play square with you?"

"You always knew what I was doing. If you had had any guts, you could have stopped it."

For the first time, he includes me voluntarily. "You see, Dave? Bet you didn't know what a sweet state of affairs you were getting yourself into. Oh, to be fair, it's been no picnic for her. But even considering the knocks I've put her through,

Sylvia still isn't what you'd call the sympathetic type. Once I hit the skids, she just jumped the fence like a mare in heat for greener pastures, and except for an occasional kick in the head since, she hasn't had anything to do with me."

"Maybe that's because there was nothing I could do to help you, and whenever I tried there was nothing there."

Duffy throws his hands up, dismissing all further debate as useless. "Anyway, another reason I invited you to this charming affair was I wanted to give you both my blessing before I left. Sylvia, for all the pain I've caused you and the failure of our marriage, I apologize, and I hope that your current flame has considerably more staying power than the others. May he bring you all the happiness I failed to. David, I wish you a safe and pleasant passage. You'll find her course changeable and on occasion cruel, but if you can stand by the helm and weather the storms, you'll find, as I'm sure you have already, that there's no finer ship afloat. But be warned: keep a steady hand or she'll toss you to perdition, and the sharks of the deep will polish your bones."

Even before he's finished, Sylvia has registered disgust. "My god, you're absurd. I get seasick just listening to you. Besides, who do you think you're fooling? You'll be back in a week like always."

I look at him closely. Not counting the stagey bravado, he still seems different. For the first time I put in my two cents.

"I don't know, Syl. Maybe he won't."

He turns to me, and something passes between us.

"You heard?"

"Uh huh. You told him to stick it."

"That's right. And that was the *nicest* thing I said." Wonder enters his voice. "I told him face to face what I thought of him: his incompetence, his stupidity, his pettiness. Spilled my guts of everything I've been choking on for years. And Lord, did it feel good."

He picks up his envelope and rises, indicating that nothing more remains to be said. "Now if you'll excuse us, Sylvia, I'd like to chat with Dave in private. He'll be back in just a few minutes."

We leave. Duffy doesn't even look back. Letting his casual words hang as an epitaph to nine years of marriage, he leads me along the glenstone rear of the clubhouse and around it to where we have a beautiful view of the golf course. Four hundred and fifty yards away, a flag waves in the sun. Dying for a smoke, I slap my pockets only to remember I finished my last one over by the courts.

"Nice day."

He nods. "Great for golf."

A golf cart pulls up to the first tee, and we watch two men disembark. The first walks onto the tee, places his ball, and goes through a series of waggles out of all proportion to the act he is about to perform. Finally, after a dozen pumps, he slowly draws his club back and commits himself to a swing, only to shank the ball wretchedly to his right.

"God, Duffy, I never meant—"

"Shhh. He's taking a Mulligan."

The man tees up another ball and goes through his act again. Waggles. Pumps. Checks his grip, his feet. Waggles again. Pumps. Then comes the agonizingly slow draw back of the club accompanied by a sense of déjà vu, and a whiplash return. This time the result's different. The ball soars straight as an arrow down the fairway. A real beauty. Two seventy easy. Maybe two eighty.

"You know, when I found I'd guessed right, I wanted to kill you."

I watch the second man tee off. "Duffy—"

Again he stops me. "For a minute inside the clubhouse, I actually thought of getting a gun. With the others I didn't care that much. After all, they were just bags of wind, balloon faces. But you were my friend and the only one I really respected. From you at least I expected better."

His words rip into me like Sylvia's tears. I remain silent, sensing it's his play.

"But then it came to me that you hadn't given in easily. For some reason I knew that. It must have been hard enough for you, damn hard. Besides, you must have felt bad as hell afterward. Right?"

A breeze stirs my hair. "So what are you going to do now?"

He gazes into the distance and shrugs. "You know," he says, a note of wonder entering his voice again, "I told him to stick it, and it wasn't hard at all."

"Wish I could have been there, Duff."

"You would have howled, Dave. He nearly fell out of his chair." He laughs. "What was it Sylvia called me, a mouse? Well, I was the mouse that roared, and that's something not even you have done."

In the distance the cart stops, and we watch one of the golfers get out.

"You know," he continues, "sometimes it seems I've been scared all my life without even knowing why. It's like fear was in my father's seed and I lapped it up at my mother's breast. That's why I always admired you. You were tough. You had guts. And yet I always felt in some odd way we were similar, that if things had been different we could have been—I don't know. It's just I've always felt a bond between us. Who knows, maybe that's the real reason I didn't come after you with a gun. In a way it was like I was cheating on myself. You were the man I might have been."

He stops and abruptly goes on.

"So I'm leaving to find myself, discover who I and what I am. You know, I never really knew. A long time ago my father decided I was going to study math, so I did. But I've never felt like a mathematician, and I don't think like one, either. Who knows? Maybe it'll turn out I should even be a writer. You know how curious I've always been about people, about what makes them tick and why they do certain things." He smiles. "And you've got to admit I can be pretty shrewd at spotting cover-ups, especially when it involves my wife and best friend."

I redden. "Your old shit detector," I say.

"Yeah, a writer," he says with shining eyes, not even hearing me. "Why not? Maybe I can be whatever I want! Anyway, what I've got to do now is go out and try to find out for myself who I am, and what's right for *me*."

I'm about to tell him I know all about searching but don't. Maybe it's because the closeness I feel between us makes it superfluous. Then, thinking of Sylvia, it occurs to me I should at least say something to separate this moment from the billion pointless ones life is made of.

"Your search is beginning, but mine's about done. I've already found part of what I've been looking for."

He nods with understanding and hands me the envelope. "Maybe this will help you find the rest."

I turn it over, finding it bulkier than I'd thought and crisscrossed by coarse brown string.

"What's in it? A bomb?"

"In a way. Remember my joke about you and Bledsoe? How you were going up against Goliath?"

"Yes."

"Well, call it an equalizer. A stone for you sling."

"I don't get it."

"Really? It should be obvious. Guts are fine, but you're going to need more than that when you challenge the artillery of the gods."

"Duff, you're playing games again."

"O.K. Let's just say being a math professor proved to have its rewards after all. At least it put me in a position where my path crossed that of Ashland's head accountant, who, it turns out, has his own ax to grind with the school." He taps the envelope. "It's all there, Dave. Facts, figures, photocopies, plus not just one but *two* secret prizes in the Cracker Jack that I promise will blow your eyes out. Also, you'll find my own summary, which a child could understand. You know, a place like Ashland can get away with just about anything. It can fail to educate, and it can grind people up like garbage. But let it get caught just once misusing federal funds, and the stench of hell will be ambrosia in comparison."

"Can it really do that much damage?"

"Bawana, what's in your hands can tear the place down, stone by moldy stone."

"In that case, maybe *you* should—"

"Un unh." He pushes it back. "Whoever uses that has got to know who he is and where he's going. I don't even know my first name yet. That's why I'm hitting the road, to find it out there."

"Maybe what you're looking for is right here, Duff. Sure you're not just running away?"

He shakes his head. "I've given it a lot of thought, and there's no other way. I've got to make a fresh start. Here there's only a dead marriage and the tag end of a career. It's either Head West, Young Man, or go under. And after going through all that fuss to stand up to Bledsoe, I'm not about to throw it away."

"But I'm not sure I want—"

"You'll do fine. You're the only one I know who cares about doing what's right and making things better. I chose the right man to give it to. Besides, you might decide not to do anything. That's all right too. Whatever you decide, I know it'll be the right thing."

"Well…" I turn it over, not wanting this new headache right now. Damn it, the thing even *feels* uncomfortable.

It's clear, though, I'm stuck. Duff takes my arm.

"Come on, you can see me off at the pier."

In the parking lot he springs one last surprise on me: a spanking new jeep. It gleams bright and snappy in the sun, and he beams with pride as I look it over.

"Snazzy, huh? Always wanted one of these babies."

"Looks great, Duff. In a way I wish I was going with you."

"And look here." Like a kid, he steers me to the back. "See? I've got all my gear stowed away. Tent. Sleeping bag. Pots and pans. Thought I'd start by getting back to nature." He pauses, eyes glistening, and holds out his hand. "Well, wish me luck, old man."

Suddenly I feel like crying. I've known him two years and haven't really said anything to him when there was so much to have said. Now, about to part, maybe never to see him again, I can't think of a damn thing. Then I remember John and Carol and start to tell him what a team we made in helping them, how if it hadn't been for his sixth sense about John's being fired and his idea of going to Courtland, their marriage probably would have shipwrecked on the rocks of John's self-doubt. I want to share everything with him, especially John's casting the gauntlet at Bledsoe's feet before the entire faculty. Bledsoe's public impotence and embarrassment would make a satisfying thought in the long miles ahead of him and in his bedroll beneath the stars, particularly since he was the one who had engineered it.

But as much as I want to, I can't tell him. It's a funny thing about life. Sometimes there's something you really should say but can't because the time's just not right or it's too late. Even now, when he's about to leave and I'm aching to tell him, I realize I can't. It's like this part of his life is already over. What remains now is the road ahead, and all I can do is awkwardly take his hand and force down the pain.

"Bon Voyage, Max. I wish you the best."

Then, anxious to leave, I walk away.

"Dave."

I turn around. He's got the door of the jeep open and stands with what I now notice is a boot raised up on the step, about to climb in. His face has lost its excitement and is now fiercely defiant.

"It's not true," he says, shaking his fist, "that a man can't change. He can. He *can* get a second chance if he wants. It's not true that we're all frozen. We *can* change our lives if we only have the strength to change ourselves."

I'm about to answer when I realize he's not talking to me but to himself or some force beyond us both. Face set in determination, he climbs in and shuts the door, and I wait in the sun as he starts the engine and shifts gears. Then, not even waving, he drives out of the parking lot and turns onto the open road.

Seventeen

I'm DAYDREAMING THE NEXT DAY when something snags my attention. I glance around, looking for a clue. Two of my students are deep in meditation. One has his nose mashed flat against a book on his desk, which he studies with his eyes closed. Elsewhere, Willie Clyde and Beulah Mae are fondling each other again. The rest contemplate the nature of things with blank expressions.

Finding nothing there, I turn back to Jackie, this year's Homecoming Queen with the delectable body half the dudes on campus would like to break into. Right now she's in the middle of an endless plot summary of one of those sex and sadism novels they grind out by the carload. The thing's a regular scumbag of perversion and third-rate writing, and I listen just long enough to make sure there's nothing that could have caught my interest before drifting back into thoughts of Sylvia. I'm just getting settled again when the discordant note returns. This time, though, I get a fix on it. Let's see, seems fourteen year old Sondra has just found a stash of dope—

"Jackie, what did you just say you'd do if you found the dope?"

She looks up with those perfect white teeth of hers and gives me a smile.

"I just said I wish it was me."

"Why?"

"*Cause*, man, it's easy money. I could unload it myself or sell it to a pusher."

"I see." I turn to a student who will probably graduate Magna Cum Laude this year and who has already been accepted into Michigan State University's law school. "What about you, Barbara? Would—"

"Heck, yeah. If *I* found twenty-five balloons of quality stuff,

I could make a real killing."

"You mean you'd push it?"

"I'm not saying *that*. Probably I'd sell it to someone."

"Huh uh. What about you, Cathy?"

"Oooh, man. The book says Brick paid her $4,000 clear for it."

"And you wouldn't feel guilty?"

"What for?" asks Dennis. "That's four thousand dollars tax free. Do you know what—"

"Yeah, but what if someone sold it to kids?"

"I know what you're saying, Mr. Newman," the law student says. "But if it wasn't me, it would be someone else."

"So you'd—"

"That's right. If I didn't profit on it, the police or someone else would. So why shouldn't it be me?"

"What about the rest of you? Do you all feel the same way?"

As it turns out, they do. Thinking about it afterwards in front of a display poster of Ashland College, it occurs to me that at least three in the class are no slouches. Unlike the vast majority of students, they at least have some spark and have come a long way in the three years since they were freshmen. And yet...

Wake up, damn it. Where do you think you are, Cloud Cuckoo Land? It's the easy dollar down here, where as long as you've got the bread, you can buy whatever you want. And forget about the Please and Thank You.

Still, their unanimity bugs me as I gaze at the poster. Labeled *Ashland College: A Challenge For The Eighties*, it consists of photos of new buildings and of a few old ones taken from favorable angles. Everything is tastefully arranged and it really looks good. Should make a nice brochure.

Outside, Sitwell and Fishbait hotfoot it my way.

"Hey, what's the rush?"

"Contracts are out!"

"Yeah, man, contracts!"

Brushing past me, they enter the Ad Building practically arm-in-arm. Talk about miracles. Imagine, here at Ashland a white guy and a black unite in pursuit of a common goal. What won't they think of next?

I'm about to continue when it hits me.

Contracts!

What are you waiting for?

Hurry up and check!

Heart thumping, I follow them into the building. Sitwell and Fishbait have already picked their boxes clean and dispersed, their brotherhood dissolved. I swallow and look around. For the moment I've got the room to myself. I work the combination quickly. Is there anything in there? There is. A neat sealed envelope. *Office of The President* in upper left corner. Name on envelope: David Newman.

Jamming it into my pocket, I head outside wondering if it's good tidings or a ticket back to the farm. How do I know it's a contract? It would be bad form to chop my head off this late, especially on the same day when contracts are renewed, but those who polish the guillotine around here have been known to do worse. Take Wooster in Biology, who got canned for trying to collect the $300.00 he'd been promised for coaching the tennis team. Or the history professor who went to his class one morning after a contract dispute to find someone else teaching it. And with a blade like Bledsoe just aching to cut, you can never be that sure your head won't roll. Like the poet says, all things are potential in the fires of the sun.

I reach in my pocket to get the damn thing when I hear my name called. Over by the Fine Arts Center Sylvia's waving from her car, and I break into a run.

"Hey, what are you doing here?"

"Taking you to lunch. Hop in!"

I oblige. "Where are we going?"

"How about the club? We can take a swim there first and eat afterward."

"O.K. if I go naked? I'm kind of low in the trunks department."

"Check in back. I brought one of Max's suits."

I reach and get it. "Mind if I try it on here?"

"Be my guest."

I turn it over. "I don't know, Syl. Looks snug and I'm pretty well hung."

"I know."

At a red light, I watch Jackie Carter cross the street.

"Know her?"

"Yeah, she's in one of my classes. Back on the farm, we used to take talent like that behind the barn."

She frowns at what I've said. "Have any of your students ever propositioned you?"

"A few."

"And?"

"Well, as it turned out, they had all the moves."

"Oh, you..." She removes her foot from the pedal and tries to kick me.

"Hey!"

"Seriously, you didn't—no, of course not. You're too much of—"

"An idealist."

"Yes."

"As a matter of fact, one was strictly business. She came into my office like a pro and said for an A she'd give me Sodom and Gomorrah and show me how much juicier black girls were than white. The others, well..."

"That deadly charm again?"

I sigh, laying the modesty on with a trowel. "Guess when you've got it, they just can't help it. Anyway, they were more personal. One even straddled my lap and kissed me before I knew it."

"Were you tempted?"

"Of course."

She's silent for a moment. "Have you ever... made it with a black woman?"

I consider a diplomatic lie but reject it. "A couple. You know, it's amazing what some white guys think about them. I met a redneck once in Holly Springs, Mississippi who swore that no white man ever screwed a black girl because she screwed *him*. Said that they liked to go all night, so the rewards were all on *their* side. Claimed they just wore you out."

"Maybe he knew something."

"Naw, he was just sucking air. The libido's an individual thing, not racial. I've known plenty of white gals who'd bury you with your pants off if you'd let them."

She snaps me a look. "Hope you've put all that behind you."

I stroke her thigh and pat it. "You know I have. Anyway, you know what I've often wondered?"

"What?"

"What it would be like if a man could experience thirty orgasms in one night like some women. Ever consider the implications? I mean, maybe history would have been completely different if men were multiorgasmic."

She laughs. "It sure would be hard to get you boys out of bed."

"Or off to the wars, for that matter. Ever think of that? I mean, we'd be so busy humping we just wouldn't have the time. Besides, we'd be too tired. Talk about grinding our swords into plowshares..."

"Make more babies."

"Maybe, but that depends on birth control. Anyway, with all the beautiful women in the world, it's a shame a guy's capable of only two or three a night. 'To use it is to lose it,' as they say. Sometimes I wonder what the Old Boy was thinking when he gave us the weapon but short rationed us on the ammunition."

"Well, He wasn't stingy with *us*. Sometime I'll tell you what it's like to have thirty in one night. Poor boy, you just don't know what you're missing."

Now it's my turn to feel jealous, but before I can follow it up I get an idea.

"Hey, Syl, turn left here."

"What for?"

"Never mind. Just do it."

Overruling her protests, I direct her across town toward the Pee Dee River, which we reach by driving up a dirt lane into a bumpy parking lot.

"Here we are, end of the line!"

"End of the line? What are we doing *here*?"

I grab my suit and check the place out. The river sparkles in

162

the sun, and the air's filled with the sound of kids playing.

"Looks great, Syl. Let's change."

"You mean you want to swim *here*?"

"Sure, why not? It's more fun than the pool, and we can eat at the club afterward."

"But they're black!"

"So?"

"But we're the only white people here! Are you sure it's safe?"

"Safe? Why wouldn't it be?" I coax her toward a small building made of concrete blocks. "C'mon, we change in here."

"No thank you. You go in if you want, I'll just watch from here. Besides, I've heard about this place. There's been trouble in the past."

I take her arm. "That's ancient history, Syl. Besides, whites swim here now and then and everyone gets along fine. No one wants any trouble."

"But we're the only whites here *now*. Wouldn't it be better to come some other time?"

Surprised and disappointed, I steer her along. "C'mon, where's your sense of adventure, the *Bhagavad-gītā* and all that? Take my word for it. Once you get in, you won't want to come out."

As soon as I change, I pound her door.

"Hey!"

"What?"

"Shake a leg!"

"I'm doing the best I can. David?"

"Yeah?"

"It's so bare in here. They don't even have a shower."

"It's just a place to *change*, Syl."

"But at the club we'd at least—"

"Step on it, Syl! Time's a-wasting."

Finally she comes out in a wicked two piece and we take our duds to the car.

"You look smashing."

163

She blushes and takes my arm. "I feel like they're all watching me."

"That's better than having them watch *me*."

"That's not funny."

"Sorry, just hold on."

Which she does. Like I'm a lifesaver. Real snug and close around my arm, against my side. As we move toward the water, for the first time I know what it's like to feel protective toward someone you love.

Although it's mid May, the water's nearly freezing. I tug her arm, acting like I'm going to pull her in.

"Don't, please!"

I laugh, run and dive in. The shock's great and below it's a deep green. I swim twenty feet and burst the surface yelling like Tarzan.

"Stop it!"

"Why?"

"Everyone's looking."

I swim back and draw her to me.

"Oooh!"

"Cold?"

"I'll say."

I back-paddle. She shivers against me as the water rises and wraps her legs around my waist. I drop my hands and hold her bottom close.

"Come on!"

"I'm tempted!"

"It's getting hard."

"Take a cold shower."

"I am, but it doesn't help." I move against her.

"Hey, that's enough."

I grin into the eyes of a nubile young native and give Syl my best shot beneath the surface.

"We can be *arrested* for what we're doing."

"Un unh. I'm still under the speed limit."

"Just barely."

Water laps at our chins as we head downstream. "Ain't life grand?"

"Wonderful!"

On both sides of the river, cypress trees dripping moss pass us by. When it gets too deep, I reluctantly let her go and we swim along side my side. She turns out to be really good. I try to pass her, but she stays even without any trouble.

"Say, you're good."

"That's because I'm a Pisces."

I point up ahead. "See that big metal barrel just after the bridge with the rope running through it from one bank to the other?"

"Yes."

"Well, let's stop there. O.K.?"

Gradually the current gets stronger. We've left the children and most of the adults behind, beyond the rope that separates the "family" area from this part of the river. They've got no lifeguard here, so it's swim at your own risk. Swimming beneath the bridge, we reach the barrel and hold on to the rope, feeling the drag of river which has become irresistible.

At this point the river narrows into a channel, creating a rapids that extends for maybe fifty feet. Beyond the rapids the current is mild again, but for that fifty feet it churns green white and offers a real ride.

"Ready to try it?"

"Sure."

"O.K., just stick to the center of the stream. When you get beyond the rapids, you can paddle over to the right bank and come back through the cypress trees. Oh, just one thing."

"What's that?" she says, her eyes shining.

I point ten feet ahead to our left and right. "Watch out for the suck holes."

"Suck holes? What's that?"

"Small whirlpools that drag you down. If you should get caught, just remember not to fight it. Let it pull you down and when you get to the bottom, just step out to the side. But there's no danger if you stay in the center of the river."

"Anybody ever get drowned here?"

I shrug. "Last year a kid got caught in a suck hole. They don't show up too well against the water, you know, and he probably fought going under and tired himself out. Anyway, just follow me. Check?"

She nods. I test the pull of the river, letting it carry my whole body forward. Lying full length on my back, I do a couple horizontal "chins" on the rope. Then I let go.

The rapids takes me. I bob and bounce in the swirling water, howling all the way. Then I'm out of it and dog paddle over to the right bank where I climb onto a fringe of smooth sand. Sylvia joins me a moment later, laughing as I give her my hand.

"It's divine!"

"Want to do it again?"

"Sure!"

We weave our way back through the cypress trees, avoiding their hard roots or "knees."

"David?"

"Yeah?"

"Any snakes here?"

"Just water moccasins."

"Thanks for telling me."

"Don't worry, I've never seen any. Besides, snakes attack only if threatened."

Entering the river near the barrel, we shoot the rapids again and again. Finally, after a dozen times, she comes out of the water and embraces me like a hungry mermaid. Against me, I can feel every inch of her skin molded in a continuous flame. I get the message at once and draw her back into the trees, out of sight of the river. In seconds we peel our suits and as soon as we hit the sand I'm inside her. She cups my buttocks and presses me into her in time with my thrusts. Then before I know it, she turns me over without separating and sits astride me in total command. Her powerful thighs nudge mine apart.

Above her shoulders, sunlight of late spring dapples the leaves and branches and plays in their rich shadows, making where we lie seem like a primeval swamp billions of years old. Pterodactyls sail above the moss on graceful wings. Nearby the ancient river murmurs. Twigs dig into my back and where we join is an ache a mile long. Suddenly she moans and a convulsive shiver runs through her body like an electric charge.

"That's just once," she breathes into my ear. "Hold on, I'm going to shoot the rapids twenty-nine more times."

Whether she goes downstream thirty times, I don't know. I stop counting after a half dozen. By then she's sobbing loudly, and I raise my hands to caress her erect nipples. She moves above me. Then I go over the edge. My heart heaves, my stomach falls through, I shoot the Thunder and Lightning Gods out of the sky, destroy their Cave of Winds. Sylvia stays with me till the end when she too can rest, lie down upon me and close her eyes.

Silence. Gradually our breathing slows and merges into one. Somewhere a bird hoots.

When she moves the spell is broken. Eons roll back in an eyeblink and when I open my eyes, it's South Carolina again. No pterodactyls. No eternal river. The sun filtering through the moss is as newly minted as our sweat, and my calf has a case of terminal cramp.

Still, the last time I felt half this high was at a rock concert in Georgetown. I rise and head upriver again.

"Adam? Aren't you forgetting something?"

I look at her, not grokking. Then I catch on and break out laughing. My suit! No sir, it wouldn't look kosher for me to leave the Garden of Eden without a fig leaf on. A fella can get busted for a sight less in this postlapsarian town, and at the very least the news would make sour reading at Bledsoe's breakfast table.

So sticky wet, I struggle back into my false skin and return to civilization. Along the way my stiffness reminds me that I'll be thirty-nine next week. Reaching the stone wall above the river, I slip her a wink.

"Care to shoot the rapids one more time?"

"Sure you're up to it?"

We laugh and dive in. At the barrel we cling to the rope for a minute, letting the cool water clean and refresh us. The air is warm and sweet. I squeeze the coarse woven rope as hard as I can with both hands, so hard it hurts, and flex my muscles against the pull of the current. Never before have I been so happy, felt so alive. This is the high point in my life. The absolute peak.

Finally, since no climax can last forever, I reluctantly let go, celebrating enroute by turning on my back. Above me a black kid stands on the bridge. He says something to me which I don't catch, so I give him a jaunty wave and roll back on my stomach. Seconds later I collect Sylvia and return.

This time we cross the bridge instead of entering the river. On the bottoms of my feet, I can feel round rivets baking in the sun. Upstream, kids squeal, their brown bodies gleaming as they chase an overthrown beach ball. Reaching the other side, I remember the kid on the bridge and look around for him. But he's not there. Probably he went to play with the other kids.

I'm about to forget him when I hear a cry. I turn but don't see anything. Then something snags the corner of my eye. Just beyond the rope and near the opposite bank, an object bobs in the water. Something dark and round. A head. Hands beat the water frantically.

In three strides I'm at the water and swimming as hard as I can to reach him, but without success. Then I realize I'm fighting the current and let it carry me to the rope, which I use to pull myself along. On the other side of the barrel, the head's already gone. I dive.

The suck hole takes me down like a giant mouth. I feel rocks and sand but nothing else. Pushing to the side, I thrash to the surface, look around, dive again. Again the suck hole. Everything's a murky green. Damn it, where's the kid? He should be here. I turn around, feeling glued to the bottom. Jesus, he should be here! This is where I saw him go down. Again I force myself out to the side and rise to the surface.

Now I've got a stitch in my side and about enough left for one more dive. I've got absolutely no idea where to look. He *should* be down there in the hole, but he's not. On the far bank, someone screams. I dive.

Again it sucks me down, this time so hard I stab my foot on a rock. I grope around but find nothing. Wherever he is, he's dead. Must be minutes since I saw him.

I'm about to give up when I spot something just *outside* the suck hole. I move to it and grab. A hand.

I pull but nothing happens. What's wrong? He escaped the hole so he should come up. Must be caught somewhere. Using his body to reach the bottom, I locate an ankle and feel for the foot. It's free. Grabbing his other ankle, I find his other foot wedged between two rocks. I pull on it without success.

Bracing my feet on the bottom of the river, I tear at the foot. Come on, you fucking river, let him go! As a last resort I turn the foot between the rocks and like a miracle it slips out. Making the surface, I lunge for the rope before the current takes us and work him back along it to the far bank rather than try to climb the wall on the near side.

When I reach land, I'm gasping for air and dead as the kid, and barely manage to stagger onto the grass and drop him. Remembering something I learned twenty years ago, I straddle him and start pressing his back and raising his arms. Un unh: seems to me they gave this up years ago. Desperately I turn him over and see him for the first time. A little boy with delicate features, he looks like a piece of debris washed up on shore, a casual reject of the river. Moving to one side, I open his mouth. Then I take a breath, cover his mouth with mine, and blow in. Again and again. I gasp for air, my back in agony. C'mon, breathe!

Dimly I hear voices but don't look up. If I do, I'll quit and sink into a vast cushiony dreamland. The kid's gone for sure, and I've done all this for nothing. Hopelessly I work on him, fighting to remain conscious and to repeat the simple process. All I can do is gasp air, give it to him, and repeat. Who's that crying? Can't be me. Gasp air. Give it to him. Repeat. Gasp air. Give it to him. Repeat...

Suddenly his chest gurgles and a moment later water gushes out of his mouth. Then he's choking and fighting for air. His fists beat me like butterfly wings, and with the last of my strength I gather him up and support him against me. As I do, the outside world reels back and in a daze I see the crowd. Sylvia's face is white. Everyone's shouting. The kid's chest rattles against mine and a woman flings herself at him. I just sit, not understanding any of it and lacking even the strength to lie down.

Eighteen

Afterwards the kid's fine and my head clears. The ambulance comes and takes him to the hospital just to be on the safe side. Before he goes, the mother kneels beside me and kisses my hand.

After a while, Sylvia helps me up. I'm completely drained and my whole body aches. Feel just like Methuselah. To tell the truth, they should have left the kid here and carted *me* away in the ambulance. I'm the one who needs it. Besides, the pats I keep getting feel like body punches. One swimmer is built like Hercules and keeps working me over like one of those huge bags they pummel in gyms. Leaning on Sylvia, I stumble off in the direction of the car, wanting only to be alone so I can recover.

When we reach the car, she gets a cigarette from my shirt and lights it for me. I take a drag and draw it deep into my lungs, enjoying the strong tobacco. Suddenly I start coughing.

"Are you all right?"

"It's O.K. I can handle it."

She puts her arms around me. "Oh, David, I was so worried. I kept seeing you dive under and when you tried to revive him on the grass, you looked—"

"Easy, baby." I pat her back. "Daddy's back."

"But are you sure you're all right?"

"Sure. Feel like a million."

I do, too. The shakes are gone and the pains are those you get after a hard workout in a good cause, like that time in high school when I wrestled this kid during a team match and managed to pin him with just five seconds left on the clock. Only this is even better. I'm beginning to realize what I've done and my exhaustion tastes like fine wine. I take another long drag on

170

the Camel, enjoying even the nicotine. Sylvia looks me over.

"My hero."

"Yeah."

"You were—"

"Come on, let's go."

Anxious to make tracks, I get my clothes from the car. As I carry them to the building to change, something falls from my pants.

"What's that?"

I stoop painfully to pick it up. The President's letter. Surprised I forgot the damn thing, I carry my clothes back and dump them on top of her car.

"What is it?" she asks again.

I turn it over. *CONFIDENTIAL. Mr. David Newman.* "Could be anything," I say. "A ticket back to the farm, or an invitation to pick cotton for another year."

"What are you talking about?"

I tap it against my palm, finding it hard to take seriously. Here I've made love and saved a life all in the last hour, and now this scrap of folded paper with its licked glue turns up. I've worried about it and now it just seems absurd, meaningless as fluff blown from a dead dandelion. What can it possibly have to do with me?

Sylvia, though, senses something important in it.

"Is that—your contract?"

"Could be. I was going to open it when I saw you on campus. Guess I just forgot it."

"Well, don't you think you should open it?"

I turn it over, shaking my head. "I don't know, Syl. It's so nice and white, seems a shame..."

"David!"

Shrugging, I tear off the end and spill out the contents. Like last year, it's folded in duplicate. Sign both copies and return the white one to the President's Office. Keep the yellow one for your files. I snap it open and give it the one two.

"Well? Don't just—"

"Relax, I've got good news. You're looking at a genuine

American success story. Here I am on the sunny side of forty, and already I'm making over ten thousand dollars a year. The Colonel has done given po' David a two hundred and fifty dollar raise."

"You've been rehired?"

"Yup."

"Thank God. I bet you were worried, especially with the Dean hounding you all the time."

"Yeah, well, looks like our love affair is on for next year."

Not till I've said it do I realize how true it is. Bad as Ashland is, its money spends, and right now that's important to our future. Handing the contract over, I watch her read it and make a discovery of her own.

"David, there's something else in the envelope."

"What is it?"

"Looks like a letter."

"Let me see it."

I take it and give it a quick scan. "Well, well, the Lord giveth, and the Lord taketh away."

"What..."

"Here, read it."

She looks it over. "I don't understand."

"Really? It's perfectly obvious. The Dean has given the President a Dear Dave letter to include with my contract. When *that* expires, so do I."

"You mean you're fired after next year? But why? And what does he mean here where he says, 'Matters of which we have spoken...'?"

"That's just his sweet way of letting me know my record closes the door on any chance of appeal. He could have fired me at any time for the mistakes I've made, but instead he's given me the year's notice required by the *Faculty Handbook*. So as far as he's concerned, he's covered."

"But why do it now, on the very day when you receive your contract? It's so *cruel*."

"Exactly! That's the point. The cup of wine dashed from the lips. The good news spiked by the bad. What better way to sink the old knife in?" I hit her car. "Jesus!"

"How dreadful. Isn't there anything…"

"Sure. I can eat my heart out."

She comes over and touches me. "I'm sorry."

Despite my anger, I'm critical enough to be surprised at my reaction. From not caring at all, I've come in one minute to care very much. Also, I'm filled with wonder. "You know," I say, "despite what he's done to me, I have to admire him."

"Admire? How can you say that? He's just ripped you apart."

"That's the point." I pause, and it's like I can see clear across town into that other brain that's done this to me. For a moment that crackbrained, unfathomable mentality is no longer alien but beautifully clear, and I can see how the world itself must appear in its eyes.

"You know," I say "for sheer sadistic brilliance, there's no one who can touch him, and believe me, in my day I've seen my share of pricks. He's a real Son-of-a-Bitch's Son-of-a Bitch, the best there is. Fucking ball-cutter, I bet he's been hatching this one for months, long before I last talked to him in April."

"Maybe he *didn't* plan it, though."

"Bullshit. Of *course* he did. You know, I think I finally understand what makes the old sodomist tick."

"But maybe you only *think* you do. Oh, David, I always get the same thing from Max about how he's the Marquis de Sade's illegitimate great grandson and enjoys hurting people. Maybe he just doesn't care one way or the other."

"He cares all right. Goddamn lousy—"

"But maybe he *doesn't*. I hate to see you take it personally like Max and tear yourself apart. Maybe if you think of him as just being cold and indifferent, it won't hurt so much."

I shake off the thought. "Un unh. He meant it personally, all right. Make no mistake about that. He's just sucking it up." I start stripping off my trunks. "Come on, let's go!"

"David, not here! We're in public!"

Removing my trunks, I walk to the river and sling them in. "God damn Bledsoe, he planned this all along. Just sat there in his office and waited for the day when he could step on me."

"David, you don't have any clothes on!"

Turning, I advance up the hill, shaking my fist in the direction of the school.

"FUCK YOU, BLEDSOE! I'M GOING TO GET YOU IF IT'S THE LAST—"

"David, you're naked! What if a policeman—"

"THING I EVER DO! DO YOU HEAR ME, BLEDSOE? DO YOU HEAR ME? IF IT'S—"

"David!"

"THE LAST THING I EVER DO, I'M GOING TO GET YOU, YOU MOTHER-FUCKING SON OF A BITCH! I DON'T KNOW HOW, BUT—"

"David, please, there's children coming this way!"

Her voice finally snaps me out of it. I take a deep breath and look around.

"O.K., Syl, let's go!"

By the time we're dressed I've cooled off a little, but not much. "Give me the keys."

She hands them over and I toss gravel.

Sonofabitch! I don't *want* to start looking for work again. I'm tired of jobs that last only a year or two because I keep getting in trouble. Besides, with my record, maybe I can't get another teaching position. They're scarce as hell the way it is. And what about Sylvia? Thinking of her makes me boil. Damn it, I want to settle down! That's not too much to ask, is it? What's this going to mean as far as *we're* concerned? Fucking Bledsoe. Bet he gets a real bang out of doing this to me.

Hitting the town square, I notice for the first time what's been bothering me about the Confederate soldier. On other Southern statues I've seen, the dude's rifle points up or into the distance. This asshole points his down. If he isn't careful, he'll blow his foot off. Beyond the square, traffic's tighter than a virgin's knees, and after a minute I'm ready to climb the guy in front. Then I spot the trouble. Up ahead a store's opening, and a familiar white haired figure is getting ready to cut the ribbon. On both sides of him, a line of employees grins into the camera.

"Colonel Sanders," I say.

"What?"

"His majesty the mayor. The Honorable Peter A. Pendleton." I snort in disgust. "That's Green Town for you."

"What do you mean?"

"Read your local rag sometime. Everytime you open it, there's another picture of him snipping away. Fucking town, that's all it wants from its mayor: a glorified ribbon cutter."

"Well, that's what people want from their politicians, isn't it?"

"Sure. Someone short on substance and long on ceremony. Old Mr. Do-Nothing and Sweep-It-Away. You know, this country's never grown up. Just look at its slogans. 'Laissez faire.' 'That government is best which governs least.' 'Government is a necessary evil.'" I thump the steering wheel. "Well, all I can say is that folks deserve whatever they get."

In front of the store, the ribbon divides and everyone claps. The mayor beams and pumps the owner's hand.

"Finger lickin' good."

"What?"

"Well, look at him. He's the spitting image of Colonel Sanders. And like the ole Colonel, no matter how you photograph or view him, he looks exactly the same every time."

At the school I park next to Big Red as a student roars past us, his radio blaring one of those rousing ditties that brings you stompin' and jerkin' to Jesus.

> Heaven's just a sin away,
> Heaven's just a sin away,
> Heaven's just a sin away,
> Oh, yeah...

Lighting a cigarette, I lean back against the soft vinyl and spew forth enough holy smoke to fill half the city. "Christ!"

She puts her hand on my knee. "I know."

"I've never had it all happen to me at one crack before. Don't know what the hell I'm going to do for an encore. Maybe wrestle a gorilla or sky dive from twenty thousand feet without a parachute." I take another drag, thinking of everything and nothing. A boy crosses the lawn in front of the car, young and smiling a twenty year old smile. Cupping a portable radio behind his ear like a shot-put, he greets a brother with a ritual handshake. "You know," I go on, "the last time I went under for that kid I thought I was going to stay there with him. Maybe it would have been better if I had."

"You don't mean that."

"No."

"What was the matter, anyway? Couldn't you find him?"

"The first two times I couldn't. Then I found he'd escaped the suck hole only to get his foot wedged between two rocks." I close my eyes and I'm beneath the water again, feet braced against the bottom. Come on, you fucking river, let him—

She presses my knee. With a start, I find myself on dry land again, fighting other currents.

Parked as I am in front of the WELCOME sign, I command a view of virtually the entire campus. At the moment the sun is being especially kind to tarnished structures like Moulton Hall and the music building, working its alchemy in such a way that it seems they've received a face-lift. The library, just three years old and bearing the President's name, rises resplendent and its glass panes glitter like beacons for learning. Nothing, the whole place seems to say, can touch me. I am invincible. From building to building, clipped lawns to flowering shrubs, a smug call seems to rise. Nothing can hurt me. I am invincible. Long after a pygmy like you is gone, I'll still be here, growing bigger and more unassailable than ever.

I take another drag, taking the smoke down so that it forms a hard narrow knot in my belly. "I'd like to do a number on this place," I say.

"If only you could."

"Maybe I can."

"How?"

I stab out the cigarette, something inside me beginning to focus. "Just before Max left, he gave me something."

"What?"

"Remember the package he had with him at the club?"

"Oh, yes. It was tied up with string and he put it on the table. What about it?"

"Well, just before we said good-by, he gave it to me. Said the Head Accountant, who had his own ax to grind, had given him evidence about the school's misuse of federal funds that could bring it down like a house of cards."

"And *that* was in the...?"

"You betcha. He also said there were two secret prizes that would absolutely blow my mind, plus his own Easy-To-Understand Instructions." I laugh. "So what I've got ticking away on my apartment table is a Do-It-Yourself Destruction Kit a kid can assemble. Just open and plug her in."

"But I don't understand. If what Max found is so explosive, why didn't he use it himself?"

"You forget. He felt he had to leave."

"Oh, he's said that a thousand times." She pauses. "Do you actually mean he might *not* return this time?"

"I tried to tell you that. In the parking lot at the club he told me he was leaving to find himself and wouldn't be back." I slap the wheel. "You should have seen the preparations the son of a gun made. Bought himself a new jeep and—"

"But," she cuts in, "why didn't *he* use it? You know how he hated the people at work."

"You forget again," I say a bit irritated, "how often you've said he just didn't have the guts. Can you imagine 'Poor Max' trying to bring down an entire college?"

"Well, why did he give it to you?"

"Guess I was his only friend and he left it up to me to decide what to do with it."

She shakes her head. "This is incredible. Absolutely incredible." Suddenly she darts me a look. "And have you examined the evidence? Has Ashland actually misused government money?"

"That's what Max said."

"And who's implicated? Any teachers? What about—"

"Actually, I haven't opened it yet," I say uncomfortably.

"Haven't *opened* it? David, what are you *waiting* for?"

I take the steering wheel in both hands. "Nothing, I guess. At least not any longer. Now that they've stuck it to me, the least I can do to show my appreciation is to open Max's little legacy and see if I can get the last laugh."

"But what good will that do?"

"You kidding? I can blow the whistle on—"

"But what will that accomplish? Even if they *do* listen to you, the most that will happen is that a few heads will roll. And even if the pillars fall, what do you get out of it?"

A hundred yards away, a boy and a girl hold hands as they climb the steps of the library. Just before entering they separate, the boy turning to shout something to someone I can't see.

Something touches the back of my neck. While I've been watching them, Sylvia has moved next to me and started stroking and massaging my neck with a gentle circular motion.

"Davy, have you thought of using this to your advantage?"

"What do you mean?"

"You know. Making it work for you."

"How?"

"It's simple." Her fingers are working wonders at the base of my neck now, coaxing away the tension and helping me to relax. Softening her voice, she moves still closer.

"Honey, why not let them know what you've got in advance?"

"In advance?"

"Yes, so you can—talk terms."

"Terms?" I sit up. "You mean I should...?"

"Yes. I was reluctant to mention it because I know the kind of person you are. But it would be a *crime* not to use it against them after what they've done to you."

"But that's blackmail!"

"Listen," she says, massaging my neck again, "if you've got what you think you've got, not only can you get your job back but more money, power, security—"

"Forget it."

"No, now listen. I *know* how you feel. Believe me, I *admire* you for your ideals. But David, *David,* you can't afford to let *this* slip through your fingers. Talk about lucky breaks, this is a once in a lifetime opportunity, and you've got to act *now.* The difference between a smart man and a fool is that the smart man knows when he should act and does it."

"Then I'm a horse's ass. Look, Syl," I say with such heat that she moves away, "I'm not about to get cute with any of that Grade B movie shit. You know: all that 'I've-got-a-friend-and-if-I-don't-call-him-in-an-hour-he-goes-straight-to-the-cops' stuff. For one thing, it just ain't my style, and for another, with my luck it would probably blow up right in my face."

"Listen—"

"No, *you listen.* Last but not least, I *do* have values. All my life I've seen rats thrive and have tried to do something about them. And again and again I've failed. Either the system stamped me flatter than a tin can or my own friends let me down. And now I've finally got a chance to do something about it and change things, and...god damn it, I'm...*I'm not going to let it get away!*"

My fist shakes right beneath her nose. She seizes it in both hands.

"You're mad right now, aren't you?"

"Damn right."

"You could hit me, couldn't you?"

"Don't tempt me."

"Oh, David, I *want* to tempt you. You're a man. Not like Max. A *man.*" With both hands she presses my fist to her cheek, practically swooning over it. I stare back amazed. Suddenly she's a stranger, someone I've never seen before. "Oh, David," she says, her eyes seeming to devour my face, "if you could just see yourself right now, *feel* the emanations that are *pouring* from you. God, there's an *aura* about you, a life *force.* David. Oh, David, *listen.* Remember how I told you that most people freeze up early and *can't* change, but how with you I had the *feeling* your big moment was yet to come? Well, it's almost here, David. Soon you must decide what you're going to be! And David, you can be whatever you want, if you have the strength. So when your moment comes, *be strong. Take what you want.* The world belongs to the meat eaters, and only they—"

I yank my hand free. "What's all this crap about 'emanations' and 'meat eaters'? As if urging me to commit blackmail isn't bad enough, now you're on one of your mystical kicks."

"What I'm on," she says, immediately seeming to calm down, "is a reality kick. I've simply been trying to point out the need for constructive action."

"So that's what you call it. Well, to me it's extortion, breaking the law. Damn it, I thought I knew you. Now I find I don't. Guess Max was right when he called you changeable."

"Keep citing Max like he's an authority and you'll end up out there with him. Just another loser." She takes my hand again. "David, do you care about me?"

I gaze into her dark eyes. "Yes."

"Then do something for our future."

"But not blackmail!"

"Yes. Listen, what do you have left after Ashland? Another scratch job someplace if you're lucky enough to get it? Well, I'm too old for that anymore. I've been through it too many times with Max, seeing him get fired and moving from place to place. I'm not about to start it all over again with you."

"Are you telling me I've got to come down to their level or it's bye, bye, Charlie?"

She draws my hand against her cheek. "David, do you *really* love me?"

"Of course I—"

"Then *do* something about it!"

Feeling like I'm in the suck hole again, I gaze across the campus, seeing "Sylvia's Curiosity Shoppe" emblazoned above it across the sky. "And if I don't, does that mean we're through?"

She kisses my hand. "You wouldn't do that to us, would you? I know you wouldn't."

"Syl…"

"Just think about it, won't you? For both our sakes."

"I can't."

"David, please!" She moves next to me. "Just say you'll think about it."

"No!"

"Just think about it." She turns my head and kisses me.

I look back out at the campus. This time I don't answer.

"David…"

"Syl…"

"That's better." She pats my hand. "Just think it over and you'll see—"

"That's enough."

"Just think it over and—"

"Do me a favor," I say, "and shut up." I grip the wheel. "Just shut the hell up!"

Nineteen

Even in the dark I can feel it lying there in silent accusation. C'mon, it says, get up. What are you waiting for, an invitation to dance? Angrily I pull the covers up over my head and retreat beneath them, searching for sanctuary. God, I can't go on like this. If it doesn't let me alone soon I'll—

What are you trying to pull, Newman—a vanishing act? Well, as Joe Louis once said, you can run but you sure can't hide. C'mon, show some guts!

Finally, since man was not designed to sleep with his conscience raging in his ear, I throw off the covers and sit up. It crouches there just as it has for the past week, ready to spring like a cat. Or maybe a bomb metaphor is better. What it actually does is tick. And I'm the detonator. One way or another, I've got to pay the piper for this tune, and whether there's an explosion that rocks the county or a popcorn fart that doesn't go beyond the walls of this room, it's still my play. I can't pussyfoot around it any longer.

Funny, when you think of it, how so much of my life lately has come to depend on things you open. First the letter from the school, now this Surprise Package with its yet to be revealed mystery. Or who knows, maybe the real mystery lies in me since I'm the one who has to open it.

Speaking of mysteries, sometimes how you make a decision is itself one. Suddenly I get up so fast that I'm the last to know I've made up my mind. How about it, am I acting on the spur of the moment or have I deliberately and subconsciously incubated this decision for a week? Whatever the case, I'm no sooner launched than everything becomes slow motion. Yet my brain winds out to 10,000 RPM, clear and impatient with the tardiness of flesh. After what seems hours I gain the table and tackle Max's Gordian knot, Sylvia's nagging echoing in my head. Have you opened it yet? Honey, you can't put it off any longer... Max's boy scout wizardry inspires cowardice, for it's obvious I'll need nitro to crack this nut. My hands persist in fumbling at the door of Fort Knox and after a millenium the knot dissolves and the paper parts like the Red Sea. New wrapping appears and I assault what proves to be a square knot. Then there's a new package, another knot, and so on, endlessly and forever. Ultimately, in the "amplitude of time" as Whitman puts it, I unearth a gleaming envelope with Office of the President inscribed in its upper left hand corner. On its face is engraved David Newman, CONFIDENTIAL, and when I open it a letter falls out. To Whom It May Concern, it reads. KEEP THIS HONKY RUNNING.

At which point I wake up.

I'm still sitting on the bed and the package is unmolested. Rising, I go to the window where I find in the morning light that there are no ducks on the pond out back. From the looks of things, though, it's going to be a stunner of a day.

Something gnaws at me. What is it? Oh, yes, today's my birthday. I'm thirty-nine. The discovery drives me to the counter where I dig beneath my underwear for some cigarettes. Thirty-nine. God, am I really *that* old?

Out of curiosity I go to the john and look at myself in the mirror. I've never been one who's paid much attention to how he looks. I know my hair's too long and that a lot of women have found me sexy in a boyish sort of way, but beyond that, all I've had to go by is a general impression of my features. Now for the first time in fifteen years I take a good long look at myself. I don't like what I see. Where I should be smooth as a baby I'm a road map of wrinkles, and as I fill in the other spaces, I approach horror. Jesus, I've got a good jump on a double chin and my hair's in retreat at the temples. Funny how you can go on for years, thinking of yourself as a twenty year old only to find your body's betrayed you. Or maybe it's like Dorian Gray's portrait and there's a link between character and appearance. What you do becomes reflected in your face.

Feeling down, I come out and look around the living room. Thirty-nine, and what have I got to show for it? I make a quick inventory of my possessions, and as with my face, it's the first time in years that I've really seen things. Not counting the gorgeous accommodations, I've got a Zenith stereo, much the worse for wear, a stack of records mostly from the fifties and sixties, a Smith-Corona Electric Portable 120 with a broken letter N, a Bankers Trust checking account with $119.62 in it, three pairs of pants, assorted shirts and odds and ends. Not to mention Big Red and of course, Max's Gift, which so far has proved about as likeable as one of those Furies you find in Greek plays. All things considered, it's not much to show for a guy pushing forty.

But wait, these are just *material* things. Look at what you've acquired *lately*. For instance—

Sylvia.

Yes, and she's damn near drained the starch from my spine with her surprise blitz. For three days now she's hounded me, and yesterday she called five times. And she's made it abundantly clear that unless I do something soon we're kaput, because, you see, in addition to everything else, I've also got one more thing.

After next year, I've also got no more job.

But let us not be pessimistic, as the condemned man said. After all, you've still got your charm, your mother wit, your *savoir faire*. Jobs you've lost before, by the bushelfull, no less, and you are nothing if you are not resourceful. With a smile and a shoeshine, you should be able to figure out how to keep both your solvency and the girl in this caper. Either that, or it's back to the farm for you, bucko.

The farm. Odd that I should think of it now, when I've closed the book on that chapter for years. It's a morning for remembering and taking stock, and I'm not sure what it all adds up to. A month ago I thought I did. Then I met Sylvia, and it was like I was born again. Now the Old Boy has changed the rules and switched the dice again and I've just rolled a . . . on the tractor my father sits red-necked in blue overalls as I tell him.

Around us is the field, plowed and crying for the corn, and as I stand looking up at him, with my hand on the burning red bumper and the omnipresent smell of manure in my nose, a crow flaps his wings in the distance above his shoulder. The day is brutally hot but I go right on telling him anyway. Tell him how I feel about his farm and how I've always felt about dirt and the base thoughts of those who work it. When I reach the point in my tense recital where I've planned to tell him how I'm going to leave to seek my fortune elsewhere, it's as if something in that primal mystique of the land I've always been immune to precedes my words within him, something bred on instinct and ancient as the sun. Working the lever, he snorts contemptuously and hawks a streak of spittle across the rows. Years later I hear how he died, in harness, of a stroke, carving up the North Forty.

Come to think of it, that's another link between Max and me. His father wanted him to become a professor while mine wanted me to be a farmer. The only difference is that I left whereas he—

Enough with reminiscence. If you don't open your birthday present soon, the suit of armor or whatever's in there will get rusty and go out of style. Come on, man, move!

Feeling like I'm facing my father in the corn field again, I sit down at the table and unplug my cigarette from the socket of my mouth. Stubbing it out in the ashtray, I set it aside. That way I can have some elbow room and work the knot with both hands.

Twenty

By the time I've read everything and selected the most important papers, it's past nine and I've got to hustle to give a ten o'clock final. First, though, I make a couple of stops. Number one is at a drugstore where I get three dollars' worth of dimes and on impulse buy a cigar. The second is the town library.

Feeling paranoid, I glance over my shoulder as I slip the first dime in. In seconds a copy slides out into the tray slick as a cake off a griddle, and before I know it, I'm a highly efficient machine in my own right. Insert dime ... press button ... collect copy ... lift mat ... remove paper ... insert paper ... lower mat ... insert dime ... press button .... Copies emerge, are stacked by one hand as the other lifts the mat to remove the originals. Once I stop, Max's two special prizes are in my hand while I run my eyes over them again in disbelief. Half of me is numb and doesn't know where the other half is headed. However, it's plain from the copies I've made that whatever I'm up to, I'm making excellent progress.

Then I run into a roadblock: Ambrose A. Abernathy.

Ambrose, whose triple A rating transcends his initials, enters the place like a one-man swarm and immediately buzzes about the black girl behind the service counter. I watch him warily, hoping he'll miss me, but he catches my scent and comes into the Reference Room. Even now, after two years of exposure, meeting him calls for fancy footwork and an ear that can cope with the machine gun rat-a-tat-tat jive he uses for language. Once you adapt to his delivery, though, you find he's about the only black at Ashland you can have a relationship with.

"Hey, man," he says, "what you be doing? We don' like any *nigguhs* in here."

"That's O.K., the ban's been lifted against *kikes* too."

He gives a mock wince and starts poking me. "Now why you *want* to go an' say *that?*" he says, puncturing me with words in a style all his own that I've always had to lunge a bit to grab onto. "Don't you *know* us Jews has gone through *thousands* and *thousands* of years of *per-se-cu-tion?* Yet we still *try* to be *nice* an' treat you *up-pity nig-guhs* like you ain't *scum!*"

"That's O.K.," I say, feeling like my chest's been tattooed. "Go ahead, get mad. After all, I did tell Bledsoe that for a hundred dollars more, we could have gotten Sammy Davis, Jr."

Quick as a chipmunk, he darts his head to the side and rubs his nose in what passes with him for laughter. Jewish. That's a laugh. He's about as Jewish as Anwar Sadat. Still, he does look like Davis. Five feet five and bantamweight, he's one of Ashland's few top acts. Look beyond his faults and you'll find one of the state's leading artists. For twenty years, as chairman of the Art Department, he has built a reputation as a painter and become the college's one claim to fame. But if Bledsoe had his way he'd be out on his ear. Between them there exists a traditional enmity—sure proof, if any were needed, that Bledsoe's bigotry is ultimately colorblind. To The Man all men are niggers, especially when they challenge his Gradgrindian insistence on hard facts and fixed answers.

According to reports, Ashland's scrappy terrier has snapped repeatedly against the bulldog, and each time the latter has found someone pull rank on *him*. Apparently, the President himself has a fondness for Ambrose, perhaps because next to him, Ambrose has been here the longest. (Bledsoe, in comparison, is an immigrant just off the boat.) Last year, the Dean thought he saw his chance to nail Ambrose for good when an outraged mother blew the whistle on his sexploits. The President bailed him out on that one. However, recently Ambrose seems to have given Bledsoe just the edge he needed when he refused after several rejections to write course outlines to meet the Dean's standards.

Ambrose spies what I'm doing.

"Hey, what you up to?"

"Nothing."

"Then what's all those papers?" Feisty with curiosity, he snatches one before I can move and starts reading it. I watch him helplessly. Maybe it's best this way and I should give it all to him. Maybe *he's* the one who really deserves it.

"Ambrose!"

He turns, the paper flapping in his hand, and looks toward the service counter.

"Who's she, Ambrose? Your protégé?"

"Black *honey*!" Caught by other matters, he restores the document to me. "Well, *du-ty* calls."

"Watch it, grandpa," I say with relief. "Young poon like that can kill you."

"Shoo! Boy, I been puttin' *that* down with a spoon before you was born." He leaves with a wink and a nose rub, leaving me behind schedule.

It takes just a couple more minutes to finish up, so I've got plenty of time. As I turn Big Red onto Wade Hampton, I find that the old Southern RR is heading to block the crossroads. Still, there's no reason to fret. After all, when you figure how slow they are plus the fact that it's a final and they've *got* to wait, I can stop off for a beer first and then just stroll over.

My foot, though, has different ideas and floors the accelerator. Gripping Big Red by the horns, I take off after him. Christ, what am I doing? Just for once, I'm going to beat the sonofabitch. This is going to be one time when I *don't* sit like a stooge on the wrong side of the tracks watching him drag his tail behind him like a mile long insult.

Wind blasts the windshield. I'm passing a lot of railroad cars and can catch him easily. But that's not enough, I've also got to turn right and cross the tracks in *front* of him. And to do that, Big Red's got to go flat out and transcend his limitations. Rattling like he's about to fall apart, he winds out past eighty and approaches his apotheosis, his absolute, final, and glorious transfiguration. Now I can see Engine Jack's sunburned elbow on the window ledge and scream at myself to stop. You damn fool, I shout, Sylvia's face filling my mind. What are you doing? It's not worth the dying!

When I enter his peripheral vision Jack casually turns his head to check me out, and for the first time ever we see each other. We make it a good long look, one that lasts a lifetime. Then he senses I'm trying to head him off at the pass and blows his whistle while at ninety miles an hour I remove one hand from the wheel and give him the finger. Sweat fills my eyes. Then the turn's ahead and somehow I'm into it, braking and clutching the wheel as the train shrieks over my head like thunder. For an eternity we freeze, a reflection in a cosmic eye, then time unlocks and I become unglued from the front grill of the engine and slam over and across, fighting for control as I skid toward the pedestal at the entrance to the school. Swinging the wheel, I miss it by inches and slide past, hitting the speed trap hump so sharply my head pounds the roof. Feeling dazed and like William the Conqueror, I stop at the WEL-COME sign and get out, my legs wobbly as Jell-O, and the envelope in my hand.

Naturally, I'm about five years early. There's not a soul in sight. I have plenty of time to gaze out the window at the tracks and reflect on the wisdom of risking my ass for nothing. By the time the first students trickle in, my sweat has begun to dry. I lift my eyes past a white splat of bird shit and squint into the flashbulb sun. Going to be another hot one.

At twelve past ten only two-thirds of them have arrived. Deputizing someone to distribute the tests and semester grade slips, I explain where the date goes and how they should write their names. After answering the same questions three or four times, I finally get them bedded down, at which point Rinehart the Magnificent comes in. Superior to all the scene, he stands at the door in his shades and three hundred dollar vest suit and preens his feathers. A couple of brothers look up, give him a cheer and watch him strut his stuff over to me and receive his directions with a smirk. Sitting down, he slaps a couple palms and slips a brother a handshake.

Somewhere a student starts banging a piano.

Leaving the room, I head toward the front of the Fine Arts Center where the names of trustees and dead dignitaries are spiked to the wall in neat black letters. At the top the President's name crowns the list. In the center of the building, two flights of marble steps rise and curl in opposite directions to offices on the second floor. Beneath them, Blanchard's Black Literature class has set up a display. Moving to it, I find Douglass, Wright, Ellison and others staring at me with lumpy noses and brief biographies lettered in crayon beneath their faces. Gazing at the modern, ceiling high windows, I think of how the banister in the Ad Building always feels sticky with the residue of a century of climbers and how you can rub yourself into it to join them. How when you go to class, sometimes you find your students just sitting there silently in the dark. How you can write notes on the boards to teach your classes and weeks later they're still there like undelivered messages.

All at once I get to thinking of last year's graduation when we formed two lines in the center of campus and complained about how ridiculous and medieval our regalia were. Those stupid tassels, and our gowns and hoods just wouldn't button or lie right! After fidgeting half an hour, we had filed into the Fine Arts Center through its two front entrances and entered the auditorium where the President sat in state in cardinal red robes, easily the gaudiest peacock of us all and the possessor of an honorary doctorate which entitled him to be addressed as "Doctor." Marching up on stage to join him, we had perched like freak birds so the descendants of slaves could gawk at our plummage. Here you are, folks, get your book learning in a rainbow of colors!

What I remember best of those two interminable hours is the smug, congratulatory look shared by the President with black Methodist ministers next to him when the speaker had stressed the virtues of hard work and perserverance by recalling how they had all once lacked shoes. Later, his face dripping, he had ended his sermon to a hot, overpacked house of flapping Commencement programs and squalling babies by exhorting the graduates to work hard and "Be Strong! Be Strong! Be Strong! Be Strong!"

Graduation Day. No matter where you find it, it's vulgar and asinine. And tomorrow will be my last one. My very last. I'm not alone on this May morning. On the other side of the steps where they can't see me, Happy Ray, Oldcastle, and some other white teachers have just gathered and are excitedly shooting the breeze about the faculty meeting. Closing my eyes, I soak in the gossip along with the sun, working on a tan near one of the windows which functions as a massive reflector, and listen as John's name and mine pepper the air again and again. They're really buzzing away about it, and if they're any indication, we've knocked the entire campus for a loop.

Suddenly someone else joins the bull session and is warmly greeted. Dame Rumor.

"Have you heard the news?" Farnsworth says. "John Hart's been rehired."

"No!"

"You've *got* to be joking," says Ray. "After marrying Sanford's daughter and publicly daring Bledsoe to make him shut up?"

"Well, it's true, I can assure you. The President's secretary confided it to me not five minutes ago."

What do you know! So John has his job back! Hallelujah! The news almost makes me break out in a wild cheer. Well, maybe the good fight's doomed anyway and you can never turn the tide for long, but now and then you can win a battle and keep them from taking you completely for granted. At least they don't reap all the spoils by forfeit. Yes, and occasionally a John Hart rises up where you would least expect and the serfs find themselves with a new champion. It may not be much, but at least it's something.

I'm so euphoric because of the news, that I've failed to notice it's my name being bandied about now. A voice I recognize as Oldcastle's suggests I'm the one responsible for the newspaper item.

"I agree," Ray says. "Newman's a born organizer. Two to one the whole thing at the meeting was *his* idea."

"Well, you've got to admit," someone else says, "it sure worked."

Oldcastle laughs. "Newman caught them with their pants down, all right. Imagine Sanford putting the screws to the President that way! Shows who's *really* got the say around here. Anyway, from what I hear, no one's seen the Dean or the President since yesterday."

"Hiding out, I guess," says yet another voice. "Well, let them. It's about time a white man got his way around here for a change."

"If it was me," Oldcastle says, "I'd be so embarrassed I wouldn't show my face for a month."

"One thing's for sure," says Farnsworth. "At least they know now black isn't *always* right."

"Uh huh," Ray says. "But you fellows want to know something? You could have knocked me over with a *feather* when Hart pulled out that newspaper."

"Me too."

"Same here."

"That's nothing. Bledsoe turned *white!*"

Suddenly they're all laughing.

"Yeah, and what about Sanford? How do you think he feels about his son-in-law?"

"Wonder what the full story is behind that anyhow?"

"Dunno, but whatever it is, Hart sure hung tough. Did you see how he stood up to the Dean? Gutsy. Mighty gutsy. I would never have thought he had it in him."

"What I want to know," Ray says, "is what's going to happen to Newman. Maybe they had to hire Hart back, but I can't believe they'd let Newman get away with this thing."

"Ah, as to that," says Farnsworth, "it looks like I've double-scooped you this time around."

"What do you mean?"

In the silence the top of Farnsworth's lighter snaps open, sounding just like an ejected grenade pin. Without looking, I know he's got his pipe out.

"Simply," says Farnsworth, "that Newman's contract has been renewed for just one year. After that he's a free agent."

"Why didn't they fire him now?"

"Probably because it's too late. They're supposed to give him a year's warning. Anyway, Newman's involvement with Hart probably didn't have anything to do with this. The Dean's been down on him for a long time now."

"True enough," says Ray. "But this thing didn't help his cause any. After what he did, they'd have to give him the ax sooner or later."

This observation wins a round of assent. Then a teacher whose name I don't know speaks up.

"You know," he says, "in a way I admire Newman and Hart for what they did. It took spunk. If the rest of us would just stand up that way, maybe this place would be different."

"Or maybe we'd find ourselves on welfare," says Oldcastle.

"That's more like it," says Ray. "Besides that, maybe it's best for *us* that Newman goes."

"Why?"

"Well, after this mess, a little saber rattling seems in order. When the brass gets stung, they've got to sacrifice a soldier or two just to keep order in the ranks and to release their hostility. Better they settle on Newman rather than us."

What do you know. It's save-your-ass here-let-me-hold-your-coat-while-you-walk-the-plank-time. Or as Tonto said to the Lone Ranger when they found themselves surrounded by a tribe of bloodthirsty Indians, "What do you mean *we, paleface?*"

"Sounds a bit cynical to me," the man who spoke before says.

"Maybe, but it's also realistic," says Farnsworth. "Anyway, Ray's right. After what's happened, they're going to want somebody."

"Besides," offers Ray, "it's better all around this way. Listen, I also have to kind of hand it to Newman for what he did, but let's face it, he just doesn't fit in here. To be frank about it, I just don't like him. He's always criticizing this school and causing trouble. As far as I'm concerned, it's good riddance."

"Couldn't agree more," says Farnsworth.

"I'm inclined to go along," Oldcastle says. "There's just something about the guy—"

"Maybe you've got a point," the former holdout adds.

"Yup."

"Anyway, from what I've heard, this isn't the first place he's caused trouble."

No, it's not. It sure as hell is not. Lighting a cigarette with a safety match, it occurs to me that I've spent my entire life on the outside looking in, always the faultfinding observer barred from the circles of those who do belong or who do wield the power and make the decisions. What do *I* know of such things? For the first time ever I feel real pain.

"Any of you hear that?"

"What?"

"Dunno, sounded like somebody lit a match."

Uh oh, I've blown my cover. Taking a deep drag, I move out from behind the steps and approach them.

"Howdy, gents. Nice day for a lynching, ain't it?"

Farnsworth's teeth clamp down on his pipe. Oldcastle's mouth falls open. All of them look a bit like boys who have just been caught diddling themselves behind the barn. Even Ray, bless his heart, has the good grace to turn a deeper shade of pink. Course he also recovers first and camouflages matters with a smile.

"Dave! How's everything?"

Huddled together, they're all watching me, and suddenly I find I can't wisecrack like I've done in the past when I've been canned. The best I can do now is shrug.

"You're making it O.K., then?"

His face has settled into a benevolent mask, and it's only at this end that the venom comes through. Slowly, I remove the cigarette from my mouth and favoring them all with the most gracious smile possible, present them with my middle finger held upright.

"See that, gentlemen?" I say. "I want you all to stick it right up your ass." Then, thinking of Duffy, I add: "Stick it all the way up, just as far as you can reach: right where the sun never shines."

I hold it up there a few seconds longer, just to make sure they get a good shot of it and can savor the sentiment, and then leave with a wink and a wave.

Back at the ranch the desk is littered with test papers and only three students remain. Gathering the tests, I find myself wondering when Sylvia will call. Five times yesterday and not once today. Maybe she feels that if she hasn't gotten her message across by now, she never will. Anyway, right now there's the matter of waiting for these birds to finish so I can get out of here.

At which point Rinehart glides in.

"Hey, teach, when you gonna have them tests graded?"

"*What* did you call me?"

"Uh... Mistuh Newman."

"That's right. *Mister* Newman."

He gives me a bemused grin. "Hey, man, what's this jive you handing me?"

"I'll tell you what this jive is, Rinehart. Just for once, I'd like you to remember I'm a teacher. Get that? A *teacher.*"

He opens his arms, all injured innocence. Suddenly I realize who he looks like: a black Errol Flynn.

"O.K., O.K., just take it *eas-y.* Don't blow your cool. All I want to know—"

"You'll be informed in due time, just like everyone else. No special favors."

"Yeah, Mr. Newman, sir. But you see, I'm kind of worried, ya know? If I don't get a B—"

"Hey, Rinehart, just take it *eas-y.* Don't blow your cool, ya know?" I give him a pat. "You run along now, you hear? And don't let the door bruise your threads on the way out."

As soon as the others finish, I leave. There's almost no one around outside. Tomorrow the campus and especially the Fine Arts Center will be packed with folks in their Sunday best carrying cameras. And ten minutes after graduation, grads will be loading their stuff into the trunks of cars, anxious to make tracks. After all, who wants to stay at Ashland a minute longer than necessary?

In front of Moulton, a student stands with the middle finger of his right hand presented upright to a colleague across the street. "What's that?" he shouts. "Your I.Q. or your sperm count?"

Outside my office, something crunches underfoot. More plaster has fallen from the ceiling. One day this whole condemned rattrap is going to collapse like the House of Usher. In the darkness I fiddle with my keys and finally manage to find the right one. After dropping the tests on my desk, I take a deep breath and leave, and as if on cue, the phone rings. For once somebody decides to answer it. Farnsworth. I can see his pipe glow in the dark as I approach. "Mason Hall...Who?" But I already know who, even before I swing past him and he calls after me. So she finally got around to it, did she?

I come out into the day with the envelope under my arm and set my course into the sun. March. March. Left foot right foot. Looking neither to the right nor to the left, mind blank, heart numb, I step over a chain between two posts without even breaking stride, the envelope wedged like a knight's lance under my arm. A car crosses in front of me but I keep going, eyes fixed on my destination. When I reach the door I enter. Climb disembodied. Listen to my shoes on the steps. At the second door someone passes me going out, and behind the counter Mrs. Sharp glances up like a bright bird.

"Yes, Mr. Newman?"

"I'd like to see Dean Bledsoe," I say.

"Just a minute." She disappears into his office.

Now that I'm finally here, I'm so primed that I almost commit the unpardonable sin of charging right in. At Ashland, white professors have been publicly humiliated by secretaries and functionaries for a lot less. But I keep my cool. After all, this is my big scene, and I'm not about to queer it by getting my knuckles rapped.

"You can go in now," Mrs. Sharp says.

"Thank you." Lance in place, I take a deep breath and enter.

I find him behind his desk just like last time. Only now he doesn't get up but fixes me with an expressionless stare from behind the steel-rimmed disks of his glasses, as much as to say: *What are you doing here? Your account's closed with us.* There's not a hint of curiosity or speculation as to what I'm doing here. He just sits silently awesome like Buddha or one of those statues you find in oriental temples, waiting for me to get to the point of this gig.

Since he doesn't offer me a seat, I provide my own invitation and quickly accept, choosing one of his soft cushioned chairs instead of the stiff wooden one he grills his victims on. "Nice weather," I observe.

He lets that pass. Apparently climate is of no interest to him.

"Bet you're pretty busy around here since graduation's tomorrow," I continue.

That elicits a slight response. Somewhere beneath his sphinx-like features a cog engages and a wheel starts turning. "We expect a record turnout," he says.

Beyond the door, I can hear Mrs. Sharp's typewriter carriage. Outside a car honks.

"I guess you're wondering what I'm doing here," I say.

"I imagine it concerns your future dismissal," he says flatly.

Suddenly I remember what Sylvia said and realize she was right. He really doesn't care. I'm nothing to him. The letter he wrote was just an impersonal hatchet job, and for all he cares I was a turd he flushed down the toilet bowl.

For a moment it's too much and I have to struggle to get my head together. How could I have been so dumb? I'm not even important enough to be offered a chair!

It takes a moment but I make it, and where my illusion and vanity used to be I feel a cold clean hate settle into place that makes my anger toward Ray and Godwin seem like temper tantrums. This is different. This is pure, unlike a kid's mere impulse to hit back. I want to strip that indifference from his face and make him see me, tap that impervious tranquility with an ice pick and watch it radiate into a million pieces and ultimately collapse. I want to carve him up like food for the gods as delicately and deliberately as a surgeon, so that I can savor each morsel as he disintegrates.

But how to do it? Seems to me if I hit him with the goods all at once, I'll blunt and cheapen my attack. If Ray and Godwin were unworthy adversaries, they should at least have prepared me for this. No, I've got to do it with style and finesse if I'm going to pull off this Hat Trick.

I surprise myself by taking out the cigar I bought and unwrapping it. Could I have had this in mind when I went into the drugstore? It's one of these big gaudy jobs and after waving it around a little, I ignite a safety match with my thumbnail so that it bursts into flame like a torch. After it stops flaring I light up, puffing and rotating the cigar till its end is a bright engine red. Then I toss the match into his ashtray and leaning back, expel a cloud of smoke at the ceiling.

The whole bit's like waving a red flag before a bull. "Mr. Newman, if you don't mind—"

"Man, I'm tired," I interrupt, exhaling again toward the ceiling. "It's been a hard day. You know—"

"I'd appreciate it if you'd put that—"

"You know, I'm sure glad the year's about over. Know something? Once I get my grades in, I'm going to tie one on this town's never going to forget." I lean further back and lock my hands behind my neck, cigar jutting skyward as I stretch my legs out luxuriously. "And you know something else? After I—"

"I don't like cigars in my office, Mr. Newman. Dispose of it at once."

The cigar comes out and delicately, I tap its ash onto the carpet.

The room gets quiet. Very very quiet. The dam cracks and I can feel the force of the man gather like the Red Sea above both me and my flame. Just one more moment and—

"Mr. Newman, I'm not going to tell you again."

Sitting up, I take the cigar out of my mouth. "What's that?"

"What?"

I wrinkle my nose. "That—smell."

"It's your cigar. Now if you don't mind—"

"No. It's not the cigar." I twist around in my chair, sniffing like a hound dog. "It's—mendacity."

"*What?*"

"There's a powerful odor of mendacity in this room. Don't you smell it?"

"I don't know what you're talking about," he says, but it's plain his guard's up and he's getting strange vibrations. Clearly, I'm not acting like I should. "What—"

"Mendacity," I smile, "is the system we live in. It's a fancy word for—lying."

His eyes go on red alert.

I tap more ash onto the carpet and take the package out from under my arm. For the first time, like a flushed quail, he seems to notice it. Behind the disks of his glasses his eyes widen, and it's as if he's the one sniffing the air now. Opening the package, I extract the records I chose back in the library for the opening kick-off.

"Now here's some intriguing items," I say. "As you can see from the copy with the fancy seal at the top, Ashland received over $200,000 last year from the Federal Government to support its ACT program. As you know, ACT is an important source of revenue for emergent schools charged with educating backward students, and if you'll examine the attached photostats, you'll see that approximately 60% of this amount was allocated for 'the maintenance and extension of present facilities.' That is to say, repairs of classrooms, the purchase of audio-visual equipment, that sort of thing." I toss it on his desk. "There you go, counselor. Consider it tagged and submitted as Prosecution Exhibit A. Now, if you'll direct your attention to Exhibit B, you'll see that in point of fact only $4216 was actually spent, and that primarily for the purpose, which is outside federal guidelines, of extending the air conditioning in the A.S. Henley Science Building to accommodate a certain influential chemistry professor's laboratory which is on a lower level than that covered by the regular system. The rest, despite the claim made in Exhibit A, is mysteriously unaccounted for. In addition—"

"How did you get this? Who authorized the release of these records? This is the property of—"

"That's not the point."

Wham! He hits the desk. "Mr. Newman, your possession of these records constitutes a felony, and if *I* have anything to say about it, we'll prosecute!"

"Look—"

"I might add that I consider your misrepresentation of their contents to be not only malicious slander but treason. As an employee, it is your duty and responsibility to serve the best interests of Ashland and not violate its trust."

Treason? Who the hell does he think I am, Benedict Arnold? Doesn't he remember, *he* fired *me?* For a moment, as his crackbrained power rolls over me, he's got me switched. Who knows, maybe he's right. After all, these *are* state secrets. A crazy image leaps to mind: me on my knees in a cotton field, begging forgiveness. Then sanity wobbles back. Damn it, he's not going to blow this by me! Lifting the envelope, I shake its contents onto his desk, strewing it with papers. "Now, don't bullshit me," I say. "No more god damn crap. You want felonies? I'll give you Grand Larceny." I run my eyes over the carnage. Where to start next? How about the supposed use of federal money to pay fifty-seven Work Study students who had in fact been laid off at the time for trumped up reasons? There had been a real stink about *that* one. Or what about— suddenly I spot the real smoking pistols in the lot, Duffy's secret prizes. Talk about second story men, it must have taken a real cat burglar to steal *these* babies. I snatch them up and drop them in front of him.

"Take a look at this one," I say.

Reluctantly, he looks at it.

"I won't bore you with details," I go on. "Let's just say there are certain authorities who would love to know what you did with the $40,000 that was transferred to your keeping by the Business Manager and what both your roles were in such an unorthodox procedure. They might want to have it made plain to them why no record of the transfer appears in the regular accounts." I lift a page. "Also, there's the matter of an equal amount consigned to the President."

"That's enough!"

"No, that's *not* enough!" Damn it, how can I get through to him? "Look at this crap," I say. "There's enough evidence here to fry you and half the administration a dozen times over. Proof positive of a conspiracy to rip off Government funds."

"These records are stolen!"

"Listen!" I lean over his desk, trying to establish contact and dripping cigar ashes over everything. Never before have I been so close to him. "I'll give it to you one more time. You're dead. The President's dead. The Business Manager's dead. London Bridge is Falling Down. Get it? What you see is *prima-facie* evidence that you've defrauded Uncle Sam."

He pauses, seems to reflect. As if by accident, he opens his drawer about six inches. "And what do you intend to do with it?"

Suddenly I remember the stories about The Gun In The Dean's Drawer and turn cold. "In case you've got any ideas," I say quickly, "please notice these are all copies." I think of the originals, crammed into Big Red's glove compartment. "If anything should happen to me, a friend will go to the authorities with the originals."

The whole thing sounds corny as hell. What if he laughs and plugs me, claiming I attacked him because he'd fired me? No, that would be stupid. But with someone like Bledsoe, you can never be sure. He just might do it and actually convince them.

But he buys it. At least, I get the feeling we're looking at things from the same angle now.

"So what do you want—money?"

"No."

"Your job back? A promotion?"

"No."

"Then I don't understand. If it's not money or your job, why see me? Why not simply—"

I lean close to him again. "Just this. I wanted to face you man to man with this shit. You know, five weeks ago you gave one hell of a sermon in this office. Remember? A lot of pious bullshit about duty and integrity. Well, I just wanted to know about yours. Come on, tell me, where is it? I'd really like to know how you can help students who so badly need an education when you steal the money that makes it possible."

"The money hasn't been stolen, only temporarily reassigned in accordance with what *we* deem to be in the best interests of the school. It's hardly your prerogative to question our judgment."

His voice rolls on over my frustration. Somehow I've got to extort some concession of guilt from him, make him *see*. But of course he can't see, and no matter what I say, he's always got an answer. In his mind everything's justified and makes perfect sense. He and those who run the school can do no wrong, and anyone who attacks them is the enemy. Like the Rock of Gibraltar, he's impregnable.

Not quite! If he can't understand his hypocrisy, he can at least recognize brute force when he sees it. Angrily, I break in.

"Well, at any rate, you can be assured of one thing. You *will* have your day in court and an opportunity to share your unique perspective with federal auditors."

"Then you're going public with this?"

"Exactly. And just in case I forget, let me give credit now where credit's due." I wave my hand at the wreckage on his desk. "See this trash? Well, Max Duffy says hello."

His head snaps back and for once his calm explodes. "Damn it! That punk!" Then he catches himself, but not before he's given me the edge I'd hoped for. Not victory, since ultimately he's unconquerable. Call it a decision. For the first time ever I'm ahead on points.

Now that I've got clout, he becomes conciliatory. "I hope you're not leaving."

I stop at the door. "As you can guess, I've got things to do. I'll leave these here for your enjoyment."

"Please." Instantly he's up, towering over me and cajoling me back to my chair. "Please, sir, one minute if you will." He sits down and picks up the phone. "Mrs. Sharp, get me the

President...yes...he's not in? Then try his home." Pause. "Busy? Yes, I'll hold."

Why am I still here? I flick more crud onto his carpet. After a minute there's a click and a voice at the other end. Bledsoe shields the receiver, talks low and fast. At one point I think I hear the other voice ask how much I've got. Bledsoe turns his face away from me. "Everything." There's another pause and then the voice at the other end continues. The Dean nods his head. A moment later he hangs up.

Reaching behind his desk, he lifts a brown satchel and with a giant hand gathers everything on his desk into it. Locks snap. He looks at me.

"Mr. Newman, would you accompany me to the President's residence?"

"What for?"

"Please. The President would consider it a personal favor."

I get up, aware of a new wall between us, a new and terrible wall. I flick more ashes on his carpet.

"Mind if I smoke?" I ask, not giving a damn.

"Whatever you prefer, sir."

Twenty-One

WHEN WE GET OUTSIDE the Manicure Boys are breaking their ass getting the place ready for tomorrow's graduation. Some are mowing lawns and clipping hedges, others are planting caladiums in front of the Fine Arts Center and dismantling Blanchard's idiotic art display.

The Dean leads me to his Chrysler Imperial and opens the door on the passenger side. I'm not about to cooperate, though. The taste of power is sweet and I feel giddy.

"Looks like a nice day. Let's walk, shall we?"

Expressionless, he closes the door.

"As you wish."

So now the whole plantation is treated to a scene out of dreamland: me with a circus cigar stuck in my kisser strolling with the Jolly Black Giant. Hey, kids, look at me. Meet my new pal. How about it, should I link arms with Luther, slap his back? I look up at him marching ramrod straight at my side and looking neither to the right nor left. In his satchel the Great Equalizer is locked safely out of sight.

We follow the walk that bisects the campus. A song pops into my head: We're off to see the Wizard, the wonderful Wizard of Oz. Is anyone watching? I look around, resisting the urge to strut. On the library steps, Solomon Wise stands gazing at me again. As tall and expressionless as Bledsoe, only his head and eyes turn as we pass him. Something stirs inside me, something I can't name. What's he doing here? Is he *really* here this time? And if so, what does he think of this pomp and circumstance? I stop, try to—

Bledsoe nudges me on.

For the first time since I've started seeing Wise, he moves. He bounds down the steps, hand raised, and opens his mouth as if to shout something to me. He's too late, though. The A. S. Henley Science Building comes between us and we reach the street.

Westminister, the President's mansion, sports a gently curving driveway and an emerald lawn trimmed to perfection. Though I've been to receptions here both for the faculty and Miss Black South Carolina, it's as if I've never seen it before. Now it looks like a palace that has been wrested brutally from the land and political opponents in some sweltering banana republic. So this is what it's like for one black man who has really made it in America: the face of respectability and power with all the bloody skeletons tucked away in king-size closets.

We cross the street and march up the front walk. Bledsoe presses the doorbell while I struggle against a feeling of unreality. Is this really happening? Have I actually gone this far?

The door opens. Bledsoe motions for me to enter, and I step past the negro maid into the living room. Words are exchanged. Bledsoe presses my elbow with a giant hand and we cross the living room and move down a hallway. I have a fleeting impression of a Chippendale chair, china in a cabinet. Before we reach the door at the end of the hallway, it opens and the President comes out beaming.

"Well, Mr. Newman. Come in. Come in please, sir!"

I enter and find myself in a long walnut paneled den with built-in bookcases along two of the walls. Bledsoe remains at the door and extends the satchel to the President.

"Will there be anything else?"

"Thank you, Dr. Bledsoe, I'll handle matters from here."

He closes the door and goes to his desk. Suddenly I'm reminded of how seemingly innocuous the President is. The Dean is 6'6". I'm 5'11". The President, though, is a plump bald little man in his early sixties who is barely 5'6". When he turns his head, I notice a bulge of fat at the back of his neck formed between two creases.

"Please sit down, Mr. Newman. Make yourself comfortable."

I sit in a luxurious leather chair while he snaps open the

satchel and places the contents on his desk, which is of a heavy walnut like the walls. Gold pens in holders pierce the air. Sitting down, he sorts through it like he's merely checking the Dean's inventory and doesn't care what he finds.

"Well!" he says, "you are to be commended. You certainly have done a thorough job."

"Thank you."

"If you don't mind my asking, how did you come into possession of these records?"

"Is that important? The important thing is that I've got them."

He leans back and smiles. "Just curious. You don't have to answer if you don't want."

Something in his borrowed Oxford air gets to me. "To be precise, Mr. President, I don't have to do anything I don't want. But since you ask, Max Duffy gave them to me. He, in turn, received them from the Head Accountant, who I understand has left for reasons of his own."

"As did Mr. Duffy," says the President. "His departure this semester has been quite an inconvenience to us. But that's beside the point. Oh, I'm sorry. Would you care for an ashtray?"

What do you know, I've still got my cigar. The President gets up like an impatient pimp and brings me an ashtray. I've lost my taste for the thing, though, and besides, it's out of place here. I tamp it out in the ashtray while he holds it. Setting it down, he returns to his chair where he leans back and laces his fingers on his stomach.

"Well, sir, what are we to do?"

"It's your invitation. You tell me."

"All right. Might I ask what you intend to do with these records?"

"Oh, I don't know. Turn them over to the Feds. Or perhaps try the newspaper again, as I did with the Harts. I haven't decided yet."

"I see, as you did with the Harts. Yes. Yes, indeed. If I may say so, Mr. Newman, you've proved to be quite a cross for me to bear."

"The pleasure's been all mine."

"Doubtless. But to return to these documents. Might I ask further if anyone else knows about them?"

"No, but a friend's got the originals and he's been given instructions."

"In case something should happen to you?"

I wave my hand, surprised at the ease with which I pull this bit of malarkey off. Hell, I'd make a dandy blackmailer. Then I see he doesn't consider it far-fetched at all but is taking me seriously. Ice freezes my spine. What is this, the black Mafia? Is he their Godfather?

"Since you haven't decided yet what you're going to do, may I make a suggestion?"

"Sure."

"I suggest we come to some kind of accommodation."

"But you don't have anything I want."

"Are you sure?"

His eyes probe me. I lean forward.

"All right, there *is* one thing."

"What?"

"An answer."

"To what?"

"To the same question I asked the Dean. Maybe you can answer it better."

"I'll try."

"All right." Blood pounds in my ears. "I know this may sound näive and stupid to you, but I really would like to know how you justify this stealing."

"I'm afraid I don't—"

"I'll make it plainer. Ever since I came here I've heard you described as a paragon of virtue, a pillar of the church and all that. In particular, I've heard you praised at assemblies as a President who has devoted his life to this school, who wouldn't do anything to harm it in any way."

For a moment he just looks at me.

"Your question, Mr. Newman?"

I swallow. "Well, I want to know—I really want to know—just how you square all that with what's in front of you. Tell

207

me, how can you help students who desperately need an education when you rob them blind?"

He's never faced such chutzpah before, and he's not used to it. Muscle pounds against his soft cheeks. That's the real man, the one beneath the facade of plump benevolence. Suddenly I realize he's the one who really calls the shots, not Bledsoe, and that even with all my evidence, I'm walking a tightrope.

But he deigns to answer. "I'm afraid you just don't understand."

"Understand what?"

The muscle pounds again. Apparently even the thought of discussing this with a white underling is enough to heave his gorge.

"What you don't understand are the dynamics involved in running Ashland."

"And you do?"

"Yes, along with a handful of others who have been here nearly as long as I have." He leans forward, exuding immense energy. "You see, Mr. Newman, sometimes it's essential that we make certain adjustments. In order to take maximum advantage of our allocations, it occasionally proves necessary to reassign them."

"Sounds illegal to me."

He shrugs. "Call it bending a few technicalities. Nothing of substance."

"I doubt the Government would agree."

He snorts in contempt. "The Government. What do they know? Bureaucrats. Outsiders. What can they possibly know about the needs of a private black Christian college whose only other source of funds is the Methodist Church and the contributions of a few individuals?" He rises and comes around the desk. "Come over here, please, I'd like to show you something."

On the back wall there are photographs of Ashland in various stages of development.

"Now this," he says, pointing to the first, "I had taken twenty-eight years ago, the day I assumed the Presidency. As you can see, there were only nine structures then. All of them were in disrepair and badly in need of renovation. We had no modern Fine Arts Center or Henley Science Building. *They were to come later, due largely to my efforts.* Incidentally, it may interest you to know that if you had been an employee here at that time, you would have missed a pay check or two. We were so poor then. But I'm happy to report that for the past twenty years we haven't defaulted on a single payroll or failed to meet our responsibilities to our employees. For twenty straight years we've operated consistently in the black. How many other institutions of higher learning can make *that* claim?"

If there's a message in his proud recital, and there is, it comes through as a patronizing rap on the knuckles. *Who are you, boy, to question me? I was saving this place from extinction when you were in knee pants, and if it weren't for me, you wouldn't have had a job here in the first place.*

I open my mouth to hold up my end, but he takes my elbow and steers me along memory lane, stopping every foot to point out a milestone he helped to erect. The Fine Arts Center...Moulton Hall...The Dudley Student Union...Leadon Dormitory... His face develops a sheen. His energy drenches me as the decades pass. New buildings rise, facilities expand. At one point we see him grinning at a ground breaking ceremony with a shovel in his hand. Finally we reach the present, Ashland as it now is with its twenty-one buildings and a peak enrollment of eleven hundred. With that, he turns me around to an easel where there's an artist's sketch of a building complex.

"Know what this is?"

"The future Phys. Ed. Building?"

He nods, eyes shining. "That's right. It's an artist's drawing of the Physical Education Center, which will be constructed along Wade Hampton. It will contain an Olympic-size swimming pool, a new gymnasium, and handball courts. For years it's been a dream that we've looked forward to." His eyes snap at me. "But dreams cost money, Mr. Newman. In this case nearly four million dollars. And a private black college like Ashland doesn't have a chance without a President who's willing to perform the thankless task of raising funds." He pauses, his muscles hardening in his cheeks again. "You come in here, comfortable and well-fed, and talk to me about account book irregularities. Well, let me tell you about the realities of traveling constantly about the country and prying reluctant fingers from stingy contributions, the broken promises I've received, the indignities I've had to—"

He breaks off, aware that he has revealed more about himself than he wants, and then goes on. "Oh, I suppose from your side of the desk my job looks pretty glamorous. Just snap my fingers and people jump. But it's not that way at all. There are sacrifices I have to make. Ashland isn't Clemson, you know, or USC. We don't have the multimillion dollar endowments those people do. What they can do overnight takes us years to accomplish."

"If you can do it at all."

"Oh, we'll do it," he says, eyes glistening as he gazes at the picture. He jabs his finger at it to emphasize his words. "Make-no-mistake-about-it! This-center-will-be-built! Maybe not this year or next, but in God's good time. And with His guidance I will make it come to pass!"

Jesus, now he's Christ and Ashland's his church, and he who threatens one threatens the other. Never before have I felt so outgunned. Even Bledsoe doesn't have this man's power. He's a born preacher, and if I don't get on the scoreboard soon, I'm a goner.

"You're forgetting one thing," I say.

"What?"

"Me."

His eyes prick me like knives. "I was hoping what I've said would change your heart."

"Yes, I'm sure you did." I turn away for breathing room and run my eyes over the tiers of expensive volumes. Real or phony? Will the gilt covers crumble if I touch them? Are the pages blank? Does he read them? I turn back. "Unfortunately, when you talk about Ashland you leave out the most important thing: people. Especially the students. What about them? What about the quality of their education? I listen to you and I get numbers, objects, *things*. All this place is to you is money and swimming pools and enrollments. But enrollments of what? Enrollments of *students*. Is there any place in your accountant's view of things for them?"

"That's who it's all for."

"I don't believe that. I don't think you care at all about them. What these students need right now are new classrooms, not handball courts; better teachers with advanced degrees, not the cheap, local, inadequately trained variety who are often little better than they are. You want facts? Over ten percent of the faculty here are teaching subjects in which they don't even have degrees, and teachers are given almost no incentives or encouragement to improve their professional skills by engaging in research and publishing. Not only that, but the counselors, the very people who are supposed to guide and help our students, are incompetent and completely unorganized. They operate out of different offices and under different programs, and no attempt is made whatsoever to coordinate them. And the upshot of it all is that this year just three percent of our students passed the National Teachers Examination. That's three percent! And yet you persist in crying racism and cultural bias even though they can't read or write!"

"Are you finished?"

"No. All *that* I can take. But what I can't stomach are your lies about the money. You forget—I've seen the evidence. We're not talking about technicalities. We're talking about thousands of dollars that was to go to help the students. There's evidence on your desk that proves $40,000 of it was siphoned off to a private bank account in *your* name. That's money that went into *your* pockets. What I don't understand—what I've never been able to understand about people like you—is your blindness to the gulf between what you preach and what you do!"

But he hasn't even heard. "So what are you going to do?"

"Mr. President, if I have my way, I'm going to tear this place down. Stone by moldy stone!"

"And what will that accomplish?"

"Clean this mess up!"

"And what about the students you claim you care so much about? What about the thousands who would never have had a college education if it weren't for black colleges like Ashland? What about the hundreds who have currently invested years of their lives here? Are you willing to see their hopes go down the drain?"

This checks me. I haven't considered that angle before.

"Well, maybe it's for the best when you consider the rotten education they get."

"Then you belong with those who are trying to kill black education in this country. Those who are using the National Teachers Examination and any other ruse they can lay their hands on to destroy us." He snorts contemptuously. "You come in here like a crusading knight, and your first and only act of reform is to *destroy*."

"Well, maybe they should be in *white* schools."

"Listen, Mr. Newman, ninety-seven percent of our students are on Government aid and seventy per cent come from families with incomes of less than seventy-five hundred dollars. If it weren't for schools like us, they wouldn't get an education."

"Some education."

"All right, maybe Ashland isn't Harvard, but don't blame *us*. Blame it on the injustices in this country. Blame it on poverty and prejudice and the second-rate education they get from the first grade on up."

"In this school it isn't even second rate, and it's your fault. You could make it better!"

"And by God, it *is* getting better. Make no mistake about it. We may not be the best, but at Ashland the business of education is going on. Maybe not good or fast enough for dreamers like you who can't see beyond a few irregularities in a ledger, but going on nevertheless. And it's—"

"Look, maybe your problem is you just don't want to know. Let me tell *you* something. *You* don't have to teach them. You don't have to go in there day after day and face students with a sixth grade education who couldn't care less what you have to say, students who have never even heard of William Shakespeare and who can do everything with a basketball except sign their names to it."

"And you want to help them?"

"Right."

"By destroying?"

"If it's necessary."

We stare at each other, both of us breathing fast. Then he explodes.

"Then by God, you just go ahead. In a quarter century I've been attacked many times. I've faced them all, and ground them all into the dust." He steps close and jabs my chest. "So you go ahead, white boy, you just try to stop me. You won't be the first, and I'll be here performing my mission long after you've returned to the ash heap you came from!"

"You really think you can survive this?"

He grins in mockery. "Did you really think you could stop me? Boy, you don't know *anything*. The system doesn't work that way. I have connections in high places, and there are people whose interests would be ill-served by certain revelations. Oh, I don't deny it would be inconvenient, just as your assistance to the Harts which you take such obvious pride in. There would be even more adverse publicity and the appearance of an investigation. Some of our people would have to go. The trustees would be obliged to ask their questions again, and for a while we'd have to tack to a different wind. But destroy the school, destroy *me?*" He shakes his head. "Let me tell you something, boy, despite occasional appearances to the contrary, *I'm* the one who really runs Ashland. Not a handful of white trustees. Not even Sanford. Oh, now and then they may think they do. But I can assure you, they're wrong. And in a matter of just a few hours I can eliminate the worst effects of your disloyalty simply by transferring certain funds. In the end you would have accomplished nothing but to hurt those you say you want to help."

I look at him in frustration. "I don't believe you."

He grins again. "Don't you really? Come now, Mr. Newman, you've been around long enough. Consult your own experience. One man against a system: when does it ever work? You've tried to change things before, have you not? What have you got to show for it?"

I open my mouth but sawdust comes out. He glides in and takes my arm.

"Listen, you want to improve things?"

"Yes."

"Very well, I can respect that, even admire you for your ideals. But if you wish to help, there's just one way."

"How?"

"By working *with* us, within the system."

I laugh. "You forget. I've been canned."

He flaps his hand. "Consider yourself rehired, with a six thousand dollar raise and a guarantee of tenure."

"You think you can bribe me with sweet talk and a fat job? Is that what you think I'm after?"

He shrugs. "To have influence, you must have a position. One doesn't go without the other. Of course, you understand, it would also be necessary to make you Chairman of your department and eventually Division Chairman."

"I don't think Dr. Farnsworth would like that."

"Let *me* worry about Farnsworth."

"Forget it."

He drops my arm. "I thought so. I should have known. I've seen white liberals like you before. You come here, take our money, stir things up and expect to have things your way. And when you find you can't, you cry 'Unfair!' and run off. Instead of cooperating a little and fighting for what you believe, you just give up!"

This cuts very close to the bone and something must happen in my face, for he backs off.

"Look, don't you *dare* say that to me! All my life I've fought bastards like you. And you're right, I *have* learned from my experience. Only what I've learned isn't what you think. I've learned there is no cooperating or compromising with people like you. As you've made amply clear, I'm a white 'boy' in a black school, and I've already put my ass on the line by coming forward. How long would it be before I found myself neutralized or stamped flat?"

"Stamped flat?"

"I'm sure you have your ways."

He brushes this off. "We're not the Gestapo. Besides, don't *under*estimate what you have. Believe me, it would be awkward if you disclosed it."

"But according to you, hardly fatal."

He shrugs again, a mannerism I'm getting used to. "There are no guarantees. Part of it would depend on how fast you learned—how should I put it—to use your leverage. But make no mistake. You *would* have a voice, and as President I assure you I would be obliged to listen. Now, isn't that better than creating a lot of unpleasantness that wouldn't help anybody?"

Somewhere in the room a clock ticks. I wait till it reaches five before answering.

"No."

He sighs and goes to his desk. Opens a folder. "When Dean Bledsoe called me, I pulled your file. Very interesting. Seems you've had quite a number of jobs in the past few years."

"What of it?"

"So unless I'm wrong, Ashland should be about the end for you professionally. With your record and the academic job market being what it—"

"Good-by, Mr. President."

"Wait."

I turn at the door. He comes over, a short, harmless-looking little man.

"Indulge me one more minute, please, because I think I know you and feel you're making a mistake. Isn't it about time you stopped moving around and settled down somewhere? What are you afraid of? Stop running away. Stop trying to change the world and come to terms with it. What have you got to lose? If you stay you can make a difference, and you owe it to yourself to help *yourself* for a change. What's wrong with a little success?"

I force a smile. "You could talk a bull out of its balls."

"Maybe you've already convinced yourself," he says softly.

"What do you mean?"

"Don't you know?"

"No."

He pats my shoulder. "Mr. Newman, why did you really have duplicates made of those records?"

"For insurance, so that when I saw the Dean—"

He shakes his head. "No, there's something here that doesn't fit. If you wanted to expose us, why didn't you simply go to the authorities? Why see him first?"

"Like I told you—"

"No, I'll tell you. You did it so you could get something for yourself."

"Go to hell."

"Listen, there's nothing wrong in that. What is wrong is not being honest with yourself. You know, for a half-hour I've listened to your platitudes, but the real reason you came here was to make a deal. Admit it and accept my offer."

All at once I hear the clock ticking again and try to find it. But the sound seems to come from everywhere and nowhere. I raise my fist, and before I can stop myself, move forward and hit him, knocking him back against the desk. I watch his head strike the edge of his desk and spatter blood across it like a ripe watermelon. A hundred times I watch him fall, and when it's over, find I still haven't done it. Instead I'm standing, my whole life gathering into a ball as events from the past flood my mind. The lost jobs. The failures. The kid vomiting blood at Kent State who looked at me with those eyes. The loneliness of going nowhere, never belonging or fitting in. Then I see my father hawking his spit across the rows and the times I tried to kill myself. At last comes Sylvia urging me to commit blackmail and a voice like a hammer in my brain.

Why not?

Why not get something for yourself?

Why not think of Number One for a change? If anyone's paid his dues, *you* have.

I try to find the clock again, but the voice goes on.

Think of what you'd have.

A job.

Power.

Status.

A future.

Something at last to show for nearly forty years of life. And above all—

Sylvia. And maybe a family.

Like an old friend, the President guides me back down the hallway, telling me how smart I am and how we should stick together. Odd that he should think I made the duplicates so I could sell out. Not that it would be a completely bad idea. At least that way I'd have a chance to do some good here, especially with men like Hart on my side. Still, it's not my style, and he should know better.

Because we're so close, we have to go slowly. The hallway is tight, and as I struggle down it toward the light a bizarre conceit flashes across my mind. For a moment I see the hallway as a vagina, a birth canal, and the President as a doctor laboring to give me birth. And when I reach the light what will I be born as? Or will I be reborn? Perhaps as something new?

We reach the living room, which is unaccountably bright, and cross the floor. He opens the door.

"You think it over," he smiles, "and I think you'll see I'm right. But there's just one thing."

Almost imperceptibly, his voice hardens.

"Let me know in twenty-four hours," he says.

Outside it's a furnace, and as I near the curb I find myself thinking of the tennis players at the Country Club. Funny, I beat Ray and Godwin and finally even managed to outpoint Bledsoe, but it *really* takes some doing to get past this little man with the chummy smile and the eyes that can see right through you.

A truck rumbles past, imparting a solitary breath to the

day's perfect stillness. The street is hot, and as I set out across it, I find I can't see. Sweat fills my eyes and I try to wipe it away. Then I find it isn't sweat. At the same instant, a horn roars almost on top of me. The truck turns me with it, whipping my clothes scaldingly against me and driving me to my knees with the force of its passage. I kneel on the sun-blasted pavement, blinded by the dust as it heads North, which is *his* direction and any direction his heart and will takes him. Left behind, I gaze after until he fades away and starts to climb a hill in the distance, rising toward the clouds and another land for all I know, another country.

"Max," I say, laughing through the tears, "I sure hope you make it."